Also by Onia Fox:

Covid Blues And Twos (Jessica Taylor) – Lockdown Erotica

Listless In Turkey (Jessica Taylor) – Travel Suspense Thriller

Alexa – humorous, coming of age, short story

Enemy Closer

By

Onia Fox

Jessica has no intention of returning to Turkey after her previous brush with the law, but circumstances conspire to dilute her resolve. Her friend, and senior colleague, calls in some favours. An old dalliance makes a welcome appearance. And her husband sidles up to his attractive colleague.

To the backdrop of the real-life shooting down of a Russian jet fighter on the Turkish-Syrian border, and the many infighting groups involved in the ongoing Syrian civil war, Jessica charges in.

Enemy Closer is a factually accurate, believable, page turning procedural suspense thriller.

keep your friends close, but your enemies closer

Contents

Chapter one

'Mrs Pebbles?'

'Grab a seat, Jessica. One minute.'

Jessica sat in the leather chair across the expanse of desk from her team manager. Amara continued to tap on her keyboard and scrutinise the hidden desk monitor. She wore contact lenses in the office, a security device to prevent visitors reading her screen in the reflection of spectacles.

'I prefer you in glasses Am, they make you look dead sexy.'

Amara broke into a grin. Without looking up from her monitor, she raised a finger to her lips to silence her friend and junior colleague; Jessica aware that the office was likely sound recorded – either bugged by security or by Amara, or both.

Jessica let her eyes drift around the office. The window behind Amara looked over Portsmouth's historic dockyard, heavily tinted to prevent snooping from outside. Only senior managers had office windows, the open plan work areas sealed from the outside world. Jessica studied the photographs Amara hung from the walls and displayed on her desk – otherwise empty except for a blank monitor she used for visitors and a small vase of dried wildflowers, ideal for concealing a microphone. The photo subjects interested Amara but gave away no personal information; to comply with Company policy. No family portraits, no pictures of the outside of her Guildford house, no car number plates.

Jessica studied the scene from a Californian Gay Pride march. Some protestors marched bare chested or naked, with various slogans against subjugation and the shackling of women's bodies by male invented restrictive underwear, inked across their breasts – bra burners. The sun shone brightly; the faces all smiled back at the camera. A female officer from the San Francisco Police Department brought both hands to cover her embarrassed but beaming smile.

'Nice pussy.'

Amara looked up briefly from the monitor.

'Bengal Hunting Cat. But then you met Jeffrey, when you came to mine for supper.'

The photograph of Amara's cat hung on the opposite wall.

'So, how is your Elizabeth Class *Naap* project coming along?'

Jessica opened her notebook and slipped in the aluminium sheet to stop her notes imprinting onto the following page. Before the end of the shift, she would enter all notes onto the secure computer vault or project file and shred the paper page. Jessica locked away the blank notebook each night, but security still made checks to see no hard notes remained.

'I can't tell you much that isn't already on file, Mrs Pebbles. Last five per cent of the project is twenty per cent of the effort and all that, but it will be ready for sea trials to meet the milestone.'

'Nervous?'

Jessica laughed.

'How do you do that, Am? Nobody gets in my head like you do!'

Jessica was to use Amara's surname at work, but they were close friends, and talked more informally when alone.

'Talk me through it, as if I don't already know everything. Assume you are moving off the project; tell me the nugget of information I will not glean from the file.'

'Everything is fine, Mrs Pebbles. It is only my personal insecurity. The NATO Anti-Aircraft Platform system fitted to the two UK aircraft carriers is operated off-ship. The captain can prime the system or close it down, but the actual firing of the cannons and missiles is completely remote and automatic, instigated from the benefitting country. The carrier becomes an air-defence system for those countries benefitting from the system – namely Israel and Turkey, for now.'

'Why those two specifically? And why use carriers?'

'We need the carriers because of the physical size of the system. NATO worries about Israel arming with more battleground nuclear weapons against Palestinian and Arab threats. The two parties signed the *IPCP* back in 2017 and *Naap* enables Israel to step back from escalating the arms race with her neighbours.'

'*TMBAs*?'

'Sorry Mrs Pebbles?'

'Too Many Bloody Acronyms.'

Jessica laughed.

'*IPCP* Individual Partnership and Cooperation Program. It is in NATO's interest for its non-NATO ally to remain secure. Sorry, I mean North Atlantic Treaty Organization.'

It was Amara's turn to smile.

'Turkey is more cold-war-old-school. NATO is sensitive to the Russian threat from the motherland, Iranian soil and the Black Sea Fleet, against NATO bases in Turkey. Turkey recently took delivery of the Russian-made air defence system S-400, because America wouldn't come up with the goods. NATO is seriously pissed – there is no way the Russian

President hasn't included an off button for the defence system. If he attacks NATO air bases in Turkey, Putin will flick a switch hidden under his desk and turn off Turkey's air-defence. They might have already secretly programmed it to ignore any direct Russian attacks. NATO needs Turkey, and *Naap* is our way of keeping control of Turkey's defence if the worst happens – without relying on the aggressor supplied system. When operating from the Mediterranean or Black Sea, HMS Queen Elizabeth or HMS Prince of Wales can put an umbrella of smart ordnance over Turkey or Israel in a moment. An impenetrable wall of lead.'

'And why are you so nervous?'

'*Naap* uses intelligence and surveillance from the benefitting country's own systems, onboard equipment and even interrogates the Russian supplied kit. A conflict of interest. But I have a much more immediate concern.'

'The nugget?'

'Yep. This is an anti-aircraft system controlled off ship and bolted to our aircraft carriers. What if, the first time we test it live, it shoots down a friendly aircraft returning to the carrier? What if the info from S-400, which we only half understand, conflicts, corrupts, or derogates our own intel? We can run any amount of models you like, but I would not want to be that pilot returning to the carrier for the first time and looking down the barrel of a gun controlled by Turkish and Russian intel.'

'Think of the paperwork.'

'Seriously, Am, I wouldn't let my nieces go for a joy ride in an F35 Lightning Jet on test day.'

'The entire project is your responsibility, including efficacy. But your software team are the experts and I know you ensured Quality has checked and double checked.'

'Exactly Mrs Pebbles, which is why I haven't raised it. Perhaps I am punching above my weight on this project – it is so technical.'

'I hope you are not challenging my selection of Area Project Manager Mrs Taylor.'

Both women smiled.

'Between you and me Amara,' Jessica still mindful of the conversation being recorded, 'I may have turned down this role if it wasn't you who had selected me. I have had more than one sleepless night.'

'I will make a note of your concerns. But I can also assure you, we are more than happy with your diligence and professionalism. You have done a good job. And by the way, you don't have the option to turn down roles.'

'Ok. Thank you. I guess.'

Amara held her colleague's eye for a long moment.

'Talking of which, you are on the move. I shall close out the construction phase of *Naap,* ready for commissioning. I want you to head up a new project.'

'Wow. Ok. I wasn't expecting that, Mrs Pebbles.'

'It is not actually one of mine. You are seconded to Sam Smith's team from Monday.'

'Am, no. I want…'

'I cannot give you any details about your new project, as I said, it is not one of mine. Good luck and thanks again for your good work on *Naap*.'

'Am …'

'Let us leave it there for now, Jessica.'

Amara returned her gaze to the monitor. Jessica left the office.

Chapter two

Friday was always Date Night. Jason worked from home most Fridays and already had the Butter Chicken bubbling in the slow cooker, when Jessica arrived home late afternoon. They went straight to bed. Jason kicked off the duvet and lay on his back, panting. Jessica lay on her back across the bed, her head resting against his hip. Her body still shuddering from their lovemaking, each shudder bringing a smug grin to her lips, her eyes closing in a lazy blink. They both catnapped for a few minutes.

‘Amara has dumped me onto another team. I’m not sure if I should feel proud or rejected.’

‘Really? I thought you two joined at the hip. In fact, you did once.’

Jessica slapped his stomach with the back of her hand.

‘Jace! We slept together one time, years ago. I never should have told you.’

She found his hand, and they locked fingers.

‘You haven’t told me the details yet Jess, why not start from the beginning.’

Jessica noticed him becoming aroused again. She squeezed his hand until his knuckles cracked.

‘Pervert.’

‘I’ll be the judge of that. I have some work news as well, but you go first. I will need your advice on my news.’

‘I have no idea why she did it. I report to Sam on Monday. The teams do not talk to each other – sometimes one team is working on a defence system for one country while the neighbouring team is working on the attack system for the hostile country. Where there’s muck, there’s brass. Am does not know what my next project entails. Perhaps they selected me because of my performance on the last project; I really don’t know. So, what is your news?’

‘Your lot has approached me for some consultancy work.’

‘My lot? What, Company?’

‘Yep. A small chemical fuel additive plant at a military airbase.’

‘But we don’t do petro-chem.’

‘Presumably, that is why they approached me.’

‘But why you? How weird.’

‘Oh, thanks for your vote of confidence. I have completed a similar installation at a fuel distribution plant in the UK, so I am guessing they got my name from one of the professional or trade bodies, or perhaps from ExxonMobil. Good money.’

‘What? Is this new job not in the UK?’

'Turkey. Dalaman airport, they have a military base attached.'

Jessica shuddered – not from the lovemaking. Her grin disappeared.

'No Jace. You can't go to Turkey, not after everything that happened.'

'Nothing happened to me. I hardly knew you when you were getting yourself into trouble. You're the one being monitored by Turkish military intelligence, not me.'

'I don't know, Jace.'

'It's unlikely I will fall in love with a Turkish soldier, only for our love to *fall off a cliff*. I will be fine.'

Jessica sat and turned to face her husband.

'You can be a prize dick sometimes.'

'Sorry. I am trying to be funny, don't get annoyed.'

Jessica moved to get off the bed. Jason grabbed around her shoulders and gathered her against his chest.

'Please don't storm off. I've got a prize dick here just for you, look.'

'Piss off Jace.' She relaxed a little into his chest. 'And get me a glass of wine or you'll have no more loving from me this weekend. Let me think about your Turkey job; I retain my veto.'

*

Colleagues thought of Amara as the *big picture* manager, an out of the box, blue-sky thinker. Junior staff sometimes criticised her, privately to each other, for not *completer finishing*, setting bars too high and stretching imaginations. Changing direction and rethinking strategies late into projects. She and Jessica made a perfect team, with Jessica tracking the ebb and flow of projects, predicting bottlenecks and identifying when specialists and engineering disciplines struggled. She had a forensic approach to meetings, drilling down on detail.

Sam Smith acted more like Jessica, a *details* man. She was part of his team when he had held her current position, and they clashed. She did not need someone checking on her work – she needed a boss with a clear roadmap for Jessica to follow, a conductor, not a driving instructor. She looked at his face as he sat turned away from her. He had a neat beard, which, unusually, thought Jessica, made him look younger. He always appeared relaxed when chatting detail with the techies and IT crowd in his team, more like a Silicon Valley anorak than an international arms dealer. He left school to join the ambulance service as a paramedic, before realising selling stun grenades to foreign police was more lucrative and just as much fun.

For a short period, he was the talk of the office - rumoured to be a cross-dresser, much to the amusement of the alpha males who dominate the Company. On dress-down Fridays, he dressed up. On one particular Saturday, he came to the office to sign-off a consignment for shipment, dressed in a tight tweed skirt and white silk blouse. He wore no makeup but did wear hosiery and a pair of size nine sensible heels. The following week he took holiday leave and by the time he returned to work, it was all yesterday's news and today's fish and chip wrapper.

Jessica stood respectfully in front of his desk; she declined a seat. She noticed he wore men's brogues, but with black tights under his suit trousers. She could see his salmon camisole under the thin white, man's cotton shirt. She wondered if the panties matched. He looked at his computer monitor. Jessica studied his policy compliant non-personal photographs, mostly monster trucks and his pet snail collection, a repeat of the situation with Amara of the previous Friday. Jessica studied a photograph of juggling hands.

'Jess, good to have you on board. May I call you Jess, now?'

'Thank you, Mr Smith. I'd prefer Jessica, to be honest. But you pay this piper, by the hour, so whatever.'

Jessica now worked as a self-employed contractor. Although Sam's total renumeration package far exceeded Jessica's, with a list of perks, long paid holidays, bonuses and an industry beating pension for when he burnt-out young, his after-tax take-home salary was no bigger than hers and this niggled him. He did not like contractors.

'Of course. You are coming on board at a crucial stage. I have arranged for a senior software guy to run you through the big picture after lunch. Until then you can familiarise yourself with the file, say hello to your area team and hopefully hit the floor running. Any questions, Jess?'

Sam came to Jessica's side of the desk and sat on the polished glass and leather surface. He encroached on her personal space; way too close. He meant to intimidate her, but she held her position without stepping back. His shin brushed against her calf as he crossed his legs.

'Is that you juggling, in the photograph?'

'I meant about work, Jess.'

'No, not really. Other than, why did you ask for me. I am hardly your type.'

'What is my type?'

'A career staffer. Not a fly-by-night mercenary like me.'

'Like you, I do as I'm told. Possibly similarities between your previous project and this one, perhaps.'

'What do you know about my previous project? Do we need to discuss this with Mrs Pebbles or security?'

Sam fixed his expression.

'I'm not having this conversation with a junior contractor, Jess. You are being most unreasonable. I am pleased you are seconded; we need you here. And my welcome is genuine. Make room in your diary for a follow-up meeting later this afternoon, after you have familiarised yourself with the role. And for goodness' sake Jess, lighten up.'

Sam stood, his face almost touching Jessica's, before returning to his seat. Jessica stopped at the door.

'Sam. I am sorry; I have been rude. I will do my best for you on this one.'

He did not respond.

*

Jessica speed read the Project Plan and File. Sam had compiled the file, and there was no Project Manager or Area Manager shown. Jessica added a note to the file to run this past Quality; it was not best practice. But Sam had done a good job; detailed and concise. She ran down the list of team members, noting those who now report directly to her. She saw a familiar name under the *Disciplines* section, a software engineer who started with the Company at the same time as her. She smiled to herself and felt her cheeks blush.

She had Trish, the Floor Secretary, book a meeting room and invite her team along to say hello – starting at shift finishing time, to keep it short. Trish also cancelled Jessica's planned leave without asking and sent Jessica invites to a selection of forthcoming meetings. Jessica knew who really ran the Projects Departments, and Trish was good. Jessica left for an early lunch.

Upon her return, she saw a jet-black mop of hair sat at her desk, swinging in the guest seat.

'Onslow Dalliance! Look at you all growed up.'

'Jessica Khan, sorry, I mean Taylor. Good to see you again.'

They shook hands but did not release the grip. Eventually they sat, still holding hands. Jessica grasped his with both of hers, squeezed, and released him.

'Don't tell me you are my Senior Software guy, you're just a boy!'

'I certainly am he. I may not have had the meteoric rise you have, but I hold my own.'

'Well done, Ons. I have heard only good things. I'm glad you are on the team.'

'Likewise, Mrs T. I'm afraid we must press on; Trish has only managed to squeeze me in for ten minutes. How can I help?'

'I have read the file; all I want is your synopsis of the project. No detail, not technical, not just about the software – the entire project in a sentence or two – especially the politics that I have missed out on, and which won't reflect in the notes.'

'Yes ma'am. Ok, President Erdogan of Turkey has been asking America for a missile defence system and there has been some inertia.'

Onslow watched a flicker of recognition cross Jessica's face. Having read the file, she now realised why they seconded her.

'And so, our maverick ally popped to the shops and bought an alternative from his new mate President Putin of Russia, the S-400. Company believes Vladimir all but gave the system to Racep.'

'Why?'

'The S-400 was developed with a specific requirement in mind. It is designed to shoot down the American F-35 Stealth Jets.'

'What? No way! A NATO member has a Russian anti-aircraft system designed to shoot down NATO planes?'

'It will shoot down anything, Scuds, Exocets, MIGs, seagulls, but yes, specifically American Stealths.'

'And we think Putin has maintained some control over the system? He could shoot down F-35s, from Turkish soil, as they took-off from Turkish NATO airbases?'

'What was your previous project about, Jess? Some defence system on the carriers, wasn't it? Are we the flip side of your coin?'

'Loose words sink ships. Walls have ears, and all that.'

'Ears? Makes a change from sausages.'

Jessica smiled, crinkling her nose. Feeling herself blush again, she nodded for him to continue.

'This feels strange saying it out loud. It is so secret for so long. I had Trish check with security and with Stacy in Amara's team, before I agreed to talk with you.'

Jessica shrugged and waited.

'Ok. The UK wanted Turkey out of NATO and America wanted to nuke them. But the Turks have us over a regional barrel. They very nearly aligned with the Arabs after World War One and the Russians following World War Two. Their NATO army is massive, airbases strategic and regional influence far-reaching. A deal was dealt. We provide a plug and play to add to the Russian S-400 defence system in Turkey, hopefully raising no software warning flags with the Ruskies. We can then interfere with any attempt to use the system against NATO and interrogate the Russian kit to provide operational information to our Mediterranean fleet, to your carriers. Perhaps you know more about that, than I do. And we gather information about the Russian S-400 workings, Turkey keeps its hacked Russian defence system, Putin thinks he is being clever, and NATO remains intact. Simples.'

'Wow.'

'Jess, I've got to go. Drink sometime?'

'Sure. Thanks.'

'Soon?'

'Why not? Sure.'

*

Jessica reclined into the bubbles. She prepared the bath for when Jason first arrived home. On the way home, she grabbed his favourite takeout beer from the local pub – a draught Golden Bolt ale.

'This is nice Jess, thank you.'

Jessica ran her foot up his chest, resting it against his shoulder. He massaged the sole with his thumb before bringing it to his mouth and sucking on her toes. She sat upright to keep her breasts out of the bubbles and on show; she knew how to keep Jason in a light mood.

'I like treating my husband after a hard day of boiling oil and making petrol, or whatever you do. I want to talk about your Turkey job, but first – guess who I bumped into today?'

'No idea. Your mother?'

'No Jace! Be serious. I mean, at work. A senior member of the team, who I will work closely with over the next few months. Go on, guess.' Jason shrugged. 'Only Onslow Dalliance! Onslow, Onny, Ons, Dally; you remember.'

'If I had ever known somebody called Onslow Dalliance, it is unlikely I would forget the name. Go on then, what about him?'

'He is lovely. Capable, professional, hardworking, good laugh. I met him in Barrow-in-Furnace on an ethics course. He was on a grad-scheme when we had both just started with Company. There was a group of them. I mentioned him.'

Jessica leaned forward to top Jason's glass with beer. She stopped to kiss him.

'I wonder how many girls you have kissed without telling me. You know, in a moment of passion. Perhaps after a couple of drinks. No harm in it, just saying.'

'What are you going on about?'

'I'm just saying. Onslow and me, for instance; as an example. I remember telling you.'

'Right. Now we are getting somewhere. How well do you know this *Ons*, and how close are you now working together?'

‘Oh, hardly at all. Well, we might have pecked a kiss goodnight, once, and stuff, or something.’

‘You slept with him?’

Jessica leaned to fill her husband’s glass again, but it already brimmed with beer.

‘How do you mean? What, me and Onslow, sleep together? You really think that? Um, yes. I think we did once. I knew I had mentioned it.’

Jessica concentrated on scrubbing her foot with a flannel.

‘And you haven’t been seeing him since? Since we have been together?’

‘God no. Honest. But I will be spending a lot of time with him over the next few months, and I wanted you to know. We don’t keep secrets, so I just told you about him. See?’

‘Well, you kept this particular *previous* a secret from me, didn’t you? Any more you aren’t telling me about? How long were you seeing him?’

‘Just once. A one-night stand. A dalliance.’ Jessica looked up from scrubbing her feet to pout at her husband. ‘Don’t look annoyed. It was the first time I had stayed in a posh business hotel on expenses, and the course was boring. The grads and I got on really well in the classroom and in the evenings. I didn’t realise he was to be based in Portsmouth; I assumed he was staying in Barrow.' Jason held his poker face. Jessica scrubbed her second foot. She looked up again and smiled; he smiled back.

'No harm done. And thanks for letting me know. No regrets, I hope?'

'None. It was good fun. And when we realised, we were both to work in the Naval Base, he didn't go around bragging or anything, even though he was only young and quite immature in other ways and I was quite a catch. Although to be honest, I made the move on him.'

'You still are quite a catch, Jess.'

'Yes, I am. Thank you.'

Jessica straddled her husband, giving him a long kiss and knocking the full beer glass into the bath.

Chapter three

Jessica sent a work's email to meet Amara in the canteen, mid-morning for coffee. Amara brought Stacy along – as a witness and scribe to the conversation. They sat in the booth away from other colleagues.

'Jess darling. It is great to see you, but strictly not work, please.'

'Amara, it kind of is. But I am happy to go on record if necessary. Let me start, then we can continue with HR, Security, Contracts, Ethics, Janitor's office, you name it.'

Amara shot Stacy a glance. Stacy nodded and closed her notebook; she spoke.

'We all know the rules. Keep it general Jess, and let's take it from there. No mention of any projects, past or current.

'God, Stacy, this is like working in a George Orwell book.' Stacy opened her notebook again. 'Right. First, I shall tell you something only us three here already know. I found myself in a spot of bother in Turkey during the 2016 failed military coup. A soldier I dated died and his father arrested for plotting the assassination of the Turkish president. The Turks tried to accuse me of being involved in both incidents. While the Turkish jandarma tried to sort its shit, amongst the chaos, you two helped me slip out of Turkey and back into Greece and home.'

'Jess, I am going to stop you there. If you repeat any suggestion or inference that Mrs Pebbles, myself or any contractor, employee, or officer of Company, was involved in anything illegal or conspired to avoid lawful scrutiny, this conversation is over, and I will report you. Understood?'

'Christ Stacy, you were fucking there.'

'In that case, Jess, you don't need to fucking say it, do you?' Stacy spat back her answer, the professional veneer gone.

Amara leant back in her seat and sipped her coffee. A sign to her best friend that she had no intention of reining-in Stacy.

'Last year, I applied for a holiday visa to visit Turkey. See my beach shack that I still own. They refused my application. Now Company has approached my husband Jason to consult on a petro-chem job in Dalaman, Turkey. We don't even do petro-chem contracts. Something is going on. Company is putting Jason at risk.'

Stacy moved to end the conversation, but Amara silenced her with a raised hand.

'So, tell him not to go.'

‘Amara, I can’t tell him. He has spent years building his consultancy. He will ignore me; he is ignoring me.’

Amara leaned back for a moment, her head resting on the back of the bench seat.

‘Then let him go. The Turks are not interested in Jason. He has not even been to Turkey. Why would anyone try to get Jason in to trouble?’

The three sat in silence for a long moment. Stacy noticed Jessica’s eyes well and studied the notebook in her lap. Amara spoke with a barely noticeable shake of the head towards Stacy. Stacy closed the notebook again.

‘I love you Jess, we both do. Here’s the deal. I’ll look into why they invited Jason into the *Damp* contract, if you promise to ease back on the theatrics. You must stop criticising your managers and Company. You know how quick we can *let you go*, especially now you are a contractor.’

‘*TMBAs* Mrs Pebbles. *Damp*?’

‘You mentioned the Dalaman Additives Military Project.’

‘Not by name Amara, no. I didn’t know the name of the project. And are you and Sam talking? What makes you think I criticised him?’

Amara sat back again, looking deflated and pushing out a sigh.

'Christ, Jess, you are not an easy one to help, are you?'

Without a signal, Stacy took notes again. Amara continued.

'Mrs Taylor, I believe you are genuinely concerned about your husband, following the traumatic events we all know you suffered in Turkey. As a responsible employer, your long-term informal mentor, and until recently your team manager, I have made a decision. I hope you are in agreement. If not, we will need to escalate to HR and Ethics.'

'Ok?'

'There is a connect, a bridge, between your old *Naap* project and your new S-400 Compatibility project. I am sure you already realise. I want you involved Jess, there will be a big push on these soon. We, I, need you on board. Sam, especially, has asked for your involvement in commissioning both systems. It is a challenge and I want you to step-up. If it helps you to clear your mind and concentrate, I am prepared to talk with Contracts about deselecting Jason from *Damp,* in Dalaman.'

Jessica's chin shot-up and she stared at Amara.

'You fucking threatening me, Am?'

Amara laid a hand on Stacy's notebook.

'If you ever talk to me like that again, you ungrateful cow, I will personally ensure you never work in this industry, ever. Now get back to work or leave your ID card with reception on the way out.'

Chapter four

Jessica sat in bed; her secure work laptop open. She taped across the camera lens in case the rumours were true. Unusually for Jessica, especially following Date Night, she wore pyjamas – or an old rugby jersey she used as a security blanket, as it was. Many years ago, on her second wedding anniversary to Jason, she shared a shower with the owner, nothing more. If she had ever known his name, it was now forgotten. The smell, texture and taste transported Jessica back to hot summers and naughty games.

'Morning Bambi. I always wondered what it would be like to wake next to a rugby forward.'

'Mmm. There's an idea.' She smiled at the screen.

'I thought you couldn't bring this work home, not even on the *secure.* So, what is the real reason for the late nights and early starts?'

'Mmm. Not really. This is mandatory training and other office stuff. I still have to do it; life goes on. Then I can concentrate on the cloak and dagger during the week.'

The jersey stretched to her knees. Jason ran his hand from her shin, over her knee, towards her inner thigh. She gently raised her knee off the mattress and tucked her foot under her bottom – blocking his hand.

‘I was thinking, Jess. The last time I wasn’t laid on a Friday night, I was probably still in school uniform.’

‘Mmm. Me too.’

A minute passed. Jessica’s work iPhone beeped, and a calendar request popped open on her laptop. It was a meeting request from Jason. Jessica looked over as he returned his iPhone to the cabinet.

‘Oh Jace, I’m sorry. Come here.’

She closed the laptop and snuggled into her husband. He tried to find her bottom through the jersey; she pulled it up to help. She tugged the collar into her mouth and chewed, her voice muffled by the obstruction.

‘I normally have a break between projects. I have gone from a busy period of one, straight into a manic part of the next. I will make it up to you afterwards, promise.’

‘Good girl. But it is *us,* not just me.’

‘I know, love. Let’s have a bubble bath and a relaxing afternoon, just as soon as I finish the mandatory. Something else is stressing me. I can’t think of the words to explain it, exactly. But I have messed up with Amara.’

‘Oops. Never mix work and pleasure.’

‘I have been really rude and accusing of her and my new manager, Sam. She would have sacked anyone else who spoke as I did. Shagging the boss has probably saved my job – we may have only done it the once, but I am good. I even swore at Stacy, and you know how lovely she is.'

'I don't want to state the obvious Bambi, but yes, you are good, from what I can remember.' Jessica tilted her head to see her husband's smile. 'But seriously Jess, you need to apologise to Amara; I know how important she is to you. And not one of your *Oh I'm Jessica, everyone knows what I'm like* apologies. A proper one, including never doing it again.'

'I can't tell you what this is about, but it is not all my fault. Thanks for taking her side.'

'I don't care who's at fault. You need to *say* sorry and *be* sorry for being rude. End of. Don't lose the love of your life over a work issue. Who really cares what size bullets are best in your new cannon or who makes the best sights for your howitzers?'

'You're the love of my life, after the dog. Anyway, cannons don't have bullets and you don't aim howitzers, they aren't guns – dumbo. I am not saying this is connected, but where are you with the *Damp* work? Shit, forget I said that Jace – I mean the Dalaman job.'

'Well, well. What a complicated web we weave. I have already started.' Jessica tensed. 'I didn't mention it, partly because you are never here and because you have enough on your plate. But I might now just do the procurement from the UK. They are splitting the order for onsite construction. Perhaps they are using a bigger engineering house or a local Turkish engineer. But my offer is still in the frame.'

Jessica relaxed again.

'I'm thinking of spending a few nights in Pompey each week. It will let me concentrate without having to commute. Obviously on expenses – they owe me that much. I could also tie-in with Amara for an evening out when she stays in Portsmouth next. Stacy lives in Portsmouth as well. I might also get a couple of my team out to network and bond.'

'Don't do that, Jess. Let me drive you in early and pick you up each day. I don't mind a couple of late nights if you go out.'

'That is so sweet. But it also means I don't have to apply the mental agility between home and work; I am so overloaded.'

Jason moved his hand to the small of her back, tickling her tiny down hairs with his fingertips.

'Whatever. But not too often; we don't live all that far away.'

'I've had another thought, Jace. I like being all dirty with you. Do me now and forget about the bath.'

Jason rolled over to face his wife. She grinned wide, pushing her cheek-bones high, with eyes twinkling. He scrunched her friend's rugby jersey up her body.

'Only if you call me stupid again, for not knowing about armaments. I love it when you tell me off.'

*

Jessica threw herself into the new role. Following the meeting with Amara and on advice from Jason, she knuckled down and concentrated on the new project. She started earlier in the morning and worked later in the evening. Her direct area team was supportive and both Trish and Onslow guided her towards those parts of the project which needed her attention. She even took an old snail shell, which her dog Brian had brought to show her from the garden, into work for Sam; it spiralled anticlockwise. He asked to keep it.

Jessica called in a big favour. Phoning Stacy at home, she asked for a warning when Amara next went to the canteen. Taking a late lunch, Jessica waited by the stairs and followed Amara from the lifts. Stacy had opted to accompany Amara to stretch her legs. Pushing into the queue for salads, Jessica stood behind her colleagues.

'May I join you?'

'Hey Jess! Yes, sweetheart. So glad to see you.'

The three women sat together.

‘Not that it’s any of my business, but I hear you are doing an excellent job. Keeping the guys on their toes and impressing Sam. Go girl.’

Jessica beamed back.

‘You taught me well, Amara.’ Jessica dropped her gaze, looking at her lap. ‘And can I just say…’

‘Jess, let’s say nothing. Love means never having to say sorry.’

Spontaneously, the three women held hands across the canteen table.

‘But I am sorry, to you both.’

Onslow cleared his throat.

‘Sorry Mrs Pebbles, ladies, may I join you? I never normally use the canteen and don’t want to sit alone. I haven’t had time to cook at home since Mrs Taylor took over!’

Onslow did not report to Jessica directly, but she set the targets he needed to achieve.

‘Go for it, young man.’ Amara slightly over pronounced her words. A second-generation Nigerian, whose parents expected her intonation to cut crystal. ‘And you are?’

Onslow sat with a bowl of salad. Jessica spoke.

‘This is Onslow Dalliance, Mrs Pebbles. We go way back to grad-scheme days and now find ourselves on the same floor. Ons is Mr Big in software, on my project – an absolute godsend.'

'We have met, Mrs Pebbles. You took two training sessions I attended. I remember you well, a wonderful speaker. You won't remember me.'

'Sorry son. I am the only black lesbian working for Company, I have an advantage.'

She laughed at her own comment. Jessica and Stacy raised a hand to their mouths, and Onslow blushed deeply.

'Oh, grow some balls, you lot! I must leave you now; I only popped down for a takeout.'

With a huge grin and patting Jessica and Onslow on the shoulder, Amara stood, followed by Stacy. Jessica smiled and winked at Amara. Onslow continued to blush. Before leaving, she spoke to Jessica.

'Jess love, I had a chat with Contracts. Remind me to update you. It is looking good.'

Amara and Stacy left with lunch and coffee.

'Wow. That was awkward. Not as PC as I expected her to be.'

'She is great Ons. But don't underestimate her – she breaks balls. We fell out recently and today I think we cleared the air. God, I hope so; she is so special.'

'Tell me to mind my own business, Jess, but rumour is you two …'

'Mind your own business Ons!'

They sat in silence, except for Onslow chewing on his Caesar Salad. The quieter he tried to be, the more noise he made.

'Jess, that drink. I was thinking …'

'Tonight? Sure. Shall we invite a few from the team? Will your other half come along?'

'I'm single. But we could …'

'No probs. Just us two then. Do you know the Pilgrims Bar in Old Portsmouth? Say eight o'clock? I'm staying in Pompey tonight, so I will only have this to wear. But…' Jessica tailed off.

'Perfect. See you there.'

Jessica shrugged and played with her phone.

Chapter five

Jessica arrived at the meeting room a couple of minutes early. Onslow's software engineer and Jessica's project engineer sat at the table. Onslow pushed his chair back, so it impinged on the space around the adjacent seat. Rather than select another, Jessica sat in the chair close to Onslow. She smelt the nutty oil he used in his hair and had a rush of memory from their first encounter. She realised she wore a cheesy grin and, as she tried to stifle it, worried she might giggle.

'Don't you just love these model reviews, goodness I can't wait. I realise the protocol is for the projects department to run the models, but as software is so painfully boring, Mr Dalliance has agreed for his people to hold our hand.' Another smirk crossed her face, and she straightened her laptop to distract herself. She gestured to the young project engineer. 'We will still add notes ourselves and agree actions – I am not relinquishing control.'

Her audience laughed. Onslow spoke.

'Thank you, Mrs Taylor. To interpret Mrs Taylor's introduction – projects department just isn't clever enough to understand this model.'

There was more laughter, and the young project engineer held up his hands in mock indignation. Engel was British from German parents; he preferred his name, Engelbirt, shortened following years of fun-poking at school. The software engineer spoke. Her accent thick Punjabi.

'Today, we are looking at the firewall system between the Russian's S-400 software and our own.'

The software engineer tapped her laptop and parts of the model showing on the huge HD screen tumbled away, leaving the computer-generated lines and boxes of the firewall section under review. Jessica spoke.

'Sorry Pun, I must be getting old, can you speak extra slow and clear for me please?'

Pun's face lit up with a toothy grin as she replied in an exaggerated London accent.

'Sure Mrs Taylor. I'll do you me best cockerney.'

The others laughed again.

'And my last interruption before we delve into this black art. Why is there only around three per cent action points from the previous review? I mean well done and everything, but that seems unusually low.'

The two experienced engineers looked to Onslow.

'Well spotted Mrs Taylor. I will give you my version of events. Sam Smith may confirm or clarify it further. Basically, our team manager, Mr Smith, took a tremendous interest in the earlier model reviews and actions. He allocated resource to mop up early, he wanted it *right first time.* Wait for it, he actually sat with us and helped to make program changes.'

Onslow looked to his software engineer, who nodded in agreement.

'And that made commercial sense, resourcing the work so early as the system was still in development? And is he even skilled enough to touch the bloody thing?'

'No and no Mrs Taylor. But hey-ho. We spent more time checking his contributions than we saved by him helping; I even raised a separate cost centre for the extra work. But it is his budget at the end of the day.' Jessica made to speak, but Onslow continued. 'And I will say two more things. It has turned out to be a good call, in this instance. The project bounded ahead of schedule as a result. And also, our Mr Smith is actually a very competent programmer. I will still raise it in my closeout report, but the proof of this pudding is in the eating. Fair play to him.'

Jessica's lips moved as if she were about to ask more, but in the end, she just shrugged.

'Oh well, who needs software and project departments when you have Sam Smith running the show.' More laughter from the meeting. 'Ok folks, lets engross ourselves in a load of squiggles and boxes. At least with a model review of a ship, we can see which way the pointed end goes.'

*

Jessica sat in a dingy booth to the rear of The Pilgrims Bar in Spice Island, a historic part of Old Portsmouth opposite the Anglican Cathedral. She ordered herself a large prosecco and added a double brandy – not really a school night drink. She also ordered her guest a Sol Lager with a slice of lime pushed into the bottleneck. She asked the bored bartender for a damp cloth and rubbed the smelly rag over the sticky table and brushed over the worn bench seats. Returning the cloth, she went to the lavatory to wash her hands. Deciding to remove her bra from under the work shirt, she also wiped under her arms with a damp paper towel. She removed an Impulse deodorant from her bag, as two local girls entered and staggered towards the single cubical.

'Excuse me, love. Can I just say?' The young lady gestured to Jessica's buttons. 'You are all lopsided.'

A little unsteadily, the girl unbuttoned and re-buttoned Jessica's shirt as her friend watched, hiccupping.

'Not Impulse love, save that for your husband.'

Hiccupping girl roared with laughter as button girl produced a bottle of Jean Paul Gaultier and misted Jessica's neck, pulling forward the shirt to add a squirt to her small cleavage.

'There! Your bit on the side will be gagging for it. Good luck. But he'll never leave his wife, you know? Because of the kiddies …'

She tailed off, taking a step back, before leaning forward and loosening Jessica's top button.

'God, is it really that obvious? It's just a drink with an old friend.'

The girl shrugged.

'We don't get posh totty like you in here, unless they are keeping out the way of their posh friends. Now you have yourself a fun night.'

The two disappeared into the cubicle.

Jessica sat back in the booth facing towards the bar. In the bar mirror, she saw the pub door open and Onslow enter; his arm extended around a young woman to reach the door handle. She stood taller than Jessica, willowy and confident. She stopped for a second to speak with Onslow in the opened doorway. Jessica thought they might kiss.

Jessica realised she was grinding her teeth. She looked at the Sol beer, feeling stupid; Onslow and his friend would think her little joke ridiculous. She sat in a slightly see-through blouse with no bra, in a seedy Pompey pub a short walk from the dockyard, smelling of another woman's perfume; her mother had a name for married women like her. If the couple moved to the snug bar on their righthand side, Jessica would make her escape; she would have to move fast.

Instead, the couple made their way to Jessica's side of the bar, towards the booth. Onslow loitered a little behind his companion, swiping his phone. The woman stopped at the bar immediately past the booth, placing her bag on the counter and making a joke with the bartender. Onslow walked into her back and they both laughed as Onslow stepped backwards, apologising. Jessica saw a tiny window of opportunity to slip out behind them, but her phone chimed and Onslow spun around.

'Hey Jess! I just texted to say I'm early, but you are even earlier. You ok, looks like you've seen a ghost?'

Jessica nodded. Her heart pounding. Onslow pointed at the Sol and roared with laughter.

'You remembered, that is so funny. I haven't drunk that for years. Don't tell me you are still on Archers and Lemonade?'

Before Jessica could respond, his companion squeezed between them and leant over the table. Jessica instinctively stood to meet the woman halfway, put her hand on the woman's shoulder, and kissed her cheek. The woman froze as Jessica sat back down.

'Hi. I am Jessica, please call me Jess. I work with Onslow as you probably know.' She forced a weak smile.

The young woman slowly straightened.

'Hi. I'm Dusky. I will be your bartender for the evening. I'm just lighting your candle, then I'll leave you alone to enjoy your colleague. I like your perfume.'

Jessica clasped both hands to her face. Muffled through her fingers, she shrieked.

'Oh no! I'm so sorry. I thought you two were together.'

The evening bartender smiled sweetly. Onslow laughed; so much so, he took an involuntary step backwards before clasping Jessica in both arms and pulling her into a hug from where she sat.

'Oh Jessica Khan! Never a dull moment.'

*

'Onslow, I feel such a fool. I saw you in the doorway and assumed you knew each other.'

'I reached to pull the door open for her, but it is a push door. We ended up closer together than I intended. That is the extent of our relationship.'

Jessica clasped her hands to her face again.

'Why me? Life is so unfair and always when I am trying to impress.'

'Impress who? Me?'

'No, no. Not impress as such. I mean, to appear normal. Did I say impress? I meant to say, act normal. And where are you living now, I guess you live in Portsmouth?'

‘I’ve been in Pompey since first moving here after the, our, training.’ Jessica nodded, willing her cheeks not to blush. ‘They were renting dead posh flats in the *lipstick* tower to critical workers. A nurse rented, claimed her right to buy and then sold it on. I don’t mean to show off, but really impressive.’

‘Wow. In the Gunwharf development? That is so cool. I’d have loved to have one of them as a bachelor pad.’

‘We’ll have to pop in later; you can have a look around. It doesn’t overlook the harbour, but still quite a view. Next time you need to stay in the city, you must stay at mine.’

‘That’s lovely. Thanks. How many bedrooms?’

‘Just the one, Jess. You’ll love it.’ Jess nodded. ‘And you all settled down? Where is your place?’

‘I am Mrs Domestic. Late eighteen century brick and flintstone cottage, two beds. As in two bedrooms, I mean, not like two separate beds. Well, two beds as well, obviously, like one in each bedroom. Anyway, big garden, semi-rural, climbing rose, dog, bread maker. Near Chichester, not normally too far for work. But just at the moment …’ Jessica gestured at the gap between them. Onslow frowned. ‘As in the busy project we are both on.’ She made the gesture again to clarify.

‘Understood. Husband?’

‘No way Onslow! Congratulations. I had no idea. Well, after we first met, why would I …’

‘I’ll stop you there, Jess. I already told you I am single. I was asking if you have a husband. I assume you have, or had, with the name change to Taylor.’

‘Sorry Ons. My head is all over the place. So busy at work.’

‘You were saying Jess? Husband?’

‘Sorry. Yes. Lovely guy. No kids, or none that I know of.’ Jessica laughed at her own joke. ‘Actually, that joke doesn’t really work for a girl, does it?’

‘Go on then. Tell me about the lucky guy.’

‘Oh, I don’t know, Ons. He’s ok, gets on my t …, nerves sometimes. He is chasing a job I don’t want him to take. But he is nice. A few years older than us. Dead funny and loyal, even though he is actually quite hot and could have any girl. Like really handsome. Plays guitar. Doesn’t like my mum, but then neither do I. Don’t know what else to say, really. He makes me feel safe. He puts up with my shit. He told me to make-up with Amara. Brian, my dog, loves him. He offered to drive me to work every day, because I’m so busy and tired, but he doesn’t want me to be lonely in a hotel room. We laugh so much; he’ll laugh at the barmaid thing when I tell him. He is so cool. Sometimes I can’t decide if I am on my life’s journey with him, or if he is my destination. Do you know, he has never hurt my feelings, ever. Except when he called me Tess on our first date.'

Jessica looked to see Onslow smiling. She smiled back and took his hand across the table.

'As it's a work night Jess, I think a nightcap, and then I'll walk you to the hotel. You must see my flat – text next time you and Mr Taylor are shopping at Gunwharf.'

*

Jessica left her desk and weaved diagonally through the various project sections towards Sam Smith's office. Amongst the general office hubbub, she saw Onslow making a similar trajectory from the opposite corner. She regulated her speed to arrive at the gatekeeper's desk together. Trish smiled but did not look up from her monitor.

'Good morning Mrs Taylor, Onslow.'

Trish and Jessica were friends in and out of work – but this was business. Onslow made towards the Team Manager's door.

'One minute, Onslow. I will call you once Mr Smith is ready.'

Onslow dropped his shoulders and moved towards the waiting area seats. Jessica stifled a smirk. Trish leaned forward onto her desk and turned to face Onslow.

'No need to take a seat. He won't be long.' She turned back to the monitor.

As Jessica walked over to Onslow, he widened his eyes in exaggerated disbelief.

'Bloody witches.'

The Floor Secretaries were referred to collectively as the coven. Demarcation was total, and nothing happened without their nod of approval. They were all generations of the same person – keen, bright, female, and college educated, no graduates. They joined the company from school, groomed by the other witches, and stayed in position for their entire careers. They wore a uniform of pencil skirts for the younger women and a more relaxed skirt for the over forties, seamed stockings and high heels, buttoned blouses and jackets, which were always worn in the corridors outside of their own office floor, even in summer. Retirement parties always well attended and lavish.

Jessica previously project managed an important recruitment weekend for a fellow team member, with a rugby theme. As part of the networking, he arranged a fun five-a-side evening with various suppliers, sponsors and training providers playing against his Company teams, grouped by sections and departments. Jessica played in the project team. As a result, management cautioned Amara for allowing a culture of subterfuge and *teams within teams,* such is the paranoia within the company. However, the coven meets openly in the canteen every Friday morning for coffee and cakes – presumably to discuss how best to ruin the career of a manager or executive who is not towing their line; Jessica wondered if her previous outburst and swearing at Stacy got a mention over Bakewell Tart and Darjeeling. Both Trish and Stacy denied all of this to Jessica even after a few drinks out. Despite the negativity, they ran the huge international arms dealership like clockwork and with accountability; the department well respected and the individuals loved by others. If an employee slipped up, it was normally the witches that sorted the fallout.

There was no signal from the office. Trish had not even looked around, but at a seemingly random moment, she invited the two to knock on the team manager's door.

'Time to see the headmaster, for six of the best.'

'I'm sure you would both enjoy that, Ons.'

*

Sam sat behind his desk. Amara sat towards the end of his desk, facing the two empty seats.

'Please sit.'

Onslow sat as Jessica remained standing. Amara fired a glare; Jessica took her seat.

'Goodness. I have my A-Team together.'

'I was thinking the same, Mr Smith. You and Mrs Pebbles on the same floor, this must be serious.'

Sam and Amara acknowledged Jessica's observation with a nod of heads.

'Yes, it is unusual. I had to ask Trish to swipe and escort me in. Strange to think we are all on the same side, sometimes.'

Despite clearing the air with her best friend, Amara still acted aloof and more assertive with Jessica than usual. Her last observation aimed directly at Jessica, although the other two colleagues would not have realised.

'First, I shall address an unanswered question posed earlier by Jess. Yes, those are my hands juggling in the photograph.' Sam gestured to the picture decorating his wall. 'Which brings me nicely to why Mrs Pebbles and I have invited you in. I think it is fair to say we are all competent in what we do and in our own way. But equally, we all approach life differently.' Sam adjusted the strap of his lacy camisole under his shirt. 'And that makes this the A-Team.' He gestured to the full group of four with a grin. 'We want you both to form a small team to work within the Commissioning team. We want you to overlook the installation of a bridge between our S-400 Compatibility project and the aircraft carrier *Naap* project.'

'Sorry, *Naap*?'

Amara answered. 'Jessica's previous project, Onslow. Jessica can bring you up to speed later once she understands the extent of *Bridge* and identifies your scope, within it.'

Jessica sounded irritated.

'Hang on. A team within a team? Is that acceptable now, suddenly? Why is Commissioning not installing Bridge? Do they even know about this little *team* of ours?'

'Obviously I cannot speak for Mrs Taylor, but …'

'Then fucking don't Ons.' Jessica's neck tightened, and she straightened in her chair, pulling herself to her full sitting height, towards Onslow.

'Oh, a lovers' tiff. Do you two need to get a room?' Sam swung back in his seat. He divided and ruled with little effort. Jessica glared at Amara, disbelieving she had not called out Sam's inappropriate simile. Amara spoke.

'Jessica, you need to temper your language and we all,' Amara gestured between Sam and herself, 'need to use less inflammatory pros. And we three need to stop bickering in front of the nerd department.'

Onslow and Sam both laughed at the last comment, Amara throwing a verbal hand grenade into her professional-speak. Jessica mumbled an apology towards Onslow.

'Don't apologise Jessica, we are all arms dealers, whatever it says in the brochure.' Amara's comment brought at least three of the four colleagues closer together again. 'Onslow, we are still to hear your thoughts.'

'I was just going to say, from my own point of view, I am more than happy to give it a whirl. I work equally for development, projects and commissioning. But I realise I do not have the same demarcation, ethics and security responsibilities that you brain boxes have. I'm just a nerd, a tool in your toolbox. Plus, it will get me out of this dump for a bit.'

'I have to agree with you, Onslow.' Amara spoke again. 'This place reminds me of the Prisoner television series sometimes. Just the other day, a friend suggested it is like working in a George Orwell book. I think it is more like being in a recurring Patrick McGoohan nightmare. Sometimes a break is as good as a rest, and I actually quite envy you both this opportunity; the chance to breathe some fresh air.' Jessica realised her friend also aimed this comment her way.

Jessica stared towards the window, situated one floor below Amara and with an almost identical view. HMS Victory dominated the vista, flags and pennants blowing in the sea breeze. For hundreds of years, the Royal Navy and its erstwhile political leaders forged alliances with others, did backroom deals and when all else failed, blew its adversaries off the face of the planet. Eventually Jessica spoke her response, softly and evenly.

‘Oh, what the fuck? If Onslow is in, I am in. Excuse my French, Mrs Pebbles.’

Onslow and Jessica left the office. Onslow’s head held high, Jessica looking at the floor ahead, her brow in deep furrows. They passed Trish’s desk.

‘Just a minute, please. I have something for you both. May I have your swipe ID cards please?’ As the two unclipped the cards from the lanyards, Trish handed them two seemingly identical passes. ‘Whilst you have been hobnobbing, estates department has erected you a temporary secure office in the top left corner of this floor, with your own swipe lock. How cosy for you both. I am afraid you are still mine, though. Why not grab a long lunch? They will install your desks and computers before 3pm, all ready to go. I have cleared your diaries of the S-400 meetings. Welcome to Bridge.’

Chapter six

Jessica and Onslow walked into the June sunshine towards HMS Victory, Admiral Nelson's Flagship for the battle of Trafalgar and still a serving Royal Navy commissioned warship. Onslow had a spring in his step and Jessica looked towards the ground.

'I love it here. Sea and fresh air.'

'Or shitty seaweed and tar.'

Onslow stopped walking. Jessica took a further two steps before halting to look back.

'What?'

'Come here, Jess.'

Jessica ignored the instruction; Onslow moved to her. He placed his hands on her shoulders and spun her around until the sun shone directly into her eyes. She closed them against the glare. Standing behind her, he placed his left hand across her lower stomach, his right hand on her chest.

'I am not sure this is in the employee's handbook.'

'You're a contractor, now shush. Relax your shoulders. Seriously Jess, for once do as you are told.'

Jessica shook her arms and dropped her shoulders.

‘Now, as you breathe, can you feel your chest against my hand?’

‘If you want to feel my tits Ons, you only have to ask. For old times’ sake.’

‘I will take that as a yes. Keep breathing. Now, for the next few breaths, I want you to lower your breathing. Feel your chest still against my hand and feel your belly push my hand up as you breathe in, and my hand pushing down on your belly as you breathe out. That’s a start, but concentrate, now deeper.’

‘I said I’d let you feel my tits, I never mentioned getting in my pants.’

‘Try to shut up talking, best you can. And breathe. And breathe. That’s better.’

The couple stood in position for one minute.

‘Now, Jess, tell me what you can smell.’

‘I can smell the sea, actually, you are right. I can still smell the seaweed, sweet, like my nan’s red cabbage. I can smell the tar and hemp. And rusty steel. I can smell clay and wooden sleepers. Canvas. Coal. Seagull poo and fish, or fishy seagull poo. Something else, metallic, like clear water or something, like sunshine. Ozone perhaps. I can smell your hair.’

Onslow took his hand away from her chest. She held his wrist against her stomach as she opened her eyes and orientated herself.

'You're the boss, Jess. But I think we should walk around the historic waterfront, look at HMS Prince of Wales, walk over to Gunwharf for a coffee and panini on the front, or a coffee with a bag of crisps and a view at mine. Then walk back to our new cell of an office to lock ourselves away for a few months. And I need to ask for a favour, please boss. I need you to convince me I am doing the right thing and I am not jeopardising my career by putting all my eggs into a Jessica shaped basket.'

The couple flashed their cards at the Victory security and walked ahead of the organised group gathering at the entrance. Jessica leant back against the huge mast that penetrated the decks from above.

'Am I really being such a shit? Do you think I can't hold it together? If they leave me alone, I am fine, but they just keep goading me. I want to do things properly. Even Amara Pebbles is on my case. Even my husband wants to take risks and do the opposite of what I tell him to do. I was fine on *Naap,* I was doing a good job. Even on S-400 compatibility, I was doing fine – adding value to the project. But I am not one of his bloody juggling balls.'

'Him, her, they?'

'I am not paranoid, Ons. I am working through a few shocks. I got into trouble in Turkey back in 2016 and last year my husband was seriously ill. But I'm doing fine. I just want things to settle. What? What is that look for?'

‘Jessica Taylor wanting things to settle? That isn’t the reputation I am aware of.’

Jessica let out a long sigh. Leaning against the mast, she straightened her legs and took a dozen *Onslow* deep breaths.

‘I know what you mean. I push boundaries and whine when they break. But that is who I am and why I’m so good at my job. There is nowhere to hide when I am firing on all cylinders. This is none of your business Ons and I am not confiding in you, but I’m barely talking to the two loves of my life at the moment. That isn’t helping.’

‘Who, me and your dog?’

Jessica threw her head back and laughed.

‘My husband and Amara. This goes no further. I have said enough. I’ve never failed. I don’t want this stupid job, but I do want to succeed. Sam and Amara have made it clear; I do this or I do nothing.’ She sighed again. ‘How say we knuckle down for a month? If I feel it slipping away, I will chuck in my hand and take full responsibility.’

‘And stop kissing bar girls?’

Jessica laughed again, dropping her gaze in embarrassment. She grabbed his arms with both hands and shook him playfully, holding onto his arm as they left the Victory.

*

‘Blimey Mrs Taylor. That is what you call a big boat.’

The couple moved from the edge of the exclusion zone for the HMS Prince of Wales and continued past the historic boat yards and maritime museums. Jessica decided she would ask Onslow to accompany her around the HMS Warrior one evening, when she next stayed over; it looked impressive by floodlight. She would not mention it to Jason. It might sound too much like a date, which of course it was not.

‘You sound like my husband. It is a ship, not a boat. The Gosport ferry is a boat. Queen Elizabeth Class Aircraft Carriers are ships.’

‘Whatever. So has he got a name, or is that top secret?’

‘Not a secret that I am aware of. HMS Prince of Wales, public knowledge. Although I think technically, it is still a *she*, even with a man’s name.’

‘I meant your husband. Has your husband got a name, other than Mr Taylor?’

Jessica giggled and shook his arm again.

‘You are so funny, Ons, of course he has. But we must brush up on our communication skills. And when we get all security isolated together and in close quarters over the next few weeks, we must still maintain formalities. Still Mrs Taylor around the office. I know it's silly. Especially after we, well, everything and that, but that's the way it is. Obviously not after work.' Jessica tailed off.

They continued in silence, both waving to children on the water taxi.

'Right, one more time. Jess, what is your husband's given name, please?'

'Jason. Shit, Jason.'

'Ok I…'

Jessica let go of Onslow and performed a high wave to a couple sat outside a café. The man waved back and stood. Jessica recognised the woman from Contracts. Onslow followed her to the table.

'Jess! I have been keeping an eye out for you. I was actually in your building earlier.' Looking at his companion, he added. 'If I'm allowed to say that. This security is so complicated.'

'That's fine.' Both women answered together.

The woman stood and offered a hand to Jessica.

'Mrs Taylor. I do recognise you. I am not sure we have spoken directly.'

Jessica smiled, studying the woman's face. She was pretty. Very pretty. She stood a couple of inches shorter than Jessica, a couple of years younger. A couple of pounds lighter. Similar features to Jessica, possibly mixed heritage like Jessica. She looked like Jessica had when Jason first fell in love with her.

'I'm Priti Khan.'

'Goodness, Khan is my maiden name. What a coincidence. This is Onslow,' looking at Priti, she added, 'he is one of us. And this is my husband, Jason.'

As hands shook across the table, Jessica took Jason's hand to shake. Realising, she gripped it harder and shrieked with embarrassed laughter. Leaning across the table, she gave him a peck on the lips, trying hard to control her giggling.

'You must think I am mad Onslow. If I'm not kissing bar girls, I'm shaking hands with my husband.' All eyes looked at Jessica. 'I'm not sure why I said that. A long story. Anyway, what are you guys up to?'

Jason looked at Priti.

'I'm not sure what we can say, Jess.'

'You can answer your fucking wife without permission, for a start.' Jessica's answer a growl.

Priti and Onslow looked down at their laps. Jason looked directly at Jessica.

'As you know Jessica, I am doing some consultancy for Company and I was agreeing some supplier invoices with Priti in Contracts. After lunch, I have a milestone meeting. All I meant was, oh forget it.'

‘That came out wrong. Sorry everyone, I was just messing with my husband. Not very professional of me. Ons and I are on our way to his, on our way to Gunwharf for lunch if you want to join us. Actually, forget that. I’m heading back to the office. Nice to meet you properly, Priti. And I guess I will see you men, later.’

Chapter seven

'And so, the charade for the day begins.' Onslow sat at the meeting table in the secure Bridge office; Jessica at her desk. 'I invite you to another model review and copy Trish. Trish books our own office for us, that only you and I work in, and sends a confirmation. I then explain something you don't understand. You authorise me to take the actions I have told you I need to take. Madness.'

Jessica moved to the seat next to Onslow, opposite the HD screen.

'There is an alternative Ons. Get yourself a job at Currys PC World and leave all this to the grownups. These protocols are in place to ensure we follow best practice with nothing missed. And they protect Company and us if something goes wrong. Also, our replacements can pick up the pieces and continue the project if we both get run over by a bus or fall off your balcony, doing goodness knows what. Now, what have you got for me?'

'That told me. Today, Mrs Taylor, we are looking at the firewall protecting Bridge from S-400 Compatibility and *Naap*. Crucially, this also protects Bridge's location and existence being detected by the other two systems, their operators and the Turkish and Russian spies, blah di blah di bloody blah. Except we are the spies, I guess.'

A section of the project flow diagram spiralled dramatically and filled the screen, showing only that part under review.

'A couple of questions, please. Do you guys stay up late playing with the graphics to look like something from Star Wars? And second, why is that line in amber?'

'Shame on you, Mrs Taylor. There is a sequence to follow. I run various scenarios and together we watch, enthralled by my genius. Then we look at anything which needs looking at, against the job specification. We don't just zoom in on something because you like the shade of yellow.'

'I have a reason for asking. And strictly speaking, it is I who drives the model, I just don't know how.'

Onslow sighed dramatically.

'If there are no objections from the meeting?'

He strained his neck to look around the empty conference table, before hovering his curser over the line showing in amber.

'That is odd. It is a utilities, but it has no designation. We will get to it again during the review, but I will need to run a diagnostic.'

'Utilities? What, like your software has hot and cold running water and a flushing loo?'

'Mmm. Something like that.'

‘Ons?’

‘Sorry, Mrs Taylor, that really is odd. Anyway, a utility might run a warning light or turn a fan on. Mundane, but still important. Oddly, this seems to run out of Bridge, but doesn’t go anywhere. You said you had a reason for asking?’

‘There was a similar undesignated amber line going nowhere on the S-400 firewall review.’

Onslow tapped his laptop.

‘No there wasn’t Mrs Taylor. Nothing on the actions.’

‘I am telling you there was. I was there, remember?’

‘You need to get out more, Jess, and not just to that Pilgrims dive. Even I don’t remember reviews in that much detail.’ He tapped a message on his laptop. ‘I’ve asked our guys to pop in.’

Almost immediately, the door knocked. Onslow closed the Bridge diagram from the screen and switched off the engaged light for their office, calling in the guests.

‘Take a seat, guys. Mrs Taylor and I are having a bet. Be careful how you answer. This could cost me dearly. During the one hundred per cent S-400 Compatibility firewall review, did we look at an errant utilities line leaving the system and going nowhere?’

Jessica's project engineer, Engel, moved to open his laptop. Onslow continued.

'No cheating, no looking at the actions. From memory only, please.'

Pun spoke. 'Yes, Mr Dalliance. It popped up at the start before we drove the model. In fact, you made a comment about it being a poor start to the review. We would have checked it when checking utilities. There will be an action, probably a diagnostic.'

'And you remember the action? Did you run the diagnostic?'

Pun thought for several seconds. She made to speak before scrunching her forehead into a frown and hesitating.

'I am sure I would have; why not? But no, I can't remember doing it specifically. The model was so up together, I don't remember running any diagnostics, just straightening a couple of command dead legs. No utilities.'

'Damn Pun. The magnum of champagne is coming out of your wages. Off you go now, back on your heads. And I guess Mrs Taylor wants this conversation recorded onto the project file please.'

Jessica nodded towards Engel.

Alone again, Onslow opened the firewall model.

'Shall we press on with the review proper, Jess? Beer is on me, on the way home. Good call.'

'You laugh at me for staring at stuff I don't understand. Actually, I am probably staring at you, more.' Onslow smiled. 'All of you, I mean, Onslow, don't flatter yourself. I pick up on the things you all react to. Normally nothing to worry about, but every so often alarm bells ring. You had mentioned the erroneous line on the previous review, and Pun looked surprised back then. Teamwork.'

Onslow ran the scenarios through the model, and Jessica added comments to the action report as they progressed. The review took six hours and when they emerged for coffee, most of the main floor had left for home. They returned to close the review, hopefully getting away before ten o'clock.

'That utilities error did not show during the body of the review. Take me back to the overview again and let's have one last look, please.'

Onslow tapped on the keyboard and mumbled to himself.

'The boss wants to look at an error, which doesn't actually exist, and boss always gets what she wants.'

The initial view vortexed onto the screen, without showing the original error.

'Now that is weird, Mrs Taylor. My guess is, the error is from another section of the system, say controls which are full of utilities. It was resolved during development of, say, controls, but a ghost image remained on this section until we ran this part of the model. Still odd though.'

'Oh well, Onslow, if that is your guess, we will go to production on that assumption, shall we?'

'Yeah, I guess so, boss.'

'No Onslow, we won't! I want your resource plan by tomorrow afternoon, please, for me to take to Mr Smith for additional funding. We might have to involve the Chennai office. I want that error found and a guarantee it is sorted. You better have deep pockets, I'm thirsty.'

*

'Prosecco and brandy?'

'Ons! You will get me a terrible reputation. I will just have a pinot, please? Make it large; you owe me. Actually, make it a bottle.'

Onslow laughed before responding.

'Oh, sorry. You mean it.'

He returned with a bottle of beer. The bartender followed with the wine, ice bucket, and two glasses. One was to remain dry.

'You know how to spoil a girl. This place is lovely, better than the dump I took you to. I'm guessing by the name, this used to be a customs house.'

The bartender spoke.

'I'll leave you lovebugs alone. Just shout if you need anything, Onny. Punching above your weight tonight sweetheart.'

She wiggled her hips as she walked away.

'Not funny Cath! My boss, actually. Sorry Jess, this is my local; she thinks she is being funny.'

Jessica leant up to Onslow's ear, her lips brushing his lobe. She placed one hand on his neck and whispered.

'This will get her thinking, then.'

Before sinking back into her seat with a smirk.

'You are such a live wire, Jess. At work, you stare me down for any informality. Out of work you are like a teasing sister.'

'Yep. Jason always says I work hard and play hard. I know I compartmentalise as well. Work/play. Home/out. Wife/lover.' She grinned before her expression froze. She clarified, 'I mean a wife and lover to Jason, obviously. You know, homemaker and whore …'

'Jess, I understood.' Onslow looked around the bar for inspiration to change the subject of conversation. 'Not running tonight? Where do you go, normally?'

'Too late tonight, even for me. Let me think. Monday, I stayed on the base. There is a kind of informal road track around the perimeter, which the matlows run. I was following a gorgeous marine around. He thought I was racing; I was actually just trying to keep up. I love a military type.'

Jessica laughed, before realising she had brought the conversation back to sex again.

'And Tuesday and Wednesday I turned left out of Unicorn Gate.'

Unicorn Gate was one of the three Naval Base main security gates. Turning left signified heading towards the Portsea district, the inner city and housing estates. Turning right, headed towards the historic hard and Spice Island, aspiring Gunwharf Quays and gentrified Southsea.

'I ran the badlands of Buckland, Landport, Fratton, Somerstown, Eastney and back along the beach to my hotel next to you. A long run, but I needed it. We've been holed up in that office together for the best part of six weeks. And to think they promised us fresh air.'

'Jess! You can't run around those areas after dark dressed in your tiny top and shorts, flashing everything. What are you thinking?'

‘Onslow, my friend. You have just overstepped the mark.’

Jessica stood, accidentally knocking over her chair. Onslow jumped to his feet, grabbing her wrist.

‘Jess, I am sorry. None of my business; I just, care. Please don’t go.’

Jessica stared at his hand, saying nothing, until he released her wrist. She stared for a moment longer as Onslow shifted his weight. Eventually, she made eye contact.

‘Do not order me around again, ever, and show some respect. And pick up my chair; a girl doesn’t throw her chair and pick it up herself.’

Onslow rushed around the table and stood her chair. They sat in silence for a full five minutes as Jessica poured wine and gestured to the staring bartender for another beer, for Onslow.

‘Jason says I am reckless. I will run along the front from now on, but no, it is none of your business.’

‘Sorry. It won’t happen again.’ Changing subject again, ‘Are you staying in Pompey every night? You can’t live more than an hour from here.’

‘Forty minutes outside of rush hour. Probably less this time of night. I am staying down a couple of nights each week.’

‘Only a couple? You just mentioned three nights out running, and this is the fourth. Time flies when you are having fun.’

Jessica picked at the label of the wine bottle.

‘Just weeknights.’ She lowered her voice, concentrating on a corner of the label. ‘I stay here Monday to Friday night. I go home on Saturday morning. I return Sunday afternoon, ready for an early start on Monday.’

‘You are making a huge sacrifice for these bastards, Jess.’ Onslow tilted his head in the direction of the Naval Base. ‘Aren’t you lonely? Don’t you miss him?’

‘Brian the dog?’ Jessica refilled the wine glass. ‘Yes, Ons, I do feel lonely, and I do miss Jason. Especially on Saturday afternoons.’

*

Jessica lay in bed, sucking the corner of her rugby jersey. She brought the remaining third of a bottle of wine back to her hotel room, but now it stood empty on the side. She dropped her hand to her stomach under the jersey, running her fingertips around her naval. She slowly scraped her fingernail over her skin in an increasing circle – higher on her torso and lower towards her legs. With her free hand, she scrolled through her phone contacts, starting with *A* for Amara. Her thumb hovered above the contact number for Onslow. Her other hand slid further down her body and rested between her legs. She pushed dial and speaker, laying the phone across her chest.

'Jess. What time is it? What's up, are you ok?'

'Sure. I am fine. Just a bit lonely. Around one o'clock, I guess. What are you up to?'

'You know, sleeping. Sure you are ok? You sound, tipsy. I fell asleep as soon as I hit the pillow; so busy at work.'

'You sound sleepy. I've got an idea. We could both, you know, both together over the phone. Synchronise. I am tipsy, and you will remember how that makes me feel, if you can remember that far back. We can FaceTime if you like.'

'Shall I come to the hotel?'

'No, please don't. I'll be up in four hours for work. I just didn't want to, you know, alone and everything. Not again, not tonight.'

Jessica raised her knees, her feet flat onto the mattress, slightly apart. She closed her eyes; the room spun a little. Her belly tightened with butterflies. Her heart pounded. She moved her fingers to the rhythm of her heartbeat. She heard snoring from the phone.

*

The knock on the door was soft, but persistent. It jolted into her consciousness. She sat-up and looked at the hotel clock in one movement. It told a little after two o'clock. Half dragging the duvet from the bed, she rushed to the door, peering through the peephole, seeing a bunch of carnations.

'Wait. Two secs.' Jessica shouted through the door.

She pulled her rugby shirt over her head and discarded it towards the bottom of the wardrobe. She pulled on the silk top of her pyjamas and hopped into the matching briefs as she made her way back to the door. Jessica flung open the door. The night porter waved from down the corridor, confirming she was safe. The carnations lowered, and Brian pushed in, wagging his tail.

'Jace! It's you!'

'Sorry? Who else are you expecting at two in the morning? Sorry, but Brian is missing you. Sorry about the petrol station flowers. Sorry I fell asleep on the phone. Sorry, but you are choking me. Don't cry, love.'

Chapter eight

'Hey Mrs Taylor! You are looking perky this morning. You obviously didn't finish that bottle of wine from last night. Seriously Jess, you look, I don't know, radiant.'

'Radiant? What is that supposed to mean? I hope you are not suggesting I am pregnant.'

'No, no. Not at all. Of course not. No Mrs Taylor. You just look glowing, on less than five hours sleep.'

'I must agree with you there Ons, a lot less than five hours.' She shrugged.

Onslow went for coffee but stopped at the door; turning to face Jessica.

'You shoot home last night, Jess?

'No! Now, fetch the coffee.'

'Visitor?'

'Shoo Onslow. This has nothing to do with work.'

'You drink more than me, exercise more, work longer, get laid and still have more energy.'

'Seriously Onslow, piss off. I am not having this conversation with a male colleague; especially during office hours.'

Onslow stood his ground, waiting for eye contact. Eventually, Jessica raised her gaze from the screen, flopped back into her chair, and stared at her colleague. After a few seconds of neither blinking, Jessica smirked a huge, embarrassed smile and crinkled her nose. Onslow watched her grin push up her cheekbones, narrowing her eyes.'

'I forgot how lovely your smile is Mrs Taylor. Welcome back.'

*

Both laptops pinged a message.

'Headmaster's office, boss.'

The couple walked the floor, negotiating Trish's barriers, and took seats in front of Sam.

'Hi team. You are looking, relaxed, Jess.'

Onslow glanced towards Jessica.

'Anyway. You need to clear a few days and warn loved ones you may not be home for a bit.' Jessica bristled; she had already sacrificed her recent home life. Sam continued. 'Commissioning is starting initial trials on your old *Naap* project, Jess. I say old, but you seem to have kept your finger in that old pie.' Jessica bristled again. She remained involved in the project upon Sam and Amara's instruction. 'Hand over any urgent actions to Pan if technical, remembering she is not part of the Bridge inner sanctum,' Jessica's hackles rose at every passive aggressive comment. She had forgotten more about security and discretion than Sam would ever know, 'and I want you guys there to assist, please, as discussed. I especially want you to familiarise yourselves with the operation of *Naap,* for when you have to pop back and commission Bridge. Today is Friday, prepare to join HMS Prince of Wales a week Monday. Trish will fill you in, on details.'

As they rose, Onslow looked out of the window, over Sam's shoulder, and towards the empty carrier docks.

*

Jessica and Onslow boarded the Company jet at Southampton Airport, destined for RAF Ballykelly in Northern Ireland.

'Everything ok with Bridge, Onslow? Now is the time to mention it.'

'You get shitty when Sam questions you, but it is ok for you to undermine me. One rule for one.'

'I'm not undermining you. I am just asking. Is that errant utility line put to bed, for instance?'

'Give it a rest, Taylor, will you?'

Jessica spun around to face her colleague, noticing he gripped the arms of his seat. As the jet accelerated along the runway, he closed his eyes tightly. She placed one hand on his wrist and another around his arm, feeling his bicep tighten and shirt dampen with sweat. She stifled a giggle. As the aircraft levelled and engines stopped roaring, he relaxed.

'Sorry Mrs Taylor, that was rude of me.'

He pushed a clammy hand over his face, now gripping Jessica's wrist with the other hand.

'That's it, Jess. You have a good laugh. Everything is one big joke, isn't it? Is there nothing you fear?'

Her stifled giggle became a roar of laughter. She spoke between snorts.

'Spiders.'

'Really? Me too, I am terrified of the little shits. Scurrying around staring at me and running over my face when I'm sleeping.'

Jessica's laughter grew louder, now struggling to breathe.

'You're not scared of spiders, are you?'

Jessica shook her head, unable to answer through laughing. Onslow tried to shake her off his arm, but she clung on harder, laughing into his shoulder.

The flight to Ireland was empty of other passengers, the flight timed to return with RAF and Northern Irish government officials. Jessica kicked off her shoes and tucked her feet onto the seat. She kept a reassuring hold of Onslow's arm.

‘I’m looking forward to this, Jess, but you are buzzing. I thought you would hate being a captive on board a boat for over a week.’

‘Lock me up with a thousand boys and girls in Navy and Marine uniform? Yeah, I am going to hate that. I am hoping they forget I am there and just leave me.’

‘Is this a real thing, Jess? Or are you winding me up?’

Jessica looked away, hiding a smirk.

‘It is real, Ons, let me assure you. From being a teenage girl growing up on an Army base to dating a soldier during a military coup, it is real. If not always positive.

Jessica and Onslow checked the equipment bags off the aircraft. Without time for coffee, they drove to an awaiting Chinook helicopter by jeep.

‘You are joking with me.’

‘What did you expect? Did you think they would swing round in the largest ship the Navy has ever owned, to pick you up off the beach?’

‘Jess, I can’t do this.’

‘Onslow, you are doing this. Don’t make me knock you out, like Mr T from Sam’s A-Team.’

Jessica flirted with the aircraft captain for a short while, trying to obtain permission to wear a flying suit. She eventually conceded, pulling on a survival suit over her clothes; allowing herself to be strapped into the helicopter. Onslow sat next to her, repeatedly rubbing his palms along the length of his thighs. She kept her hand on his upper thigh but provided little comfort. The captain explained they would *duck and dive a bit* on take-off. Routine training. The aircraft banked hard to the left, tilted backwards and then hard to the right before accelerating towards the low clouds, releasing foil-chaff and flares. Jessica squealed, bouncing in her seat and straining on the straps. Onslow froze, eyes wide and staring.

The landing on the carrier was rougher than Jessica expected. The aircraft captain joking about his side of things going fine. It was the sea captain at full steam who was causing the problems. The aircraft was to *nip and tuck*; ship crew appeared and released the passenger's harnesses, manhandling them away from the helicopter as the rotors powered the aircraft against the deck of a rolling carrier. The ship crew recovered their equipment as the helicopter soared away from the carrier with side doors still open.

The carrier turned hard to port at full power. Looking over to her left, Jessica saw only sky, to her right the angry sea. She imagined if she slipped, she would roll across the flight deck and over the side. She dug her fingers into the overalls of the crew member leading her to the superstructure. In the passageway, Jessica could hardly stand with the angle and rolling movement – the crew walked around as with no obvious effort. As Jessica bounced and stumbled around, she tried not to laugh; she needed to put her professional foot forward. Once inside, Onslow had the better sea legs.

'And I will be your host for the day. Please call me able-seaman Able.' The crew member Jessica clung to introduced herself. 'I will walk you to the operations room, where your commissioning guys from Company are already beavering away. Our weapons boss is a chief, he is waiting to greet you. Then, I will take you to your staterooms. You'll be pleased to know this sloshing around is due to finish at the end of watch, allegedly. Trials and manoeuvres and all that.'

Jessica nodded, feeling nauseous. Able handed them visitor ID cards on lanyards. Also clipped to the lanyards hung phone size devises – walking sat-navs to help navigate the passageways, hatches, decks and mezzanines of the ship. Certain areas showed green for accessible and others red for restricted. Pins dropped into specific locations including their accommodation, mess rooms and their operation room. She also pointed out safety signs and direction signs. A full induction would follow later. Meanwhile, they were to touch nothing and if they accidentally knock or operate any of the levers or dials which littered the Pompidouesque passageways and bulkheads, they must not try to reset it, but to ask for assistance. As they spoke, the ship rolled and Onslow leant on a brass lever, turning it through ninety degrees. He jumped back, pointing.

‘Oh no, what have I done?’

‘That, sir, is a door handle for the toilet. But yes, please be careful. This lever here, for instance,’ she pointed to a valve handle protruding from the bulkhead, ‘operates the sea water valves. Operate that and the carrier sinks.’ She winked at Jessica as Onslow gave the radiator valve a wide berth.

The operations room was reassuringly quiet and ordered. Each ergonomic workstation separately illuminated. Onslow waived to some of the commissioning team he recognised. The chief stood, smiled, and held a hand to Jessica. She vomited over his sleeve.

*

The commissioning lead called the meeting with his own small team, Onslow and Jessica. All meetings also attended by Chief or his designate and a naval scribe.

‘My name is Comhgall; call me Com. Whatever our guests from projects may think, I now run the show for Company.’

The meeting chuckled. Jessica made a gesture of wiping her brow in relief. All the attendees introduced themselves. Com spoke again, with his rural southern Irish lilt.

‘Comhgall is Irish for fellow hostage.’ He glanced around the confined meeting room. Half of the attendees stood and leant against the bulkhead for lack of space. It got another laugh. 'How are my office-wallahs finding their new home?'

'We are learning the jargon fast, Com, thank you. State Room, for instance, doesn't mean state-like or even room-like, but more broom-cupboard-like. I didn't pay attention when Able showed Onslow, I had no idea we were sharing.' The team laughed and mumbled agreement. Onslow smiled at her people skills, drawing the team closer to her. 'And when Able pointed to a door and said *head*, she wasn't offering what I first thought.' This brought Chief and scribe into her huddle – forces humour. Jessica continued.

'Onslow and I have been sent along as observers to the commissioning of *Naap*. I was Area Project Manager on Front End Engineering and Design and Engineering Procurement and Construction. If you have anything to ask or feedback to *Feed* or *EPC* you are to do it through me for a fast response. We are also looking to see how to provide any add-ons the Royal Navy may require in the future.' Jessica then lied, 'Onslow will be involved with *Naap* as it settles down over the next few months – so on a learning curve. If he gets in the way, send him for coffee, he can be irritating like that.' The software engineers, some of whom knew Onslow, laughed in agreement. 'But equally, use him if you can, please. He is costing me a fortune, and I want some money left in the pot for my bonus. Oh, and I love commissioning's first name

Californ-I-A, hipster vibe; please don't hesitate to call me Mrs Taylor.' A couple of *oohs* and *ouches* were included with the laughter.

Com drew the meeting to a close, more relaxed with having head-office turn-up on his watch. There were no specific workstations available for Jessica and Onslow; the operations room crammed with the mix of Company commissioning and Naval weapons operators. Jessica felt more drawn to share spaces with the uniformed Naval personnel.

Onslow tried to follow Jessica's lead and quickly formed allegiances with the software engineers, sorting niggles and keeping Commissioning moving forward, taking some of the stress and anxiety away from the team. Jessica had less to contribute, monitored the schedule, and fitted in some general office duties on her laptop.

They worked through to the end of the watch and through the following watch, before retiring to their cabin. Able stood outside.

*

'Ma'am, sir. I have brought you some formalwear for dinner at the captain's table.' Neatly folded onto their bunks sat two pairs of overalls each, and five blue T-shirts. Looking slightly awkward, she continued. 'I know you aren't in the mob, or anything, but you need to tidy your cabin, please. Put everything away. It looks like my baby sister's room on prom night.'

Jessica laughed as Onslow apologised – for Jessica's untidiness.

'You have PO stitched above your breast pocket to show you assume the rank of Petty Officer. Obviously, you will not be giving orders to anyone, but it signifies where you stand in the pecking order. Chiefs will chat to you, ratings will keep out of your way and equally, please show some deference to officers – they go through doors before you. I will show you the PO's mess, the gyms, cinema, etc. Also, I will show you the Royal Marine's warrant officers' mess, but they are as cliquey as anything. Stick with the matlows. You will forget everything I show you, so just ask or check on your sat-navs. Please please please, don't go to the officers' mess if casually invited. They ask out of politeness, and you must decline out of politeness. If it is an official invite,' Able hesitated for a moment, studying Jessica, 'and that might happen, I will nod you the wink. Sorry sir, less likely to be a problem for you.'

'Marines?' Jessica squeaked, the response louder than she meant. 'I mean sure, thanks.'

*

'I will not keep chucking you out Onslow, but if I catch you staring, you are in deep trouble.'

Jessica undressed in the tiny floor-space as Onslow reclined in his bunk.

'And get your shoes off the bed!'

Jessica washed in the basin, set into the dividing wall with the lavatory, stepped into clean pants and continued to brush her teeth and hair. She pulled on the Navy issue T-shirt and jumpsuit, found her Sketchers pumps from her rucksack, tidied away and sprang onto her bunk; making room for Onslow to repeat the process for himself. She made less effort not to stare.

'I'd have rather worn my strappy, silk slip to the marine's mess, but never mind. I assume you are coming?'

'The marines? You are joking Jess. What have I in common with a bunch of commandos? A fear of spiders?'

'Suit yourself. We'll catch up later. How did your work go today?'

'Catch up later? You have another think, Jess. I am not going to the sailor's mess on my own. I will stay here. Work was good. I have made a list for Bridge. Not least of all – they use a different port to the standard. Our hardware guys probably know, but I will double check – that would be embarrassing. Otherwise, it is coming together as I expected. When our guys are finished and I commission Bridge myself, it will be easier to discuss stuff with the Navy guys, but so far, I am quietly confident.'

Jessica lay back, processing Onslow's contribution. She then flicked her internal switch and rolled onto her side in leisure mode, watching Onslow shave.

'Here's the deal Ons. You tag along to the marine's mess, and I bet we don't have to pay for a single drink.'

Onslow stopped shaving and studied his colleague. Her overalls zip undone to past her naval, her left-hand fiddling with the bottom seam of the T-shirt.

'Maybe not you Jess, but I am taking my pre-loaded charge card.'

*

Jessica left the jumpsuit half unzipped, but every female she passed had all buttons but two done up, or overall zips fastened to within two inches of closed. She complied. Walking into the mess, she passed individuals playing games on phones and walked to a group of marines stood around beers on a table. A guitar sat in a chair.

'Sorry, guys. We are civies. Do we just order at the bar? Can we get you a round on expenses?'

The men all moved in slow motion. A competition to show who was coolest and most relaxed.

'Our round, miss. Yours next. Come with me.'

He was white, six feet tall, nearly as broad, not an ounce of fat, no neck. He wore a Hawaiian shirt over his green marine T-shirt. *Come to bed* eyes. Jessica followed, closely. Onslow waved a hand at the remaining group. One continued the conversation. Another held up a hand, in slow motion, to silence his comrade.

‘Hey. What’s your name? What are you doing here?’

The voice gentle. Onslow almost answered that he exterminated spiders.

‘We work for the company who made this boat. She’ he gestured to Jessica, ‘asked me to look at some weapons stuff.’

The silence dragged. Onslow went to speak again, but another marine spoke first.

‘Interesting?’

‘Yeah, yeah. You know, if you like that sort of thing. All computers and stuff…’ he tailed off.

‘Gamer?’

‘Yeah. Kind of. Single, you know? X-Box is slightly more fun than keep beating one off over my Kylie Minogue poster.’

There followed a short, controlled, cool silence before the group laughed. Onslow smiled back.

‘Call of Duty, mostly.’

‘Hey Ons! These guys bought the first round. Yours next. Unless you want to double or quit, lads? May I?’

Jessica picked up the guitar and strummed.

'This is one of my husband's favourites. He's more your American Punk kind of guy. Beat you lot in a brawl with no problem. But he does like some female vocals.'

She played and sung Roberta Flack's *Killing Me Softly With His Song*. The steward turned off the background music.

'Ok guys? Worth a drink?'

They clapped. Hawaiian marine signalled for a round. Onslow saw the *gamer* marine wipe his eyes with his T-shirt. Jessica downed a shot. Onslow sipped his beer.

'Now look, guys. I am not happy drinking away your Queen's shilling.' She plucked the intro to Red Hot Chili Peppers *Under The Bridge*. So we,' she gestured to Onslow, 'set you a challenge. Give me the most obscure of girls' names. I will sing you a song with that name in the title or in the chorus or verse; you buy us a drink. If I can't, Onslow here buys you all a drink – he doesn't have an expense account.'

Everyone laughed, including Onslow. A marine slapped his back. They started shouting names. Jessica strummed intros to the more obvious songs, including *Jolene* by Dolly Parton. Some challenges were so obscure, the group bullied the nominator for being unfair. One marine shouted Maud. Jessica wondered if this was a great grandmother's name, perhaps passed down as a middle name through the generations. Another shouted Skylar - his comrades tousled his hair and jostled him. Jessica guessed it a daughter's name – perhaps born out of relationship with another *girl*, in another *port*. Jessica crinkled her nose, smiling at the marine and nodding. She saw he wanted to lose the bet, to hear Jessica sing his girl's name.

'Ok. I want to see all the drinks on the table.'

The steward obliged. Stragglers gathered around as Jessica continued to play snatches of rock solos and riffs.

'Are you ready to eat my shorts, losers?'

Jessica launched into the *Happy Birthday* song. Before she reached the first girl's name, the group began laughing, booing, and throwing beer coasters. Her majesty's finest fighting force admitted defeat and paid for the evening's drinks.

*

'How do I get a look around the sharp end of this system, please, Comhgall? I hardly ever see my projects in the flesh. I am sure the software is interesting to your nerds, but I want to see the shock and awe end.'

'We have handed over the hardware to the Navy for a period, Jessica. They will fire a few rounds manually, before handing back to us, to complete commissioning. All dates are in the schedule. They have a couple of our guys on daywork rates, just in case they need anything adjusted.' Jessica tapped her laptop, checking the contract was in place for the additional labour. 'But I can see if Chief will get you access to have a look, obviously because the contract dictates your visual sign-off.' He smiled and winked. 'Our mechanical fitter will escort you within the exclusion zone.'

'Thanks Com. And looking at the plan, the munitions dry run is due tomorrow – excellent. I am sure you have read the environmental data sheet, but it will be seriously impressive. I know this bucket has a fair amount of fire power, but nevertheless, *Naap* will blow your socks off!'

Jessica muscled in on administering the commissioning plan for Comhgall, allowing him to concentrate on managing his team, communicating progress and dealing with any concerns from the navy representatives. Onslow's strengths lay on the technical side and this unexpected joint resource from Company boosted the commissioning process. What had become slightly chaotic and reactive before Jessica arrived now progressed in a much more orderly and efficient fashion.

'I am turning in for the day, Comhgall. The marines invited me to take part in a little R and R.' Jessica saw Comhgall raise an eyebrow. 'The flight deck is closed to all ops today, so they invited me to play hardball on one of their Physical Training sessions in the fresh air; I can't wait. Don't look so surprised. I am fit, I run and kick-box. I am joining at the end of the day – I will kick their tired arses!'

'I have seen those lads eat bigger pieces of meat than you for breakfast. You be careful, they are killing machines.'

Jessica laughed. Shaking her head and locking her laptop into the office vault.

'The only thing I need to be careful of, is leaving the carrier with a reduced marine capacity. They won't be able to walk tomorrow if they try to keep up with me. If Onslow comes looking, please tell him I'm playing soldiers and will see him in the cabin later or in the mess.'

Jessica changed into PT gear, which Able sourced from stores. Able laughed at Jessica's suggestion she would wear her Sketchers pumps, and so also secured her a pair of size four steel toe-capped work boots. Jessica presented herself to the PT instructor and the group of commandos she previously conned out of drinks in the mess, with her spoof challenge. She snapped to attention and saluted, enjoying herself. The group laughed at her attempt, and she blushed deeply, pouting in disappointment.

The PT instructor spoke to the group.

'Mrs Taylor, I have heard much about you already. It looks like you are Four-Two Commando's unofficial mascot. I am quite fond of the official mascot, Lance Corporal Buttercup, our goat based back in Plymouth. I will call you Buttercup, to avoid confusion.' Jessica beamed. 'I am your PT Instructor; you will call me Pete. You will do exactly as I say, or I will send you off deck. Understood? Our WO has decided, God forbid, that you may give this group of lazy scroats a run for their money and then you may fire a few rounds from an SA80 A2 firearm – hopefully away from the ship, leaving no holes in the superstructure.'

Jessica felt both feet leave the deck as she jumped with delight; she suppressed a squeal. Pete shook his head in dismay.

'C'mon then, you lazy heaps of shit! Line up for a fifty-meter warm-up dash!'

Six of the group fell in beside Jessica along a thick chalk line. She smelt the sweat from her neighbours. They had presumably finished training for the day, and this was a few minutes of fun before showers. They took positions for the sprint. Jessica made eye contact with the Hawaiian shirt marine from the previous evening. He was sitting out the race. He tipped his water bottle at Jessica; she smiled in return.

Jessica took position. Her heart pounding. She might not beat her super fit competitors, but she would do her best.

'Marks. Go!'

Jessica was first off the blocks. She pumped her arms, leant forward into the race, and strained her leg muscles. Twenty meters in and no one had passed. She pumped her legs harder, the shock from the steel deck pounding against her shins and knees. The finish line marked with bollards and chalk. She stretched forward, extending her head and neck towards victory.

She threw her arms above her head, gasping for breath. She pirouetted in a victory twirl to face the group of six, still stood on the start line – pointedly chatting and ignoring her.

'You bunch of wankers! You're just scared because you know I will beat you!'

The group laughed at Jessica's tantrum. She trotted back to the start line. Pete, the PT instructor, shouted.

'Scared of failure, lads? Now line up. If you bottle this race, it's extra duties.'

Jessica realised Pete was part of the japes.

'This is a *man down* practice. Loser buys the first round of drinks. What does a marine never leave behind, scroats?'

'PTI! Never leave a man behind, PTI!'

The six marines shouted back the answer in unison, joined by Hawaiian shirt man and the other marines stood on the touchline.

'Marks. Go!'

Jessica was first off the line again, but this time she glanced over her shoulder to check the others were running. At that moment, the marine closest grabbed Jessica around the waist and heaved her over his shoulder in a fireman's lift. As one, all the marines, including Pete, shouted.

'Man down!'

Jessica and her assailant reached the finish line as she squirmed to release herself. The marine bundled Jessica onto the shoulder of the next marine. They all turned, sprinting back towards the start line. Jessica now laughed as she pummelled the back of the second marine. At the start line, he bundled her onto the next marine and they continued until all six had completed a lap carrying Jessica. The last marine gently lowered Jessica to the deck as she laughed uncontrollably, kicking her legs in the air and thrashing her arms. Hawaiian shirt man helped her to her feet.

'You lot are so not funny! At least give me the chance to beat you at something.'

Pete singled out the first marine who had grabbed Jessica.

'That son, is no way to treat a female subject of Her Majesty the Queen.'

'PTI! No PTI!'

Pete handed the marine a bayonet. The blade was yellow, bendy plastic. He handed Jessica a similar training weapon.

'You son, use your left hand.'

'PTI! Yes PTI!'

'Buttercup – please use your weapon to defend yourself and to attack you assailant. You may use all your kickboxing skills, which I understand you bring with you. This coward may only use his weapon. Two limb strikes or one body strike is a kill. Ready to die, son?'

'PTI! Yes PTI!'

'And attack!'

As Jessica extended her bayonet, ready to attack, the marine stepped forward and in a swirl of yellow blade, prodded both her breasts, her forehead and belly.

'Wait! That's not fair, I wasn't ready.'

The audience laughed, booing her assailant.

'You heard Her Majesty's subject, marine. Now, try again. Attack!'

This time Jessica lunged forward, aiming for his left forearm, so she could also monitor his weapon. He side stepped in slow motion, before slapping her repeatedly on each cheek with the flat of his plastic blade. As the audience roared with laughter, Jessica dropped her arms to her side and stared at the marine. He kept slapping her cheeks, despite her trying to avoid him and despite her obvious defeat.

With a smirk on the marine's face and laughter of the audience ringing in her ears, Jessica snapped. Ignoring the blade slapping her face, she stepped forward and kicked his legs away. As he crumpled to his knees, she grabbed his left arm and kicked him in his left side. He tried to twist away as Jessica delivered a stamp to his chest, followed by a second to his solar plexus. He crumpled forward, his forehead banging against the steel deck.

The audience fell silent. Jessica's hands shot to her face. She looked around to see the audience, stunned and motionless.

'Shit. Sorry. I didn't mean to do that. Are you ok?'

The marine lay silent. His chest still. Jessica knelt next to him and cradled his head. Tears streamed down her face. She looked back at Pete – he returned a blank stare.

'Don't just stand there, get help.'

The marines remained rooted to the spot; mouths open.

Jessica turned back to the *man down*, to see his face grinning back at her. The audience laughed again. The marine wrapped his arms around Jessica and pulled her on top of him as he lay on his back on the deck; Jessica's arms flaying as she tried to punch his sides.

*

Jessica and Onslow lay in their bunks. Onslow whispered he had completed some prep work on *Naap,* in readiness for the Bridge installation and commissioning. Jessica listened in silence, soaking up the information. She still had concerns regarding the subterfuge they used – she would raise it again with Sam and the Ethics Department.

Jessica's phone rang.

'Jace! So good to hear from you. The ship has been on communication lockdown during trials – I wasn't avoiding you, of course I wasn't.'

'The commissioning crew is really busy, but we in projects also achieved a bit. I can't say much, especially over the phone.'

'Yeah. Really cool. We aren't normally allowed on the flight deck, which is a real shame. I hadn't realised, but I guess it is obvious with jets taking off and whatnot. But today I trained a bit on deck, with the Royal Marine Commandos! I know, how cool. Workouts, combat and wait for this – I fired an assault rifle with live ammunition. I'm still buzzing.'

'Really cramped. But comfortable. Noisy, but the swaying sends me to sleep. Rough the first day, I threw up over the client, but steady as a rock now, since they stopped chucking the ship around.'

'More like dormitories. Little privacy, but we quickly settled into a routine. Like the Waltons *g'night John-boy*.' Jessica giggled. 'Yeah, I know everyone in my dorm, colleagues from Company.' Jessica lowered her voice and directed her speech towards the pillow and bulkhead; away from Onslow. 'You wouldn't know them. Just colleagues. Mixed. You mean Onslow? Yeah, he is one of them. And me, obviously. Let me think. Actually, it is just Onslow and me; it is hardly a cruise ship. No, of course not. Bunks, obviously. Don't be silly Jace, you are not the jealous type. Don't start, I am homesick enough as it is. I will put the phone down, Jace, if you don't stop. I promise, I will be good; you shouldn't have to ask.'

'What is your news? Still lunching with Prissy? Oh, Priti is it? Whatever. Look Jace, Jace? You there?'

*

Jessica walked with Chief to the steel stairs leading up to a mezzanine floor immediately below the flight deck. A section of the ship's side had a huge cut-out, so that one side lay completely exposed to the outside world, except for a handrail. The mezzanine extended part over the deck and part out and over the sea. Several large structures located onto the mezzanine like oversized shipping containers and connected by ducting to more container type structures on the mezzanine and still more on the deck below.

At the stairs sat a uniform behind a small steel desk. Jessica would have assumed the wearer an officer, except the sleeve carried a badge instead of gold rings. Next to the desk stood Able, loosely holding a pickaxe handle; she avoided making eye contact with Jessica.

A red plastic chain cordoned the area. On the outside corners of the cordon stood two Royal Marines in full combat gear and carrying the SA80 A2 assault rifles she had fired on the previous day. She recognised the two young, similar looking marines from her new group of friends. Pitt was slightly older, maybe early twenties. Brad was barely twenty years old – he had called out the name Skylar when Jessica sang for the group on the first night, several weeks prior; drinking the shots they bought her in return. Jessica found him extremely attractive – a younger, prettier, Brad Pitt lookalike from Fury. She flirted a little on the previous day's training, and he reciprocated. She realised she was old enough to be his mother, just; a classmate at school had a baby at sixteen years old and her son would now be the same age.

Chief spoke, handing the Master-at-Arms a self-duplicating slip of paper.

'This is Mrs Taylor, Jaunty. She works for the company that supplied our new toy. One of her own people will escort her around the kit. She needs to have eyes on the hardware and witness the munitions trial, to sign it off. If you grant access, that is.'

The Master-at-Arms studied Jessica from her seated position before checking the slip against an entry in the log and tapping her iPad. Without speaking, she handed Jessica a padlock with a green disc attached, showing the number sixty-nine. She also handed her a separate green disc sporting the same number.

'Mrs Taylor, welcome. There is nothing I like more than gormless civvies wandering around my secure areas. You stick to your escort like glue. You place the green tag against your number on the in-board as you enter the area. When you leave the area, place your green tag on the out-board. You add your padlock to the open gate or hatch bolt as you enter inside any equipment, to stop anyone closing you in by mistake. The first time you forget to take it off as you leave, I will ban you. You touch nothing. Well? Fuck off then, you are boring me.'

Speechless, Jessica glanced back at Chief, who gave the faintest of winks. A young woman stepped forward. She wore similar overalls to Jessica, except with *ARTIFICER* stitched over her pocket.

'Mrs Taylor! A legend in your own lunchbreak. I am Macey, a Mechanical Fitter for Company. Stick close to me, please, and I will see if I can't keep us both alive for today.'

They walked together past the tag boards and onto the mezzanine. Jessica produced an A2 sized high level print of the installation, showing major components.

‘If ok with you Macey, I would like to start at the top and walk the installation. I have highlighted components I want to see. All are passed-off and checked by our people. If any are removed or obviously tampered with since the navy took possession, I will just make a note on the plan – partly to check if we need to address changes at the next stage or in case there are any problems now, or in the future.’

‘Like if they put the gun barrels on back to front and blow a hole in their new boat?’

‘Exactly Macey. Can I ask a question, just between us two? I know this sounds a bit, a bit, I don’t know, immature or something, but are you looking forward to the live firing later? I mean like really looking forward to it?’

‘By immature, I guess you mean kinky?’

Jessica raised her hands to her face in embarrassment, but still nodded her reply.

‘Well Mrs Taylor, it will certainly be the biggest bang that has involved me, since joining the ship two months ago.’ Both women laughed. Jessica held her colleague’s eye, waiting for the proper answer. ‘No, Mrs Taylor. I am afraid that is just you.’

*

It was past lunch before the couple completed the walk through. Some components had been removed or isolated and Jessica made notes on her iPad as they progressed, copying Chief, Comhgall, Onslow and the commissioning plan. Nothing flagged as a concern to Macey or the others.

The women split to their own messes, meeting again at the security desk to drink coffee together in the fresh air. Before they tagged back in, a klaxon sounded to evacuate the gunnery area. Able and the Master-at-Arms checked the authority of remaining personnel on deck and Able issued anti-flash hoods, goggles, fume mask, visors, anti-flash gloves, ear plugs and ear defenders to those permitted to stay – including Jessica, but not Macey.

Jessica stood in the small group, allowed to stay. Isolated from the real world by the Personal Protective Equipment, she could hear the blood pulse through her body and heartbeat pound in her ears. She felt claustrophobic, hemmed into the small group of strangers corralled into a safe corner of the deck. Wearing her mask, breathing felt restricted, and she worried she might hyperventilate. Feeling faint, she gripped the arm of the neighbouring person.

Able turned to Jessica, lifted her visor and removed the ear defenders and mask.

'Too early, for that clobber, Mrs Taylor. I will tell you when.'

Jessica gave a nervous chuckle, realising she was the only person wearing the full PPE. Some others were only just pulling on flash hoods over earplugs. She breathed deeply. Able guided her to the front of the group. Master-at-Arms wore no PPE; she spoke.

'Sirs, ma'ams, missus,' she looked towards Jessica 'you will all stay in this group and in this position until firing is over, and I appear in front of you like this again and sound the all-clear. Until then, you will not move and will not remove any PPE. If anyone disobeys this lawful instruction, I will personally charge you, regardless of rank. If it all goes tits-up and you die, you will die in this position and wearing your full PPE. God save the Queen.' She saluted the officers present and left.

A few moments later, the PA system announced firing to commence, and the call to battle stations was to be obeyed. Three electric bleeps sounded, and the group pulled on the last of the PPE. Able gripped Jessica's hand with one hand and around her upper arm with her other. Two electric bleeps sounded on the PA. Jessica felt a surge of adrenalin through her body, her neck tingled, and her palms itched; she remembered the same feeling of anticipation from the first time she made love with Jason on a beach in Italy. She focused on the *Naap* hardware. One long bleep sounded, followed by the call to battle stations. Two multi-barrelled launchers pivoted from under domed covers and pointed slightly off vertical. Able nudged Jessica and pointed to a fleet of flying drones, headlights blazing, approaching the carrier from out at sea. Six seconds after battle stations sounded, the launchers fired a continuous volley of surface-to-air missiles and cannon shots.

The missiles were specially developed Viviparous SAMs, nicknamed baby vipers. Carrying a tiny 500g warhead and at half the length of the standard land-based Rapier, the missiles left the launchers in groups of four, the next four then launched from different barrels, the next four from the remaining barrels. The first four barrels automatically cooled enough by steam jets to launch again, and the process repeated.

Missiles hit three drones – one drone seemingly hit by two missiles.

Three longer 40N6 Russian made missiles, available on the open international arms market, fired. The irony not lost on Jessica – part of her *Naap* project included specifying the requirements for Company to develop a British manufactured alternative. The missiles initially launched using a pressurised gas system, before rocket motor ignition. The noise of the 40N6 missiles was as deafening as for the baby vipers, but the flash hugely greater, overpowering the steel containment pit and engulfing the whole lower deck, including Jessica and the group. The missiles streaked away into the distance.

Simultaneously, the cannons fired a continuous volley of steel shot to create a curtain of defence. The cannon muzzles danced around on a pivoting platform, creating waves of shot murmuration into the sky.

A further three drones veered manically to avoid the cannon shot but disintegrated into shards of aluminium and plastic on contact.

Three more drones peeled off and double backed away from the carrier.

Clouds of steam, smoke and fumes engulfed the deck where Jessica stood, digging her fingers into Able. Flash from the missiles rebounded off the walls of the steel pit and fired across the deck towards the group. Despite the double hearing protection, the noise thudded in Jessica's ears and the claps from the cannon thundered through her chest cavity.

Following just thirty seconds of orchestrated bedlam, the firing abruptly ended. Two minutes later, with the smoke subsiding to reveal a mangled and distorted cannon multi-muzzle, Master-at-Arms appeared in front of the group and sounded the all-clear from a handheld foghorn. The deck filled with technicians, including Macey.

In a battle situation, the cannon multi-muzzle would have already jettisoned into the sea and a replacement fitted by robotic arms and an automatic crane.

'Sirs, ma'ams and missus, I hope you enjoyed the show. Only approved personnel with blue tags are permitted back into the area. The rest of you can fuck off my deck.' She snapped to attention and saluted the officers she had just insulted.

Jessica discarded her used PPE into a sack provided by Able; sooty and pitted. In a daze, she returned to her cabin, peeling off her sweaty and blackened overalls. Onslow squeezed into the cabin and headed for his bunk to make room for Jessica.

'Christ Jess! I thought the boat had blown-up! It must have been amazing on deck.'

Wearing just T-shirt and pants, Jessica grabbed Onslow and kissed him hard, forcing her tongue into his mouth. He returned the embrace and kiss, stepping gently backwards towards his bunk. As he moved to lie down and pull Jessica into bed, she broke free and without speaking or making eye contact, took her towel and headed for the showers across the corridor.

*

'Ok everyone, settle down. Thank you for attending this update at such short notice.'

Comhgall spoke to a crowded meeting room, packed with a mix of Company projects personnel, commissioning, naval project engineers, logistics, gunners and weapons technicians. A staff officer sat in one corner cradling his hat – nodding as attendees entered and saluted him.

'I shall rattle around the room covering salient points from each discipline, releasing people to get back to work, as we progress.'

Individuals contributed information following the firing of the new system and raised points and concerns for addressing. Chief spoke to the remaining meeting of team leaders and senior technicians, Jessica, Comhgall and the staff officer.

'First reports are very positive. Viviparous took down three of our Unmanned Aerial Vehicles, or *drones* as you civies like to call them, which presented as enemy aircraft. Crucially, the command monitors identified the different flight patterns of three UAVs which we did not tag as friend or foe, and allowed them to retreat to safety and adopt a non-aggressive trajectory away from the carrier – with the carrier representing a sensitive installation in a benefiting country, say an airfield in Turkey or town in Israel.

'Assuming the worst, we gave three of the UAVs access to the cannon firing patterns. Even so, they were unable to avoid engagement and were downed.

'Finally, our 40N6 missiles travelled 450km across the Atlantic and destroyed target deadweights, fired from a Vanguard Submarine – at high altitude and velocity as an enemy stealth Airborne Early Warning and Control or reconnaissance aircraft might fly.

'Not a huge sample, admittedly, but nevertheless, a good day.

'I will let the rest of you go now, except logistic's lead, Mrs Taylor and Comhgall, please.'

The meeting room emptied; the tired faces smiling, saluting the officer who also left.

‘Com, Jess. A bit of an odd one. A near-miss nonconformance docket has worked its way from stores to me this morning. This is a fairly low level of concern, but one that will eventually end up in the monthly report to the staff officers and captain. We partially closed it this morning, so as not to interfere with the firing manoeuvres, but we are not especially happy. Lead, please explain to our supplier representatives.’

‘I lead on stores, including gunnery. Three months ago we took delivery of six, long range, SAM, 40N6 missiles, from Company. Three we launched today as part of the firing trials for *Naap*.’

‘*Yes*.’ Jessica and Comhgall both answered. Comhgall waved for Jessica to continue.

‘You procured six for ongoing trials, along with a battery of baby vipers, cannon shot and charges. This is exactly the munitions you will arm when operational.’

‘The serial numbers matched the paperwork, no problems.’ Jessica and Comhgall waited for the *but*. ‘The markings are all in Russian, including a Russian flag, and wait for it, a Turkish flag.’

Jessica squinted in concentration. Comhgall spoke.

‘Not really my department, parts, but what do you expect? They are Russian-made missiles.’

Jessica shook her head to silence Comhgall.

‘My colleague means to say that all markings should be in English. A union flag and NATO compass rose painted onto the casing. Why has this only just been identified?’

Nobody spoke. Eyes remained fixed on Jessica.

‘So, we purchase the missiles on the international market, brokered by Finland, with the serial numbers stamped into the casing and warhead – all other designations are inked in English. Back at Company, we etch the Jack and Rose. I checked everything today and it is in order. I don’t know what to say. I need to report back.’

‘Keep this to yourselves, onboard, please. And I want a full investigation and report. We have already escalated to Ministry of Defence procurement.’

‘We keep everything *to ourselves,* Chief. But thanks for the reminder.’

‘We are a superstitious bunch, Mrs Taylor. We are only just getting our heads around women onboard – we are not ready to have enemy explosives locked in our powder box. Our chief gunner looked like he had seen a ghost when he came moaning to me earlier.’

The store's lead looked embarrassed, staring at his hands, having let the situation go unchecked.

Chapter nine

'This is the longest we have been apart since I became Mrs Taylor. Good news on that front; I will be home within a few days. Everything will be ok and we can both stop acting so jealous.'

Jessica had her mobile on speaker but turned low and under the thin duvet. Onslow lay on his back in the darkness, catching the treble hiss from Jason's voice, but unable to hear his replies. The tone from Jessica and her mobile sounded more conciliatory than the previous conversation he had overheard, but he knew Jessica well enough to hear she stepped on eggshells with her husband. If she ever mentions the sneaked kiss he and Jessica enjoyed, he hoped Jason would not come looking for him; Jessica spoke proudly of the couple's no secrets policy.

'It is almost six weeks since you turned up at my hotel door with carnations in the middle of the night; and six weeks since we last, you know.' She lowered her voice further. With a giggle at her husband's reply, she continued. 'No Jace, they were closed bud carnations, not roses, but I just loved them. Definitely carnations. I still have the *fresh carnations reduced to £4* sticker. I peeled it off and stuck it in my journal. Don't laugh at me, they were my best bought flowers, ever in my life.

'There is a Royal Fleet Auxiliary ship as part of the Carrier Strike Group, which is expecting a visit from

a Chinook soon, and I booked us on it for home, or at least to land. All we need is to hitch a lift on a passing chopper from the carrier. I was hoping for a ride in an Apache Attack Helicopter, but apparently the gunner won't give up his seat.
'Of course I haven't gone six weeks without it, Jace! No, alone, obviously. When I last suggested that, you fell asleep on the phone!'

Jessica slid further under the thin duvet and reduced her voice to a thin whisper. She switched the phone off speaker. Onslow could make out her commentary to her husband, interrupted with quieter periods of heavy breathing. He found his AirPods and fell asleep to Alex Clare's *Too Close* playing on his phone.

*

Onslow and Jessica stayed the night in Carlton Hotel, Dublin Airport. They both had long soaks in the bath and met later for dinner. The food tasted no better than the meals they had on board; it felt strange to lose the motion of the sea and the throb of the carrier's gas turbines. Now the extra space and privacy they had both longed for felt isolating and unfriendly. At last Jessica felt able to wear her strappy dress. She also wore her parting gift from four-two Commandos – a Royal Marine's green beret complete with regimental badge and a tiny ceramic brooch depicting a posy of wild buttercups, her nickname. The beret fitted perfectly; they went to some effort to have the present delivered on board. She wore the beret partly as a joke, it hardly matched her grey silk slip dress, but Onslow saw the pride in how she held her head high and marched into the hotel restaurant.

Running her finger around the rim of her gin and tonic glass, she thought of her marine friends, the other Company and naval personnel she became close to. She remembered her kiss with Onslow, who now sat across the table. She thought of her husband as always, the love of her life. She thought of the beautiful young Brad and the hunky Hawaiian shirt Warrant Officer. *Jason, bless him, was jealous of the wrong man.* She looked up and saw Onslow, studying her from across the table. She crinkled her nose into a smile, blushing slightly.

*

Sam called the meeting on a neutral floor and invited Amara. Trish, Stacy, and the S-400 Compatibility engineers, Engel and Pun attended. Sam ran the meeting, including a debrief of events, which interested the entire team. Trish, Pun and the project engineer left, whilst Jessica ran through the non-conformance regarding the Russian markings on the 40N6 Russian made SAMs.

'They are bitching because of a hammer-and-sickle and a crescent-and-star left on a missile that was shortly afterwards blown into atoms? Nice to have a hobby, I suppose, but what's up with them? Who really cares?'

Jessica answered.

'With all due respect, Mr Smith, they quite correctly raised a non-conformance because we failed to supply the missiles marked as agreed. Why they want us to do our job properly is hardly the point. We should have supplied them correctly or raised a waiver request before shipping; not just send them wrong. And it is a tricolour – they dropped the hammer and sickle decades ago.'

'I agree with you both.' Amara spoke as Stacy scribed. 'I will follow up as the supply is directly linked to *Naap*. But I agree with you Sam – *so what*, at the end of the day?'

Jessica made to argue with Amara but decided to let it go; it had no bearing on Bridge and Amara would deal with it professionally.

Amara then asked Stacy to leave, so that the four remaining could discuss the progress with Bridge. Jessica asked for Trish to come back in, to record and comment on Jessica's concerns regarding the subterfuge involving the client and other Company teams. Sam declined the request, and it shocked Jessica that Amara did not intervene again.

Onslow listed the preparations he completed, whilst assisting the *Naap* commissioning engineers. The changes went under the Company commissioning team's radar, and that of the navy weapons and project engineers. Onslow developed similar short cuts he could deploy on the S-400 Compatibility project to accept Bridge. Jessica shook her head and protested again, asking for a meeting with Ethics.

Sam refused Jessica's request. Amara instructed Jessica to record her concerns in the Bridge project file, but to make no mention in the *Naap* or S-400 Compatibility files. When Jessica challenged that decision, Amara instructed her to record that objection also – but only in the Bridge file.

Sam closed the meeting.

*

'Vanilla, we need to talk. We are due a supervision or mentoring meet.'

Jessica raised her eyebrows. Amara had never used her nickname for Jessica at work before. It was a direct reference to the brief affair they had years previously.

'Ons, can you plough through the past few weeks of Bridge, please? We need to get things rolling again. I will join you after Mrs Pebbles has finished with me.'

The women walked to the canteen and took their usual booth away from the counter.

'You came straight to work? Not gone home yet?'

'Tonight Am, promise. Jace and I had a nice phone call the other night, but I wanted to touch base about everything here, before switching into wife mode. He says I am high maintenance – he is not such a walk in the park, at the moment, either.'

'You need a break. Both of you together. I am talking as a friend. You need less time with other men and more time with Jason.'

'That isn't going to happen, Am. I am way too busy with Bridge. We need to catch up.'

Amara lent back into her chair. She kept eye contact.

'Go away. Spend a few weeks in the sun. Take your laptop and work remotely. You have Onslow holding up this end.'

'Amara, no. Just let me do my own thing. Too much time with Jace is the last thing I need, we need, and he can't just take time off.'

'We have offered Jason the Dalaman *Damp* installation project. Priti Khan, from contracts, is going as well. She can't wait, you know what it is like at that age – to be away from home on expenses and in the sun.'

'Am!'

'You could dust down that house of yours on the Aegean. The one you abandoned after the 2016 military coup. The Turks have agreed your work visa. Company has posted a huge bond and guaranteed your best behaviour.'

'Am, no!'

'I am not pressuring you, Jessica. You can refuse my offer and stay here with Sam and Onslow, whilst Priti and Jason enjoy a few weeks on the magical Dalyan River together. Or you can tag along and prepare for your commissioning visit to the S-400 Compatibility project. Honestly Vanilla, the choice is yours. No pressure. You will make the right choice.'

*

Jessica left the office early and popped into Marks and Spencer to buy steak, luxury oven-chips, Portobello mushrooms and ingredients to make a mustard sauce. She hoped to be home waiting for Jason before he finished work.

Amara insisted Jessica spend a few nights at home. Jessica would be especially busy over the weeks leading to her trip to Turkey, to prepare for the S-400 Compatibility site review. Amara had Stacy arrange for the company taxi to collect Jessica from home and deliver her safely back each night. Jessica treated the waiting driver to a nice bottle of Merlot from M&S to accompany his supper.

As Jessica arrived home, Jason had already placed a Waitrose shopping bag by the front door and walked to the side garden to release Brian from his day pen.

'You, Mr Dog, have the most luxurious home of any pooch in England!'

Brian twisted and turned against Jason as his master petted him, rubbing his ears. Jessica leant against the corner of the cottage, listening to her husband chatting with the dog. He turned and broke into a huge smile on seeing Jessica. Brian ran to her, skidding the last two feet on his back, begging for attention.

'So, not bothered about Brian? Never wanted a dog in the first place? Or just love him as much as we both love you?'

Jason folded one arm around her waist and pulled her roughly, playfully, towards him. Jessica allowed herself to be manhandled against his chest. He kissed her firmly, his nose squashing hers. She noisily breathed through her mouth as the kiss continued. Brian backed away and sat obediently, jumping from foot to foot, waiting to be invited back into the huddle.

'Is that a marrow in your pocket, or are you just pleased to see me?'

Jason kept her firmly clamped against his hips, but allowed her to move her face from his, still too close for the couple to focus properly.

'Courgette actually. I bought steak from Waitrose, I'm cooking tonight.'

Jessica smiled at her husband, deciding to try to conceal her own purchases.

'I must spend a few weeks away with 250 marines more often – as it seems to grab your attention. So, bed then steak? Or steak then bed?'

‘Yes.’

*

Jason ground peppercorns to add to the brandy and cream sauce, the medium rare steak already resting on a warm plate sat above the vent to the range oven. He wore shortie pyjama bottoms and a heavy canvas apron against oil splashes. Jessica sat on the high stool wearing his pyjama top.

‘Amara mentioned you won the *Damp* project. Congratulations.’

Jason continued to concentrate on his sauce.

‘I know it is not what you want, Jess, sorry. But I have accepted. I know you always say Company incentives are not to be believed until signed for, but this could lead to a few years’ work and me retiring in ten years, instead of twenty. *Us* retiring in ten years. A lady of leisure at forty-six with a sugar daddy of fifty-five. Well, hardly a sugar daddy, your contribution to the pension pot is greater than mine – but it will see us through the first ten years before we start to draw down pensions.’

Jessica sipped her wine.

‘We will need to start and plan our retirement idea for emergency foster caring, if you are still up for it? Or we could just drift to Turkey and crash in your villa for a bit. What do you think? Ten years will whip past, especially if we both keep working hard to top up the coffers. How many stun grenades and howitzer sights do you have to sell to make a million pounds? But still, I am sorry for going against your wishes.'

Jessica wrapped her arms around his waist and stood on tiptoes to kiss the back of his neck. She squeezed her cheek against his back. He could feel her smile against his skin.

'Howitzers don't have sites, they aren't guns. How many times do I need to tell you, dumb ass?

He turned around to rest his forearms on her shoulders and kissed her forehead.

'I love it when you publicly abuse me, Jessica.'

Jessica crinkled her nose, before looking towards Brian.

'He's family; doesn't count.'

Jason wrapped his arms around her, pulling her closer.

'I am an employer now, Jess. I have a technical clerk and a project engineer to cover for when I am away. I might keep them on if Company offer me more work. They are really good, bright as you like.'

'Listen to you, Mr Industrialist. Well done. Even if I am annoyed, I am still proud. And is Company sending along any staffers? From contracts, perhaps?'

'You obviously know Jess, or you wouldn't ask.'

‘And how are you getting along with Perti?’

‘You know it is Priti. Don’t wind yourself up. Yes, really good, thanks for asking.

‘Priti, Perti, whatever. She will be a stunner once she grows up. You must be old enough to be her father.’

Jessica felt his chest heave as he silently tried not to laugh at her. She moved to pull away, but he held her close until she relaxed again.

‘And sorry to disappoint you Jace, but two things. First it isn’t a villa. It is a stone shack with a tin roof, if it still has a roof. Second, Company is sending me along to keep you and Pokei company.’

*

Jessica and Jason flew to Dalaman, Turkey, together on the Thursday. Jason had accommodation booked near the airport from Monday night, following a day of inductions. Jessica planned to spend some nights with Jason. They would spend the first long weekend together in the Aegean village of Koyaka, arranging for any necessary repairs to the shack, or to have it cleared if too derelict. They arrived at the Azman Oda bed-and-breakfast by taxi, just a few yards from the shack.

The owner of the bed-and-breakfast recognised Jessica and, although they had not parted on good terms, held her in an embrace for a long hug. Breaking occasionally to kiss her cheeks before continuing the hug.

'Hos geldin Jessica *bayan.'*

'Hos bulduk Sahip *bayan. Tanistirayim.* Jason, *kocam.'*

Jessica gestured to Jason. Sahip squinted, scrutinising Jason's face, before extending a hand in a soft, long handshake.

'Husband? *Gercekten?* Thank God, she need a husband.'

Sahip pulled Jason into a hug and kissed his cheeks.

'Hos geldin husband.'

Leaving the luggage at the entrance to the hotel, the couple walked the few yards to the shack. The gate was missing, but her picket fence stood in good condition. The dirt yard needed a brush, and the flowerbed was dug over and mulched with a thick layer of eucalyptus nut shells. The remaining shrubs, fruit trees, herbs, chilli plant and Pimms o'clock mint bush were all cared for. A new flower bed sat planted near the river, edged with stones – a young jasmine snaked up a steel concrete-reinforcement bar. The shack looked in good condition. Jessica pushed on the unlocked door. Jason scooped her into his arms and carried her across the threshold.

'Welcome home Jessica.'

Inside, the room was clean and recently painted. The furniture all in good order and covered in dust sheets. The bed made up, some of Jessica's scatter cushions replaced with new. Everything smelt fresh. She turned on the water stopcock and fresh spring-water spluttered and coughed into the sink. She turned on the gas cylinder, still half-full, and lit the gas fridge. She flicked the switch in the electric box and the solar panel, and the wind turbine, spinning in the constant sea-breeze, lit the twelve-volt lamps and powered the desk fan against the heat of an August afternoon. She gestured for Jason not to help her as she flung back the locked shutters. Each action deliberate, thoughtful, reflective.

Jessica ran her finger on top of the bathroom cabinet, deciding it was probably cleaner than how she left it. She traced the shadow of repaired plaster, where she had left a grotesque bullet hole.

A diesel van pulled to a halt at the side of the road. Jessica and Jason moved outside to see a teenage boy and middle-aged couple standing awkwardly, formal, the man holding his cap.

'Oglan? Is that you?'

'Hey lady! You are back.' The boy gestured to the couple. 'The village guard tell my father you arrive.'

Jessica placed her hands gently onto the boy's waist. They each studied the other. The boy brought his fingers to her face. He traced a line from her temple, gently brushing her eye lashes, tracing her cheeks, across her lips. Jessica tasted lemon cologne on his slim fingers.

'Lady, last time you were broken. I think you never be beautiful again. But now you are old.'

Jessica gave an involuntary giggle. Tears welled in her eyes.

'Elvis? Uysal, I mean?'

'Is *oldu*. He die. Do not cry lady. He is old dog now, maybe thirteen when he die. Is old in Turkey. After he go blind, he happy. He nowhere to go, no dogs or soldiers to fight. He lay by the river and sunbathe. He smell the wild boar who live across the river. One day I came past from school and he asleep by the river, asleep forever. He is still there, under the jasmine, waiting for you to come home.'

Jessica and the boy walked to the new flower bed and stood looking out to the river. Jason gestured to the picnic table and sat with the parents.

'My father own house before. You know this. You buy it from him. He look after it and sometimes tourist stay. He keep money to look after house, is ok? He said you will come home one day. He said nobody can visit Turkey just once, it is the best country in the world and he has been to Albania and Georgia, so he knows.'

Jessica nodded.

‘He said you kill a Turkish soldier. We cannot forgive you lady, but we think it was a mistake.’

Jessica whispered, her voice cracking.

‘No Oglan. The soldier died; I did not kill him. He just died.’

The boy shrugged.

*

Jessica walked Jason around the village, to the eucalyptus wooded picnic area, and back along the beach and river to the shack. The same route she had taken with her jandarma lover on their first date. Some villagers recognised her and smiled, waving. Others recognised her and pointedly turned their backs in a snub. She held Jason’s arm tightly.

‘Memories? Not all bad, I hope.’

‘Even the good memories are sad, to be honest. I don’t miss him, Cavus; I hardly knew him. In fact, I will go so far as to say I didn’t know him at all; he was a lie. I was very strongly attracted to him, physically. He was drop dead gorgeous. But we didn’t really gel in the short time we had together. Just a holiday thing, I suppose, for me.’

‘But you know his family? His father or something?’

Jessica's stomach tightened into a knot. She almost ran to the nearest toilet, but after a few seconds, the pain passed. She shook her head at Jason; too disgusted to discuss the situation she was in years before.

'I could write a book about those days, Jace. I was so listless in Turkey, I made some rash decisions; some wrong choices.'

'Will you be ok staying here alone? Why not stay in the hotel with me, work from the balcony? Hire a car and go out on day trips when you can find time?'

'That is sweet of you. But I want to stay here. You are only an hour away. I can pop over some evenings, if you are not working late. No need for naughty late-night phone calls.' Jessica squeezed his arm and giggled. 'Give me a chance to get to know Pricki better.'

'She is Priti, Jessica. You know that; Priti.'

'She certainly is pretty, Jace. Thanks for pointing it out.'

Jason sighed; he could not bother to reply.

*

Jessica sat in the Dalaman Lykia Hotel foyer, working on her secure work laptop. She parked the hire car and logged it with reception, but they were not prepared to issue a second key to Jason's room, until he returned from work. Reception kept her supplied with complimentary pastries, fruit, tea and juices. She watched the mostly business clients come and go along with the few holidaymakers, mostly couples.

Jessica enjoyed the week away from Jason, turning the shack back into a home and building bridges with her neighbours, including making trays of buttery shortbread to give to neighbours on ornate plastic plates. One by one, the plates returned with dates, figs or mezes wrapped in muslin. Jason was to return to Jessica for the weekend, but they fell at the first hurdle, and he had to work. She decided to join him Friday and to welcome their colleague from contracts due that afternoon.

She watched a young Dutch couple book in. They were awkward and the young man clearly did not know all the woman's personal details, for registration. Jessica wondered if they were on honeymoon, honey-bears as the Turks called it, or if they had only recently met or become lovers. The woman playfully snatched the pen from her partner and finished the form.

Priti Khan came through the main hotel doors, followed by the bellboy pulling her large, new, wheeled suitcase and matching cabin bag. She carried her own Gucci handbag, also new. Jessica had not got off to a good start with Priti but had no reason to dislike her. She smiled to herself as her colleague beamed with excitement. This was a rite of passage for the young go-getting professional and Jessica knew she had to lighten up and share some of her enthusiasm. Priti must have asked for Jason, as the receptionist tossed her head back in a Turkish no and pointed to Jessica.

Priti went to reclaim her bag, but the bellboy assured her it would be safe with him until her room was ready. Blushing slightly, she thanked him and tried to offer a tip, but he declined with a slightly bemused expression. She blushed deeper and turned towards Jessica, extending her hand. Jessica allowed her eyes to search over Priti's body, noting the slim tanned legs and tiny ankles, the body hugging new white dress and matching summer jacket. A new travel outfit not dissimilar to the Dutch honey-bear's *going away* dress.

After a slight pause, Jessica stood to take her hand. Priti had a firm shake; Jessica would find a way of explaining the Turkish shake was much gentler, with no pumping, for when she met clients later.

'Hi Mrs Taylor. I believe Jason, Mr Taylor is still at work.'

Jessica did not like Priti speaking for Jason, but she kept her expression neutral.

'Good flight? You certainly travel well Priti, you look quite, quite ravishing.' The women smiled. 'And please call me Jessica or Jess, away from the office – especially now you are our-girl-in-Asia-Minor. How do you and my husband normally address each other?'

Priti's blush, which was yet to leave her, deepened further.

'Um, yes. First names mostly.'

'Jason, or Jace?'

Priti dropped her gaze, avoiding eye contact. She cleared her throat.

'Um, not sure. Maybe both. Or perhaps Jace, mostly.'

'Cool. So, Jess it is then.'

The women sat. Jessica slid the pastries across the table; Priti declined. Jessica poured juices.

'Understood. That dress doesn't look like the type you can eat cake in.'

Jessica sat back in her high leather chair. Priti looked up, eyes wide, as Jason walked past Jessica from the carpark door behind. Not seeing Jessica hidden by the chair back, he walked to Priti. She stood as Jason hugged her close.

'Hey Priti! Welcome to the madhouse; you are a sight for sore eyes. Really, you are looking, looking very well. Hope the journey was ok. We are in the office tomorrow, so you can familiarise yourself and settle in before Monday.'

She pulled her hands away from Jason and signalled towards Jessica with her eyes. Jason spun around.

'Jess! You are here already, great. Let's all have a meal, then I need to pop back to work for an hour.'

He bent to kiss Jessica's cheek, but she held his chin and kissed his lips, maintaining eye contact with their colleague. The concierge walked towards the group, holding two electronic key cards in cardboard envelopes.

'Madams. Sorry to keep you both waiting. Madam Khan?'

Jessica automatically responded to her maiden name, the name she had on her first trip to Turkey. He handed her a key.

'And sorry Madam Taylor, we could not issue you this earlier, because the room is in sir's sole name.' He handed Priti the second key. 'Please enjoy your stays. You must be very pleased to have your beautiful wife with you, sir. All work and no play makes Jack a dull boy, I think you say.'

He smiled at Priti, bowed his head, took a step back, and departed.

'Well girls, that was awkward.'

'Shall we swap keys, Priti, or are you happy with a key to my husband's bedroom?'

*

Jessica and Priti arranged with contract's secretary and Trish for Jessica to have access to Jason's *Damp* project; the project not related to her own.

Priti wanted to impress Jessica with her work skills but felt equally relieved to have a more experienced pair of eyes on the detail. Jessica complimented and encouraged the young woman, gently mentoring her as Amara had for Jessica. Jessica smirked to herself, reflecting on the situation. As opposed to her relationship with Amara, her relationship with Priti was unlikely to lead to a drunken night of passion following an office party.

As an independent consultant, representing Company but not yet fully indoctrinated, Jason acted more relaxed with the expected formalities. He introduced Priti and Jessica by their surnames to clients but could not bring himself to refer to his wife as Mrs Taylor, even in meetings.

He was protective over Priti, making her run through presentations and contract awards before committing publicly. Jessica felt this endearing – he acted the big brother to a sister he never had. Jessica also appreciated the effort Priti made to support Jason fully, making this crucial project a success for him. She noticed how Priti kept a special smile for Jason and frequently, when Jason spoke directly to Priti at work or over dinner in the evening, she saw Priti's pupils dilate. She trusted her husband and colleague with each other, but only just. She wondered how she would react if it was Jason who kissed Priti, instead of Jessica having kissed Onslow. She decided she would probably stab him in the neck with kitchen scissors, as he slept – although realised she needed to consider the consequences more carefully, before acting on such thoughts.

The three spent some weekends at the shack together, Priti staying in the bed-and-breakfast. When Jason had to work weekends, Priti stayed in the shack with Jessica. Priti liked to cook for the couple and set breakfast for them both on the picnic table, if Jessica and Jason lay in bed late. When the women shopped together for groceries, fruit and vegetables at the market, Priti asked about Jason's preferences – Jessica told herself to think this sweet, rather than threatening. Amara was right to suggest Jessica work from Turkey.

Jessica had already decided to return to Turkey at some point, to confront some of her demons remaining from the 2016 visit, but the Turks refused her holiday visa and on one occasion, when she had flights booked, Jason took ill with virus. Recent events came together nicely for Jessica. She had a few weeks away from the office to concentrate on working her projects, had Jason for support but not in each other's pockets, and realised she had the strength to confront her past.

Chapter ten

'Mrs Taylor, Jess. Sorry to call you on a Sunday afternoon. Head office has called a video meeting for early evening. They want you here, please. I said you would join from your house, but Stacy said for you to drive over, or taxi.'

'Stacy?'

'I think Mrs Pebbles is attending. Should we worry?'

'Yes, you should. Is Jace still at work?'

'No, he finished before lunch. We have been by the pool. He's in bed now. Well, he said he was going to bed, so I assume he is. Presumably.'

'What has happened this week, any problems?'

'I don't think so Jess.'

'You don't think so? What is that supposed to mean, Priti? Look, wake Jason and hire a meeting room from reception. No, forget that. Select a garden table with a gazebo and set up, ready. Dress for work, make sure Jace does. No speedos. Charge your laptops. Check correspondence and the Contract file, look for any area of increased scrutiny or traffic. Priti, if you can't get Jace on the phone, send housekeeping. I don't want you going to his room. See you in forty-five.'

*

'Mrs Pebbles. Good to see you putting in the hours.'

'Jess, Jason, Priti. Thank you for attending. I like your backdrop, please tell me that is one of those zoom backgrounds.'

Jessica waited to give Priti the chance to lead, but she stayed silent.

'All genuine Mrs Pebbles and yes, the waiter really is that gorgeous. I asked Priti to set us up out here – away from prying ears.'

Jessica folded her arms, leaning forward slightly to stare at the camera.

'Good thinking Jess. So, Jason, cat got your tongue?'

Jason rubbed his eyes.

'Just got me out of bed, Amara. Started work at seven, drinking beer by the pool at eleven and dreaming about life without air-con by two o'clock.'

Jessica rolled her eyes, but Amara smiled back.

'Good for you, Jace. Now look Jason, I know this is a bit cheeky, but I want you and Priti to shoot down to Incirlic, eastern Turkey. Tomorrow, please. Stacy has booked flights from Dalaman to Adana Sakirpasa Airport. Our people will collect and drive you to the Incirlic Base. Take enough clothes for a couple of nights. Stace will explain, but you have accommodation on the base. You also Jess.'

'Whoa Mrs Pebbles. Jason is on a fixed contract, with deadlines. Priti is working for Contracts, not Projects and what are we doing when we get there? Who is paying for all this?'

'Ah, sweetheart. If you didn't challenge everything I say, I would still love you just as much. I want Priti and Jason to do a brief presentation. Marketing will send the slides. I want you there for moral support. They want a shiny new petro-chem plant added to their fuel storage facility; similar to *Damp*, but with different parameters. They are willing to pay to fast track. Our people are a bit surprised as the base hasn't needed anything before – have a poke around.'

Jason spoke.

'A presentation? I'm an engineer, not a second-hand car salesman. I have a job to run here, without enough hours in the day.'

Jessica knew not to gang-up on Amara; she does not *do committees.*

'Sorry Mrs Pebbles, we don't mean to sound negative. But why is Company pulling managers in, on a Sunday, to send a mixed team flying around the sub-continent flogging bits of oily pipework? We are arms dealers, whatever it says in the brochure.' Jessica referenced one of Amara's earlier put-downs.

'Jessica, this is difficult for me, and I need your support here. I have a contractor Area Project Manager, half on gardening leave and half working from her holiday home, already committed to three interlinked projects. I have a newbie consultant engineer, who'd prefer to drink beer and sleep by the pool. And I have a Contracts engineer, with no marketing experience. But I also have a task that needs completing. I suspect there is a security implication to the Incirlic job, so petro-chem or not, we want in. You are actually all ideally suited for this trip, just the arrangements are a little unorthodox and I do appreciate your efforts.'

'Ok Mrs Pebbles. I have voiced my concern and I appreciate you taking the time to address it.'

Jason intervened again.

'Hang-on ladies. I am agreeing to nothing here.'

'Jason, lovey. Did I mention this is a variation to your contract, so you will be effectively paid triple time plus additional hours worked to catch up on *Damp* over the next few days? And did I mention we will be looking to offer you single-bidder status if we win the Incerlic job?'

'You didn't mention that Amara, no. But now I understand, I would love to go on a sales trip to Adana, thank you. They do my favourite kebaps.'

Amara wrapped up the meeting. The three stayed looking at the blank screen for a few minutes, each with their own thoughts, listening to the cicadas chirping as the sun dipped.

‘Mrs Taylor, Jess, I have a few questions, please.’

‘Then you should have fucking asked love, shouldn’t you? Chase marketing for the slides and get on to it, tonight. Tomorrow you lead the presentation, Jason will puff out any technical component, but keep it high level and don’t get dragged into talking commercial, obviously. I will handle the client outside of the presentation. Say nothing more than you must. Goodnight, I’m off to bed.’

*

They were first shown their accommodation; Priti and Jessica sharing an otherwise empty female dorm to sleep four warrant officers, and Jason an empty twin room. Uniformed staff escorted them to a meeting room to meet Turkish military and procurement personnel. Among the uniformed staff, Jessica picked out Airforce and Jandarma representatives, including special forces JOH – the same unit as her old lover, Cavus. No doubt they were aware of Jessica’s alleged involvement in the failed military coup. Under very slightly different circumstances, Jessica would have enjoyed the simpering intensity of the good-looking soldier, but she found the black uniform menacing and it induced a rush of anxiety.

Fortunately, it was Jessica who had to speak first, breaking the oppressive spell. She introduced herself, Priti and Jason, offered a brief introduction of Company based on the more positive parts of the brochure, with an emphasis on peace and security as opposed to hostility and the killing of foreign nationals. She finally touched on the *Damp* project in Dalaman, referring to it as supporting military logistics, rather than offer any detail.

Priti took over, flashing the first PowerPoint slide onto the screen. She stuttered and froze with nerves as the interpreter spoke over her. Jason stepped in to ask her to clarify a term on the slide, and this bump started her back into the presentation. By the third slide, she appeared more relaxed and confident. Jason fielded all the technical questions, which arose during and after the presentation. The military staff had nothing to ask or contribute.

Following lunch, Jason and Priti attended a technical meeting where procurement quizzed Jason further, looking to test the petro-chem experience of a Company normally associated with arms. Jessica worked on her projects from her dormitory. She waited until they had transferred back to Dalaman late on Tuesday night, before debriefing Priti and Jason in his hotel room over beer and pizza.

*

'First of all you two, well done. That was an unreasonable ask, presenting on something we know nothing about and at short notice.'

Jason and Priti smiled at each other. Jason rested his hand on her shoulder. He often made the same gesture with his brother and friends, but Jessica was less impressed with how Priti gripped his wrist in return.

'So what was all that about, do you think? There was enough scrambled egg sat around the table to make us all a spicy breakfast of Turkish menemen. Since when has Airforce and Jandarma officers been interested in a few pumps and storage tanks? Especially Special Forces.'

Priti shrugged.

'No idea Jess, I have never been to a meeting like that before. I guess they wanted to see the whites of our eyes, not just a Company salesman with a bag full of promises.'

'Any thoughts Jace? I need to report back to Amara tomorrow. What is this plant all about, do you think?'

'Sorry, Jess, I have no idea. In fact, I have more questions than answers. Our plant here in Dalaman adds cleaning agents and antifreeze to standard military ATF as you might expect. So, you might add a few chemicals to a military grade fuel like a JP-5 which you have on your carriers, or in Dalaman here, it is adding to a base fuel of JP-8. US and NATO land-based jets would normally use a JP-8 fuel – my guess is a large NATO base like Incirlic will have shipping-tanker loads of JP-8, complete with additives, piped in from the coast. The choice of base grade is more to do with storage and refuelling than performance –

whether you intend to refuel in flight, for instance, or have pressurised systems as on the carriers.'

'And the new plant deals with what, Jace? P-5 or P-8? Or something else, like a civilian grade? And why do that?'

'Exactly my point. I asked specifically if they were processing a civilian grade, like Jet A or Jet A-1. I thought they might want security of supply, in case they lost the military grades - if the Kurds blew a pipeline, say. They would not specify exactly what they wanted at this stage – it was all about them quizzing me, but I think they are processing kerosene.'

'Kerosene? What, as in paraffin?'

'I am only guessing, of course. It isn't all that fanciful. Regardless of how many designation numbers we give it, aviation fuel is only processed kerosene. But still odd. Sorry I came back with questions, not answers.

*

Jessica spent more time on Bridge and S-400 Compatibility, liaising daily, sometimes hourly, with Onslow at head office in Portsmouth. S-400 Compatibility was largely sewn up and Comhgall moved in with his commissioning team. Bridge was a much smaller project, in physical size, hours and complexity. *Naap* was complete from Jessica's position, except for a few changes to the spares catalogue and trying to kick-off the replacement Front End Engineering and Design for the British made alternatives to the Russian long-range SAMs 40N6, currently used with *Naap*. Company committed to provide the Ministry of Defence with a reliable, viable and cost-effective alternative. Like the Kalashnikov AK-47 assault rifle before, the 40N6 was proving a difficult act to follow, for reliability, simplicity, efficacy and, importantly, cost.

Jessica's daily life appeared quite idyllic. She swam in the river or sea most mornings. Worked over breakfast in a local hippie cafe most days and normally finished by 5:30 pm British time. Jason also enjoyed his work and made good company for Jessica at weekends or when she drove to Dalaman. Priti managed to lose the cost of Jessica's hire car, in expenses.

The construction stage of Jason's *Damp* project would finish shortly after Jessica and Onslow planned to commission Bridge. Jason and Jessica talked about returning to the UK. Although the temperate Aegean winter appealed, they missed England, friends, and Brian the dog. Jessica also missed the buzz of the office and, strangely, Onslow.

With guidance from Jessica, Jason and Priti became more adept at running *Damp* to spread out the effort evenly – enthusiastically claiming progress in some areas and holding back other areas – for a rainy day. The three managed a weekend off at the same time.

Priti planned a date weekend on the Dalyan River with a friend from the client's audit office – lazy hours on pristine beaches, watching turtle hatchlings scurry down to the sea by moonlight, trekking around Byzantium rock tombs and gentle river cruises. Jason arrived early Friday afternoon for a long weekend at the shack with Jessica. They planned to explore the secluded beaches along the sides of the bay and to swim in the local waterfall; an accomplishment for Jessica following the events of her traumatic previous visit to Turkey.

The worst of the summer heat subsided, the days now pleasant out of the direct sun, the evenings warm, the nights cool. The couple lay tangled together across the bed, having spent the week apart and the previous weekend with Priti.

'I am heading east again next week, Jace. Further than Adana; all the way to the border.'

'I know I don't need to say this, but please, please, please be careful. You brought the wrath of the Turkish state and half of NATO upon you before. I dread to think what you could achieve in a war zone, amongst the largest stateless nation in the world. If the Syrians don't get you, the Kurds might. Why are you going, meeting up with your old conquest?'

'Don't joke about things like that. I will be fine. And thank you for caring.' She moved her head, rubbing her hair into his chest. 'Onslow won't be there yet, although he needs to get out here soon. I want to tie-up with Commissioning on the S-400 Compatibility. And make some friends ready for when we start Bridge. Not that I just mentioned Bridge to you.'

'Now I have sold my soul to Company, tell me what the difference is between the three projects, sounds to me like it should be one big project. And don't tell me I'm not trusted. If I kept a secret from you, you would go mental.'

'Jace, I really shouldn't be talking to you about this. It goes absolutely no further. I don't want your pretty friend hearing about it through pillow talk.'

Jessica felt Jason's hand slip between her naked legs, she assumed to start their lovemaking again, before squealing at a sharp pain when he pinched her bottom.

'You are the one who spent six weeks sharing a tiny cabin with her old sex object! And I know exactly what you got up to with me over the phone. Pretty Priti and I have done nothing wrong – leave the kid alone.'

She settled back down again.

'Ok, but I mean it. Say nothing to anyone, not even me.

'Basically, *Naap* is NATO's anti-aircraft platform. It is like a whole country's air defence system, bolted onto the two carriers. It protects two countries at the moment. I am not telling you the other one, but I am sure you have guessed one is Turkey. Turkey now has a Russian air defence system, which will be of little use if Russia attacks NATO in Turkey. If things ever get heated, we will park the carriers near Turkey in the Med or Black Sea. The UK, and NATO obviously know about *Naap*, my guess is the Russians probably know as well. It acts as a deterrent, so we want them to know. NATO is desperate to have some Turkish influence; we are hearing Turkey is moving further from NATO and closer to Russia politically, almost daily. With me so far?

'S-400 is the Russian-made air defence system, which Turkey purchased to piss the Yanks off. It is designed by Russia to shoot down American F35 stealth jets. Under threat of being chucked out of NATO or worse, Turkey has agreed for us to put some safeguards into the system, without the Russians knowing, to immobilise S-400 if F35s ever deploy against Russia. Dead secret. Turkey knows, NATO knows, UK knows, Russia absolutely does not know – it is a final defence, in the event of World War Three. A *fight them on the beaches* scenario, in case we ever fly F35s against Russia. Also, we get to monitor the S-400 system as it ducks, dives and develops itself in parallel to the S-400 system protecting Russia. In addition to military advantage, Russia sees S-400 as another tool to drag Turkey away from NATO; another reason for NATO to dilute the Russian influence. That in a nutshell is S-400 Compatibility project.

'Now, put your hand back between my legs and rub that pinch better!'

'Darling, you are so sweet. You think if you shake your booty at me, I will forget how to count to three. Your third project, which dear, dear, dear, bottom bunk, One Night Stand, Ons, has rushed to help you with?'

'It is the project that dare not speak its name. Let us just say it bridges, or spans, the other two projects. Without Russia knowing, obviously, and without Turkey knowing, without the USA knowing, without the Royal Navy knowing – at least at an operational level, without NATO knowing officially, but I will get back to that – our *Naap* carrier system will interrogate Turkey's hugely clever Russian S-400 system. Not only will we know what we know, but we will know what the S-400 system knows. We will know what the Russian's think only they know. If the worst happens and Turkey ever leaves NATO, God forbid, secret Bridge will become even more crucial for regional stability. That is Bridge.'

'Bridge is a solely UK thing, then?'

'Funny you should say that. Ons was laughing about it recently. He runs a zillion fake *attacks* against the systems. UK Military Intelligence, especially the British Cyber and Security agency GCHQ, sends Company endless amounts of up-to-date tiny micro bugs. Independent photons of information which he fires at the system, from outside or even from within the software. They have a short life of nano moments – like a bin full of burner phones. They are in themselves harmless, like the protein in subunit vaccines. He described them to me like a key to the hatch in the hull of an aircraft carrier; we were in an aircraft carrier at the time. The key opens the hatch, but behind it is still the solid hull, so the ship doesn't sink, but the key still opens the hatch. The key is like these pockets of code. With me?'

'No, not really. This Onslow sounds a barrel of laughs. Shame he wasn't on my stag night.'

'Perhaps you had to be there. OK. GCHQ continuously monitors, identifies and tracks the ever-changing traffic of cyber-attacks and hacks screaming around the ether, from friendly and hostile countries and organised crime. Even from spotty teenagers locked in their bedrooms with crusty socks. Military Intelligence then produces a protein-type representation of the code, or shall we say, dead virus of the code, to see how the system copes with the intrusion. We also fire samples of the codes we want it to cope well with – when feeding a system real-time information, for instance. And there isn't a positive or negative result to the test, it is a metadata type thing. The endless bombarding of the systems with bits of code and interactions produces endless graphs showing where and how well the system is reacting. Oh come on Jace, keep up. This is the interesting bit. 'Onslow can't help but see patterns in everything. He is a real geek like that. I remember, years ago, looking at the pattern on a hotel ceiling with him … Actually, I will tell that story another time. Looking at these reams of data patterns, Onslow actually believes they developed the system with NATO's Office of Security as the *owner*. That would make sense with the paranoia around Turkey leaving NATO. I insisted he take his suspicions back to Sam Smith, just in case NATO are covertly muscling in on our new bit of kit, but Mr Sam *know-it-all* Smith investigated it himself and gave Ons the all-clear. All a bit above our paygrade.

'Now, are you rubbing my tender spot, or do I have to do it myself, again?'

'Priti says you have a bit of a reputation at work. Care to explain that?'

'The little bitch! I have slept with two people at Company. Onslow, once and Amara, once. Priti needs to grow up and shut up. Well, three people now, including you.'

'Whoa! Easy girl. Priti said you are a legend with the nickname of *Miss plus and minus nine per cent.* She said it is complimentary but couldn't explain it.'

'Ok. I will try to keep this simple and short. I want another seeing to, please. There are lots of variations to how we do this, depending on the relationship we have with the client. But at the end of the day, the client pays for everything, whether it is the Ministry of Defence with a Term Contract, or a multinational walking in from the street.

'Right. Say the MoD asks sales for a cost to make a fleet of modified tanks, to squeeze between buildings in Amman, Jordan. This is only an example, ok? Sales ask me for a plus or minus fifty per cent cost to produce a plus or minus thirty per cent estimate. Ok? I look at the job specification, which is probably really sketchy. It might say something like *develop and produce ten Challenger 3.1 tanks based on the Challenger 3 design – but eighteen inches narrower.* I google a bit, flick through any similar projects I have done in the past and come up with a number. I am going to say one-million pounds. For one-million pounds, plus or minus fifty per cent, so for between £500000 and £1.5m, I will research and produce a full production specification for approval. Within that price, I will throw in a final estimate to deliver the ten tanks. That final estimate will have an accuracy of plus or minus thirty per cent. If they agree to spending the one-million, then I produce an estimate of, let's say, one hundred-million pounds to produce the tanks, plus or minus the thirty per cent. It will cost between £66m and £133m to produce the tanks. Are you still awake? Right, the MoD has now paid me my one-million and agree to proceed to manufacture. I then produce a final estimate, now that I have the money and the go ahead to proceed. With a lot more work, I come up with my final price, with an accuracy of plus or minus ten per cent. I offer my final estimate of £120m plus or minus ten per cent, so between £108m and £132m. From that, Finance offers the MoD a fixed price, following negotiations, backhanders, girls at champagne parties, etc. But I then have to bring my project in at cost, plus or minus ten per cent.'

'Or at half the cost, for a massive bonus?'

'Absolutely not, dumb ass. If I bring it in above or below the plus or minus ten per cent, I am investigated and warned for doing a bad estimate – unless the job scope has changed, which it often does, and I have captured all of the changes.'

'*Miss plus and minus nine per cent*?'

'If my project is over running, then it always overruns by nine per cent. If it is under running, then it always under runs by nine per cent. Everyone, from Amara or Sam to Engle and Trish, get their bonus and a pat on the back, no investigations or warnings. I keep getting the work and keep raising my charge out rate. Doesn't that make you horny?'

'Always exactly nine per cent?'

'Don't get me wrong, Jace, I am good. Like fantastic at what I do. But maybe, although nobody can prove it, I might manipulate funds – its only numbers, really. So, if a project is going well, for instance, I may book part of the team from a losing project to the costs of the over-performing job. Or I might place an order for some specialist discipline that I then use to sort-out an unforeseen problem on another project. Which is partly why I like to have several projects on the go and see them all to completion. Strictly speaking, Company might see it as internal fraud, or, if the work is on a Term Contract, then actual fraud. But nobody looks too close, because everyone loves Jessica and her spot-on financing. Amara has whispered about it always being exactly plus or minus nine per cent. I should probably vary it a bit, but you know me, once I have a target.'

'I certainly remember when I was your target on that Italian beach, Jess. It took a week to wash out all that sand from my bum!'

*

'We are only having this conversation because you are one of my least unfavourite contractor Area Project Managers.'

Jessica pictured the mischievous grin on her friend's face.

'That is the sweetest thing a witch has ever said to me Trish, I love you too.'

'I can base you in a spa hotel on Meydan Plaji, almost empty with the troubles. Or, I have found a real *Jessica gem* of a place. I'd hate it, but you are so weird and everything.'

'I'll take it!'

Both women laughed.

'It is in a small town called Sehir, south of Mount Kilic in the Turkish Hatay region. Comhgall has based his team there, as it is close to the border and the S-400 Compatibility project. It looks really spooky; it is on the border with Syria and spans a canyon. One side is a community of ethnic Kurds: loyal to the Turkish Republic, consistently voting against independence and Kurdish nationalism. Across a huge stone bridge over the canyon, with a stone medieval arcade, is a community of Syrian Turkmen. The two communities have lived together peacefully for, like, ever. The hotel is Kale Otel, built within the walls of an ancient fort, something to do with Knights Templar – not sure if they built it up or knocked it down, but now quite secure. Like I say, not my cuppa, all a bit eastern, and rundown. You will need a jumper and some proper warm underwear, not your slutty kit; the Aegean climate it is not, and they are approaching winter. Up to you.'

'My God Trish yes, yes, yes! Slutty? How dare you, it's sensual, I'll have you know. Woollen knickers it is, then.'

*

Jessica boarded the aeroplane at Milas Bodrum airport to fly the wrong way for two hours. At Istanbul, she browsed the airport shops for three hours, connecting to the flight for Antakya; another two-hour flight. By the time she climbed into the company Land Rover on arrival, she felt ready for the journey to end.

She had studied her reflection in the airport restroom mirror, rubbing off dribble from around her nose and the corner of her mouth, having slept fitfully, sat upright in her economy class seat - wishing she had waited the extra day for business class availability. The wheel on her suitcase, full of recent winter purchases, fell off. She carried the bag through the hall. Previously, Jessica had compared her looks to Priti, but remembering how her colleague looked on arriving in Dalaman several months before, she now wondered who she was kidding.

The driver helped carry and store her bag. Once away from the airport compound, the passenger unlocked a steel box, bolted in the footwell next to Jessica, and took two Glock semi-automatic pistols, handing one to the driver. The box lid closed but unlocked, containing two Czech manufactured military Skorpian machine pistols; prized for the quick delivery of firepower, rather than for accuracy.

'We have some good news and some bad news, Mrs Taylor. Our bumpy little trip should take no more than two hours.'

Jessica rolled her eyes.

'Is that the bad news?'

'I am afraid not, ma'am. It should take no more than two hours, but unfortunately, with extra roadblocks, a bridge damaged by Kurds and half the road still not repaired following last winter – it will take nearer five hours.'

The driver avoided slowing for the potholes, and Jessica left her seat as the Land Rover negotiated a bump, cracking her temple against the reinforced door window.

'Comhgall has sent you a survival pack, Mrs Taylor. In the box next to you.'

Jessica opened the lid of the gun box before the passenger slammed it shut, making Jessica jump in surprise.

'Sorry Mrs Taylor, I meant the cool box on the seat.'

Jessica shook her head at her own mistake. The cool box contained iced bottles of water, two cans of cold Efes beer, a home filled baguette with spicy cold kofta in one half and a mix of white and yellow cheese in the other, an apple, a small pack of body wipes, a bottle of refreshing Turkish Lemon Cologne, and a deflated travel cushion. She smiled at the posy of garish artificial buttercups, her nickname from the marines on the carrier, tied with hairy string. Comhgall presented as a no-nonsense toughie roughneck, who did not want head-office prying into his work; this tender and thoughtful gesture touched Jessica, already feeling tired and vulnerable in her tooled-up transport.

*

'Mrs Taylor. Mrs Taylor. Jessica Taylor.'

Jessica woke, laid across the back seat of the Land Rover.

'I must be losing my touch and slowing down. That is the first time anyone has slept on the journey from the airport. You will be pleased to know we are here at Kale Otel.'

Jessica stretched and let out a long purr, rubbing her neck. It was pitch black; the milky way clear in the mountain sky, she glanced at her phone.

'Well, that was a good journey. Door-to-door only took fifteen hours. What's that, an average of sixty miles per hour? These Adana kebaps had better be as good as my husband says. It is the only reason I came.'

'Adana is a couple of provinces back the way you came, I am afraid. But Hatay is the best place in Turkey for Yogurtlu Kebap. Sauteed goat in butter, over stale bread and soaked in sheep's milk yogurt. That will get your husband jealous.' Jessica stared at the driver as if he spoke a different language. 'Perhaps you have to be there, ma'am.'

Jessica raised her eyebrows.

'You're right though, I'm sure I will make him jealous about something.'

The driver packed up the cool bag to give back to Comhgall and snap locked the gun case. The passenger carried Jessica's broken suitcase towards the airport style security x-ray machine. As he approached the body scanners, the alarms sounded, and the plate-glass door slid shut. He waved to the security guard in a steel kiosk and patted the bulge in his jacket, returning to the Land Rover.

'Don't worry, ma'am, that machine is hyper-sensitive. No doubt we will see you again, sleep well.'

Both men climbed back into the Land Rover and waited to see Jessica safely inside the hotel reception. Jessica walked through the scanner. Her bag stood waiting with the male security guard.

'Please, madam. Open bag. This, please?'

The security guard twisted the x-ray machine screen towards Jessica, highlighting a hard item amongst the folds of her clothes. She shrugged. She just wanted to get to bed.

'Hairbrush?' Jessica suggested.

'Please.'

The guard offered Jessica a plastic tray. Sighing louder than intended, she fiddled with the combination lock and unpacked her clothes, looking for the object. A female security guard peered at the screen for a moment.

'*Yapay sik.*'

The male cleared his throat and turned to study a clipboard hanging from a nail in the wall behind him.

The female collected a silk pashmina from the growing pile of clothes. She held it to her face, feeling the soft sheen against her cheeks, before folding it neatly into a square. Jessica triumphantly produced a pink latex vibrator, tucked into a slipper with a note from Jason: *In case you miss me xxx.* Jessica's heart sank.

'Ok lady. No problem. In tray. Batteries in outside bin, please. Walk out through scanner and in again please.' She lay the pashmina over the tray.

'Problem Mrs Taylor?' The driver stood a little back from the body scanner.

'Battery hair straighteners. Here.' She handed him four AAA batteries.

'Ah, ok. Sleep well Mrs Taylor.'

'I will driver, I certainly will. If reception keeps spare batteries.'

*

Comhgall worked for two hours before driving back to collect Jessica from the hotel. She stood as he walked into reception, arm extended to shake hands. She playfully batted his arm away and moved in for a big hug, squeezing her cheek against his chest.

'Good to see you again Com, I am not stalking you, honest. It looks like a couple of our projects are moving targets. We want to stay connected for when managing updates and tweaks, especially if the relationship with NATO changes.' Jessica lied. 'Fantastic rooms here. I love the arched brick ceilings and private courtyard for breakfast. My suite is probably bigger than my house in the UK, definitely bigger than my house here in Turkey.'

'Sounds like you have an upgrade. We are all in the cheap seats, but still more than happy; it makes a big difference when working away from home. We are also close to the work face, so a big plus.'

'Are we close to the actual …'

'Let me stop you there, Jess. Why not let me fill you in on the way? We are parked on the opposite side of the town square; I thought we could stretch our legs.'

From the hotel reception, they walked out through security and across the parking forecourt to the imposing, restored, castle gates. Directly outside stood a huge pedestrian town square. On the opposite side of the square loomed a stone bridge crossing an incredibly deep, but narrow canyon, complete with a stone arcade of buildings, backdropped by the foothills of Mount Kilic.

'We don't talk about anything, in front of strangers.'

'No, of course not, sorry. How is security here, generally?'

'There is definitely a risk. Islamic-State or IS and al-Qaeda's Syrian affiliate, the al-Nusra Front, are the

biggest problem. Further west, militant Kurds are a greater risk, but just here we seem to have the centre of moderate Kurdism. I am sure they all want an independent state one day, but many individual Kurds identify more with Turkey than Iraqi, Iranian or Syrian Kurds. The Kurds hate IS and al-Qaeda. Mind you, the Kurds seem to hate most people, despite being by far the most lovely and welcoming individuals I have ever met. Historically, many of the atrocities committed against some of Turkey's neighbours, was actually committed by Turkish Kurds. It was ethnic Turks, under the Ottoman general Mustafa Kemal Ataturk, who managed, or at least tried, to keep a lid on some of the genocides.
'Sorry I digress. The other group here is the Turkmen. They are fiercely loyal to Turkey, anti-Baathist and are also Sunni Muslim like the Turks and the Syrians. They look and sound more Arabic to me. Their people spread deep into Syria in this region and even now, they seem to cross at will between the two countries and in and out of the Turkish occupied safe zones to the west of here. Safe-zone is, in itself, a bit of an oxymoron – it is only safe if you tow the Turkish line, or at least keep your head down. The Turkmen are totally against our Syrian neighbour's Baathist regime, headed by President Bashar al-Assad, bless him. They are not less than a little averse to his supporters either, especially Russia and Shia Iran.'

'Goodness. So, the Kurds are siding with the USA, or vice versa. The Turkmen are siding with Turkey. The

Russians and Iranians are siding with Assad. Islamic State is fighting Assad, Russia and Iran, but also the USA, NATO generally, and the Kurds, Turkey and the Turkmen. Turkey and the Turkmen are also fighting the Kurds. Fairly straight forward then.'

'And we haven't even mentioned the Free Syrian Army. They are fighting Assad, Iran and Russia. They are not keen on the Kurds. They look to Turkey for support, despite Turkey initially keeping them at arm's length, and they fight with the Turkmen. Qatar, which is another friend of Turkey, and Azerbaijan also support them. They have sided with the Kurds against IS and sided with IS against Assad. They have supported al-Qaeda against IS purely to divide and rule. They were supported by the USA, but no longer, and fight the Kurds who are also supported by the USA. I bet the joint Warrant Officer's mess is a ball after a day's fighting.

'Oh, and don't get the Turkish backed Free Syrian Army, also called the Syrian National Army, mixed up with Assad's Syrian Armed Forces, or the Syrian Democratic Force. The SDF is Kurd led and is in direct conflict with Assad Baathists and Turkey. But wait for it, some of the smaller Turkmen militias fight alongside the SDF; I bet they all sleep with one eye open. Armenian forces have joined SDF, partly to have a pop at Turkey and the Chechens joined to have a pop at the Russians.

'The SDF are also the official army of the unofficial Autonomous Administration of North and East Syria, a catchy name for a budding country, or AANES as we know them. Somebody really should have told them *Anus* is not a good acronym. But they are trying to operate a good secular, almost liberal, regime with an army of Kurds in land occupied by Turks.

'Are you interested in this shit, Jessica? Or am I boring you? I find it fascinating – this part of the world is all that is good about humanity and all that is bad. It reminds me of the old days back in Ireland, during the troubles there.

'Turkey wants Assad out but doesn't want a USA and NATO induced power vacuum, Iraq style, so they half support Russia, who also fear a vacuum where IS can thrive, and everyone hates IS, except when they are fighting the same targets as the Free Syrian Army and al-Qaeda! And then, in the midst of this barbarism, Turkey is hosting millions and millions of Syrian refugees, including Kurds and Christians, whilst the most enlightened US Democrat president in a generation, Barrack Obama, has dropped more bombs on Syria than any, and all, Republican presidents have dropped anywhere since Vietnam! Absolutely crazy; a cluster fuck. I wonder how many sides Company is supplying.'

A fighter jet screamed past, banking hard and releasing flares and foil chaff to distract any surface-to-air missile attacks. The noise brought back memories of Jessica's involvement with the 2016 failed military coup. She froze, squeezing closed her eyes.

‘Sorry. I wasn’t expecting that. I was ok on the carrier when I knew what was happening, but that was a bit of a shock.’

‘You will get used to it, Jess. That was a Russian Sukhoi Su-24M attack aircraft, buzzing the Turkmen. The border is less than half a mile from here. I have seen the Turkish Air Force F-16 fighter jets play chicken with the Russians – both turning away at an imaginary curtain hung from sky hooks over the border. The Turks turn a blind eye to Russian, Syrian and Free Syrian aircraft creeping over the border occasionally, especially in poor weather, but it will end in tears one day. And as if that isn’t funny enough, the Turks and Russians are like best mates on the international stage, agreeing and slapping each other on the back. There is a rumour that NATO is nervous about just how close Turkey and Russia is getting.’

They climbed into the Land Rover.

‘Do you come out in the evenings into town, or not recommended?’

‘It is absolutely fine, Jess. I will come with you, if you like, but perfectly safe – so far as it goes. No bars and more than half the restaurants are dry. You’ll be lucky to find another woman having a beer out, but I remember you being quite thick skinned. They are all out promenading with family and window shopping. Lots of security, but all good natured. You must walk across the bridge to the Turkmen side, and back. It is surreal, but again, absolutely friendly and good humoured. Oh, and buy a keffiyeh scarf from both sides of the bridge. The Kurds here only wear red and white, the Turkmen wear different colours, but have this fabulous white trimmed, beige-golden design, with splashes of maroon, beautiful. Buy your man one of each.'

*

They drove out of town and into the mountains. It seemed impossible to Jessica, an island dweller all her life, that they could stand on the roof of the Land Rover and peep into a war zone. Previously, the war had literally touched the border, with Turkish border guards and jandarma firing across ditches and through border fences to protect civilians fleeing from IS and Syrian Armed Forces. A few miles to the west stood the new Turkish fence and wall, to help control insurgents and criminal activity crossing into Turkey. Here, with the Turkmen creating a natural buffer, the border was still controlled, but less defended.

'This reminds me of reading about the Napoleonic wars, where families would bring a picnic to watch the battles, and then invite officers from both sides to drinks parties in the evening. Bizarre.'

Jessica spoke as the jandarma signalled for the Land Rover to pull over by a roadblock. Passenger snapped the lid closed on the gun box. Driver spoke to the soldier, they seemed to recognise each other. As Jessica handed over her passport and a security pass issued by the jandarma, to allow her access to the S-

400 sites, the soldier looked at her and smiled. He was young, with an open, friendly expression.

'Hey! Bobby Charlton.' Younger than Jessica, it was unlikely he knew the English football player and was performing a parody, to amuse a foreign guest to his country. She grinned back.

'Ok finish. *Just like that, not like that, like that.*'

His Tommy Cooper impersonation, probably better performed wearing the Turkish Fez hat he was famed for, earned a laugh from the group.

'Shall we fill-up with petrol and grab some water here folks?'

The driver pulled into the petrol station forecourt. Passenger unlocked the gun box again, despite the considerable jandarma presence. As the attendant filled the tank, driver stepped out to accompany Jessica and Comhgall to the shop. Passenger stayed with the machine pistols.

The mountain air felt cool, the sun bright. Jessica sipped on a water, idly watching a queue of small tankers and bowsers, some towed by tractors, suckling a huge, shining red and white Petrol Ofisi road tanker; the panting dog logo proudly emblazoned onto the side.

'What is all that about?'

The driver replied.

'The road tanker is unloading paraffin into the smaller bowsers for distribution to individual houses and hamlets, up ridiculously steep and tiny tracks; the tanker would never fit. I have seen this a lot; I guess with winter just around the corner, everyone is stocking up.'

Jessica looked at the group of drivers and farmers gathered around a water standpipe, smoking away from the fuel loading. She shielded her eyes against the sun and squinted to make out a shape against one of the small trucks eighty meters away. She took a few steps forward, still squinting at the object. Suddenly waving at the drivers, she shouted and sprinted towards the truck, arriving seconds before her driver and a young farmer from the group.

The object was a juvenile Kangal Shepherd Dog hanging by its neck from a leash tied to the truck wing mirror. The collar scrunched up behind the dog's ears and cheeks. Both back legs stood on the ground, the front legs twitching as the dog snorted in short breaths. Jessica only just managed to take the weight of the thirty-kilo dog, releasing some of the pressure from its neck. The farmer fiddled with the tightened knot of the leash. Driver produced a serrated hunting knife from a sheath on his belt and sliced the leash. Jessica fell backwards onto the concrete, the dog sprawled on top of her.

Farmer and driver manhandled the dog off Jessica and onto its feet. The dog buckled, but with support from the two men, eventually stood. Jessica sat on the ground, watching it heave for breath.

'*Vay Canina, vay Canina.* Thank you lady, thank you. He will be ok, *insallah.* Thank you.' The farmer led the unsteady dog towards the water tap.

Back in the Land Rover, Jessica sat over onto one buttock, the other side painful from the fall backwards.

'Do you need me to check that, Jess?' Comhgall asked.

'You men all have a one-track mind.' Comhgall laughed. 'No, its fine, thanks. That poor farmer, he looked in shock. And the poor dog, of course.'

The driver spoke. 'That was your good deed for the day, Mrs Taylor. The suspension looked shot on that truck. I guess the fuel transferring caused the truck to rise on the springs. That would have been a slow torture for the poor dog. Well done for spotting it.'

They pulled off the road, along a logging track towards a natural clearing. A jandarma checked their passes and waved them through.

'Oh my goodness Comhgall! It is like something out of a James Bond movie. How many trucks are here? They are huge! Where is Pussy Galore?'

'Not much of that around here; I am sad to say, Jess. But welcome to the sharp end of £150m of mobile surface-to-air missile and anti-ballistic missile system. Probably the best in the world and hopefully, when we finish, a little more conducive to standing on NATO soil.

'They throw in the 400 horse-power, ten-wheel V12, military all terrain low-loader lorry with the launcher strapped to the back, 120 missiles including your 40N6 450km types, which we use on the carriers. That 8-wheeler is the command vehicle.

'The Turks fired a ballistic missile in the Black Sea and this baby knocked it clean out of the sky.'

'Turkey is spending over £1.5b and we are, so far, looking at the four units they have taken delivery of. They obviously won't tell us where they all are and, each day, they give us new coordinates to follow around the one we are working on.

'Clever as you like. They chuck one of your 40N6 missiles 450km and have a .9 chance of knocking a spy plane out of the stratosphere or a .7 chance of taking out a ballistic missile. Again, with your 40N6, it is a semi-active radar homing device, guided to its target by an external radar from command. But crucially, it also has an active radar homing head, which means it can do its own thing; hunt and destroy over 400km from below the radar horizon. You really wouldn't see this thing coming.

'It packs a few smaller missiles as well, all with active heads. The smaller 9M96 missiles can be guided with a shoulder mounted sight for dog fight type battle situations – you wouldn't want to be in the crosshairs.

'Each separate battalion can monitor and destroy six moving targets at one time, and that hugely improves when the commands are working together. We might have the Rapier – but the Russians and their new buddies have this magnificent S-400 Triumph, which sounds like a bra and is definitely abreast of the latest technology.

'Walk this way, Mrs Taylor, and let me show you how we are tinkering around inside that eight-wheel command truck. Yesterday, the command truck sat over fifty miles away from the launchers and still remained fully operational.

'I hear your Mr Sam Smith has a bit of a fetish. For monster trucks, I mean, not the other one. We are permitted to take photographs on the Turk's approved camera held by the communications officer. They then approve the photographs and send them on to us through the Portsmouth office, no less than twenty-four hours after the rig has moved location. Wouldn't it be funny if poor contractor hating Mr Smith were to see a photograph of a pretty, smiling contractor, leant against one of these monsters in the bright mountain sun – while he is feeling all sweaty, stuck in a sealed office wearing nylon tights under his trousers?'

Jessica laughed at the suggestion, nodding enthusiastically even before Comhgall had finished explaining his idea for the jolly wheeze.

*

‘Hey Jace! How are you coping without me? Catching up on your Dalaman project after a couple of days away?’

‘Good to hear from you, love. I gather from the timing and content of your text last night, it was a long journey. I know you can’t give details, but first impression down there?’

‘My goodness Jace, I thought the *you-know-what* on HMS *you-know-who* was impressive. This shit is mind-blowing. It is nice to see Com and the team again; the Turkish contact is cool. Lovely hotel and a fantastic little town. But this is weird, I can sit on one of the hotel terraces and see the Syrians beat shit out of each other. How is your contracts engineer, as pretty as usual? Oh, I forgot to say I saved a Kangal today. Horrible story.’

‘Yes, Priti is as efficient and professional as always. I am not sure if it is good that she is dating the auditor or not. Not sure if it will keep him sweet or if he will just find more reasons to hang around the office, which I rather he didn’t. Anyway, you saved an electric jackhammer?’

‘No, a Kangal dog, not a kango hammer. You just want me to call you stupid over the phone, don’t you?’ Jessica intonated a sexy lisp. ‘You naughty dumb ass, you. And that reminds me, you idiot – you being an idiot reminds me, I mean, not the electric jackhammer. I had to get my vibrator out and show security; you made me look like a right dildo.’

‘You’ll thank me later. Later tonight, probably. Dog?’

‘Oh yes, eagle eye action girl here, saw a dog tied to an old tanker being filled with paraffin. As it was filling, it lifted on the knackered suspension. I ran in, Wonder Woman style, and saved the dog single handed from being hung. Everyone stopped and clapped. Then the mayor gave me a bunch of flowers and freedom of the city! Well, maybe not the last two-thirds of the story, but one lucky pooch who needs to learn to bark next time.’

‘My news is less canine. Amara has heard back from the Incirlik kerosene job and it is looking positive so far. I might be back out to Turkey towards the middle of …’

‘Jace, that isn’t right, is it? If the tanker was filling with paraffin, it would settle on the suspension, not rise. What if the suspension was broken on one side, would that work? You know, like a pivot or something; one side dip and the other rise, perhaps.’

‘The important thing is, the dog gets to fight another day. But no, unlikely. One side might go down more than the other, but they would both go down. Are you back out …’

‘So, what happened then, to hang the dog?’

‘My guess is the tanker was emptying, not filling. That would be the obvious scenario.’

‘Right, I have got to leave you. I have something planned for tonight, and no, it has nothing to do with my little suitcase surprise. I am off to buy you and Priti a gift. I wonder what colour best clashes with her complexion.’

*

Jessica checked out with reception, explaining the route of her planned walk around town. They offered to call her driver, but she declined. The receptionist confirmed the area inside the town, and especially the square and old bridge, were perfectly safe.

She walked along the busy side of the square, away from the canyon edge, planning to walk back along the edge later to see the flood-lit drop to the river below. She purchased a piece of antler in a pet stall, a holiday gift for Brian. There were then two rows of stalls, seemingly selling the identical selection of men’s clothes, including the red and white Kurdish scarfs. She purchased a lovely silk jamana for Priti, a traditional cotton keffiyeh for Jason and a hat for herself. Pleased with her purchases, she cut the corner of the square towards the old stone bridge to cross to the Turkmen side and buy their version; they were probably all made in China anyway, and to find a restaurant selling beer.

Three shots rang out. The first from one gun and two from another. Without a single scream that Jessica noticed, the small crowd ran to the edges of the square for shelter. Jessica turned and ran back towards the keffiyeh stall, almost tripping over a small girl, perhaps nine years old, running towards the centre of the square. Jessica reached out to grab the child but missed. Taking a few more steps, she came to a halt, knowing she could not ignore the plight of the child. Taking deep breaths, she turned to face a man stood towards the centre of the now completely empty square, other than a man lying face down and the child trying to drag him across the cobbles.

Jessica raised both arms.

'*Lutfen, lutfen.* Let me take the child away.'

Jessica walked towards the girl, still tugging on the dead, or dying man's leg. Jessica had dated a Turkish man five years before, another soldier, who called her *Kizum*, meaning *my girl* and also *my daughter.* The friend had other pet names for Jessica. She tried to remember them. Perhaps my sweet. She remembered he called her his lioness, which gave some comfort. The man screamed at Jessica. She flinched, continuing to walk towards the couple on the ground. The man wore a suicide vest, a mass of duct tape, and wires. A lamp switch held in his left hand, connected by orange electrical flex to the black vest. Another shot fired, Jessica paused, before continuing the journey, not sure what to do if she ever arrived at the destination.

'*Kizum. Lutfen, gel?*' Jessica tried to entice the girl away from the body. The body was of a young jandarma. A policeman, patrolling the square of happy shoppers enjoying the cool evening. Sirens sounded in the distance. The pool of blood spread outwards. Part of the young man's head and neck were missing. His eyelids fluttered. Jessica took the silk jamana from the plastic bag and folded it into the hole in his head. She wrapped the keffiyeh around his head, tying a single knot over the jamana. The white of the keffiyeh turned red.

'Darling. *Kizum.* You need to come with me. He will be fine, I promise.'

'He my brother.'

'I know sweetie.'

The bomber screamed *'Allah akbar.'*

The soldier's hand bent grotesquely; shot or broken in his fall. His army pistol lay trapped against the ground.

'Is it loaded? *Yuklu degil mi?*'

His lips moved, trembled, but Jessica could hear no reply. She made eye contact with the screaming bomber; his eyes wide. He levelled the gun at her face, still clutching the bomb switch. She dropped her gaze to a wheelie bin on the edge of the square and then immediately back to his eyes. Diverted, he spun around to confront whoever Jessica may have noticed, firing another shot towards the stone bridge.

Jessica grabbed the policeman's pistol. A semi-automatic, larger than the one she and her lover Cavus had played with, during their lovemaking years before and which she had fired in anger, shortly afterwards. The bomber span back around to face Jessica. She lined the single white dot of the site with the bomber's head and fired, missing her target. Tilting the pistol, she aligned the three white dots with his head and fired again. His shoulder burst into an explosion of blood, spinning him away from her. She fired two more times, one hitting between his shoulder blades, he fell forward, away from Jessica.

She dropped the gun and moved to grab the screaming girl. A riot shield knocked her forward across the bleeding policeman. Hands grabbed her knees and shoulders. With her facing the ground, four soldiers ran with Jessica in the general direction of the hotel. They moved closer to the canyon, she could see the floodlit ravine walls, but not down to the river. Her shoulder dislocated, she passed out.

*

'Jace. I am fine I promise.'

Camhgall, the driver and a jandarma officer sat in the empty hotel breakfast room, now gone midnight, watching Jessica take the call.

'I have a flight booked. I will be with you by tomorrow evening.'

'No Jace. No! I fucking mean it. I don't want you turning up with petrol station carnations and ruining my evening. I mean it Jace. Do. Not. Fly. Down. Here! The jandarma is arranging a direct flight for me, directly back to Dalaman in military transport. In the meantime, I want some space and sleep.'

'Fuck's sake Jess. You have to get involved in everything, don't you? Bloody dogs, bloody soldiers, bloody kids. You need to start prioritising us!'

'Don't swear at me.'

Jason lowered his voice.

'Sorry love. Sorry. I was so scared. I love you so much, you have no idea.'

'I have no idea? How fucking dare you? I spent a week watching you die with virus last year; no thought for me, at all. All I did tonight was hurt my shoulder.'

'It was on Al Jazeera. I flicked it on when we heard there was an incident in Sehir and you didn't pick up your phone. I sat watching my wife get shot at, and almost blown up, with a mouth full of bloody peanuts. Christ Jess.'

'On your own, or relaxing with your friend?'

'Oh, fuck off.'

The couple remained silent. Jessica stared at her phone on the table.

‘Salted or dry …?’

‘Salted. Which shoulder?’

‘My left. They were going to take me to hospital. Driver pushed his way in and popped it back. Sorted. Smarted a bit.’ Jessica glanced at her driver, he smiled back. ‘I have refused hospital; I couldn’t hack the journey, but an army medic checked me over.’

‘They haven’t released your name or mentioned that you are a foreigner.’

‘Yeah, good. Apparently, they muddy the waters to stop the bad guys coming after me, whilst they investigate. But it looks like the guy acted alone, thank God. Jace, I am going now. The jandarma want me to meet somebody. I’ll call later if I can’t sleep. Don’t call me, in case I am asleep.’

‘Sorry I swore at you.’

‘Sorry I keep shooting people.’

*

‘Mrs Taylor, we cannot make you see these people, but …’

Comhgall spoke over the jandarma officer. ‘Jess, love. See these people. I will stay here with you. We end the session as soon as you want. I am not suggesting this for them, or for the jandarma. I think it is the best thing for you, love.’

'I'm not your fucking love, Com. Please call me Mrs Taylor, you know the rules.'

Jessica ground her teeth, staring into middle distance. She addressed the jandarma officer.

'The girl?'

'Back home with her family. They are very worried about their son; he lost a lot of blood. Sorry, you know that. He is in a surgical ward. They do not think he has suffered any brain damage; they are just treating the trauma.'

'Will he live?'

The officer shrugged.

'And the other guy?'

'He will survive. He was wearing a bulletproof vest made to look like a suicide vest, no explosives. The second shot knocked him to the ground and broke a vertebra; no permanent damage to his back.'

'I aimed at his head, three times! He nearly made me into a fucking killer. And you want me to meet his mum and dad? If they had done their fucking job properly, we wouldn't be here now. I hope he fucking dies. *Insallah.*'

'Mrs Taylor,' Comahgall and Jessica made eye contact. Both smiled. Jessica looked down. 'Meet them, tell them what awful parents they are. Tell them they don't deserve a son and that you hope he dies.

But see, just see for yourself, that this demon is not what you think. It will help you sleep.'

'For Christ sake Com. Let's get on with it.'

*

Jessica stood as they led the couple into the room, showing them to seats. Neither sat. The father held a cap between his hands. She looked slightly older than him, wearing country scarfs, layered skirts and tunic. The women moved together and threw their arms around each other, sobbing. Eventually, Jessica and Anna sat on a bench seat. The man stood in front of them. The jandarma officer translated.

'He was not a bad boy. Not so clever. He loves me and his father. He loves God also, but they argue sometimes. It is difficult. I am not making excuses, but he tries to ignore the voices. Last year …'

The mother stopped speaking and looked towards the translating officer. The officer nodded her head. Anna continued.

'Last year he approached by Daesh. Islamic State? They are just dog shit.' She dropped her gaze. Her husband, Baba, wrung his cap, the stitching breaking. 'They say he serving God. First, they made him run messages. Then they made him drive kerosene over the border.' Anna looked at the officer again. 'He saw them kill a man. We called the jandarma, but he came to the square and I am not excusing what he did, but I think he like to make a fuss and then say goodbye to this world by police shooting him. Thank you for saving the girl. Thank you for trying to save the policeman. Thank you for stopping my son. Thank you for not killing him.'

*

Comhgall had housekeeping take a two-seater leather couch from reception through to Jessica's private courtyard. She sat crossed legged wearing her silk pyjama top in the warm autumn sun; Amara appeared onto the screen.

'Hey Vanilla. Sleep well?'

'Not as bad as I was expecting, thanks. I haven't been out of my room for two days, but I feel ok this morning. The jandarma policeman is slowly improving; I have lost count of the operations he has had. Apparently, a world leading plastic surgeon in Iran has offered to do the restructuring, if he survives. The little girl is so worried about her big brother, she isn't showing any signs of stress about her own brush with death. Jason is spitting bullets because I don't want him here and don't want to go back to the shack in Koyaka or the UK. He even got that girlfriend of his to try and talk me around. I actually want to be left alone and get on with the job.'

Amara released a long sigh. She was not going to join the queue of people forcing unwanted advice on her friend.

'Look, Vanilla, I have a few bits of news for you. It does not mean I agree with your wishes.' She took a deep breath. 'Sam and I talked HR around. You can stay on the job, but only if you zoom me daily and promise to be honest with me about your mental health. That, young lady, is non-negotiable.

'Our security department is heavily involved. The *exec* had to cut his game of golf short with the Metropolitan Police Chief, when you hit the news. The Turkish jandarma has impounded all CCTV footage of the incident. The only coverage is the phone video doing the rounds, but that isn't clear enough to identify you. One day you will want to watch it, you look so brave. Security is monitoring the net for your name and the shooting. Your second name was mentioned once; we think on a private Facebook page belonging to your hotel receptionist. The jandarma took it down and warned him off.

'Onslow is due out soon to have a look at the S-400 Compatibility project and installing Bridge. He has finished installing Bridge at the carrier end. You are correct, he is very good.'

'I am looking forward to seeing Onslow, but he fusses almost as much as you and Jace. I seem to attract bleeding hearts who want to mother me. Even Comhgall thinks he can call me love, now.

'Amara, I want to talk to you about the Incirlik project. Can you get me access to the project file please?'

‘Jess! You have three projects on the go, and you are sticking your nose into Priti’s. Have you not enough on your plate? I know your Christmas bonus is looming, but really?’

‘I think you might need to bring in Ethics. I have a theory.’

*

A flurry of early snow fell during the night. In a dressing gown, her heavy Mongolian wool jacket and untied work boots, Jessica stood in the middle of the tiny courtyard, tilting back her head to allow the snowflakes to land on her tongue. With her hair wet and crusty from the snow, she stripped her cold and wet pyjamas, slipping under the cool duck down duvet in the cold bedroom, windows opened, and slept heavily until the sun penetrated her dreams mid-morning.

The morning warm, compared with the chilly night. She dressed in three-quarter length linen trousers and a baggy striped cheesecloth top, gathered with a cloth tie-belt. Her hair fell longer than she normally wore it, soft, silky but disobedient from the snowflake wash and pillow dry. She pulled it back into a loose, small ponytail and crowned the outfit with a calfskin hat that she had bought on the evening of the shooting and rescued from the square by the jandarma on the following morning. She found a white crop sports bra and pulled it on, underneath the thin shirt; she would not have bothered further west or back in Britain.

Driver sat in the corridor outside her room. A large laptop bag rested unzipped on his knee. He wore his jacket indoors, complete with bulge under his left arm.'

'Hey Mrs Taylor. You are looking relaxed this morning. How is the shoulder?'

'Have you been here all night? What's with the bag, run out of violin cases? I'm going for a stroll, alone, if that is ok with you, Driver. I don't mean to sound rude.'

'I have just taken over from Passenger, but please do not feel alarmed. You are perfectly safe; this is just to give you some added confidence and to earn me some overtime. Let's keep it going until after the weekend and see how you feel. I could do with the cash.'

Jessica strolled into the square, her chin up and wearing a thin, forced smile. Parked in the centre of the square stood an armoured wheeled truck with a fixed machine gun, a small tank. Jandarma lent against the sunny side of the vehicle, smoking and chatting. Rest of the square appeared back to normal.

She aimed in a direct line towards the bridge, deciding to buy her scarfs in the Turkmen quarter before retracing her steps to the Kurdish stalls. She did not want to repeat her previous shopping trip. She skirted around the dark patch where blood stained the sandy cement between the cobbles. The impact made greater by the cobbles and the surrounding area scrubbed clean. She took a deep breath. As she reached near to the armoured vehicle, the jandarma snapped to attention, holding a salute until she had passed them. She avoided looking.

Out of the corner of her eye, she made out a figure running towards her from the area of the market stalls, clutching a plastic bag to his stomach. She froze, mouth open, unable to scream, run or defend herself.

Driver pushed in front, right hand gripping the contents of his open devices bag, left hand held up towards the intruder. He shouted.

'*DUR!*'

The man stumbled to a stop on the cobbles just a few yards away. Jessica recognised him as the owner of the stall where she had bought the scarfs.

'*Ozur dilerim. Hediye. Bayan icin.*' He gestured at Jessica, holding forward the bag.

Driver met the man halfway and peered into the bag. The contents of his own bag pointing at the man's chest. The jandarma approached from the sides in a pincer movement, assault rifles pressed against their shoulders.

'*Peki.*' Driver gave a reassuring wave to the soldiers. '*Peki. Fular. Keffiyeh.*'

Driver flexed his hand, gesturing for the man to approach Jessica. She swallowed hard.

‘Lady. I have replacement for shopping. Sorry I scare you. I am fool.’

Jessica laid her hand on the man’s shoulder, too shaken to speak, and nodded. Opening the bag, she saw the same two scarves, which she had previously bought for Priti and Jason, and a beautiful silk pashmina in the pattern of a peacock butterfly. The pashmina had formed the centrepiece of the stallholder’s simple display. She swallowed hard again and nodded her thanks. He smiled, bowed, took two steps backwards and turned towards his stall. The jandarma returned to their positions.

‘Shall I walk you back to the hotel Mrs Taylor?’

She shook her head. ‘Thank you for ignoring me and following.’

Driver shrugged.

‘May I walk with you, Mrs Taylor? I am good at carrying shopping. He held out a hand to take the plastic bag of scarfs.’

The bridge caught a breeze running along the canyon in an otherwise still day. They rested against the stone balustrade, between two stone shops in the bridge arcade. Jessica shivered, driver stood closer, half his broad chest and shoulder covering most of her back to share body heat.

‘I am sure you will tell me to mind my own business …’

'Mind your own business.'

'… but why not pop back to your husband or at least let him come here?'

'Have you got a wife or girlfriend?'

'Boyfriend. Passenger and I have been dating for over a year. Well, more than just dating, I guess.'

'And do you not worry about him, especially in your job?'

'We are both professionals. Both ex-special forces. But yes, I do sometimes.'

'Today, you stepped forward to protect me. If Passenger was there, you would have stepped away from him, to protect me. I just cannot concentrate on myself with Jason around. He is my good-time husband. When I am down or scared, I become emotionally single again. A lonely spinster of a wife.'

'Don't leave it too long, Mrs Taylor. Don't be a stranger.'

'Like I said, Driver, mind your own business.'

He ran his hand around her waist and pulled her firmly back against his chest in a reassuring hug. She felt his bicep, solid and bulging, against her underarm.

'These scarves won't buy themselves Mrs Taylor.'

They continued over the bridge and browsed the market and trinket stalls in the Turkmen quarter. As they passed each stall, the owner stood or walked out onto the path to stare after the couple. She selected a golden and red keffiyeh for Priti and a Palestinian style black-and-white pattern for Jason. The stallholder refused to take the money. On the walk back, each stallholder stepped forward to give her a small gift from their stall. Glass jewellery, sweets, scarfs, lace, even a pair of slippers to match the colours of her top. The blacksmith stepped forward with a huge toothless grin and handed her a pair of sheepshearing shears, wrapped in newspaper.

Back in the hotel, she called in to Amara.

'Hey, Am, just checking in as promised. Nope, a quiet day. I popped to the shop, nothing to report, I feel fine.'

*

Jessica's work email and live messages went into automatic lockdown following the shooting. She had full contact with her managers, Sam and Amara, HR and security. Amara arranged for a special dispensation to keep her email access open to Jason. They redirected all other incoming emails to Trish, for triage. Following her conversations with Amara, the access to project files was reinstated.

She walked a lap of the square and crossed the bridge. Taking a couple of hours to soak up the mountain sun. Stepping over the low stone balustrade which protected the edge of the canyon, she picked a posy of late flowering mountain Kalmia.

The jandarma, positioned with the armoured vehicle, stood and saluted as she approached. She smiled at the soldiers before tucking the stems of the flowers into the vent slots at the end of the heavy machinegun.

Over the following days, locals added to the flowers until the vehicle appeared to float on a floral carpet, which extended over the blood-stained cobbles.

'Jessica! How are you? What has happened, why the email lockdown? I thought you got yourself sacked, or in hospital. Trish wouldn't tell me, and I emailed your husband, but he would not explain either.'

'Onslow, good to see a friendly face. Welcome to the next stage of the project.' She held both his hands. 'Long story. Hopefully remaining restrictions on my profile will go this week. I guess you know we had an incident a couple of weeks ago. In the square outside. Security threw a blanket over me, but things are fine now.'

'I had a fairly generic brief from security about avoiding public meetings and military targets. I guess the floral installation with the army tank is relevant?'

'Ons, come and sit in my room for a minute and I will fill you in.'

*

Driver now stood down from his position in the corridor, as Jessica grew in confidence and normality returned. The parents of the shooter relocated to a small Kurdish community in the Black Sea region of Turkey for their own protection. The shooter and the injured policeman continued to recover; the little girl returned to school.

'Let's sit in the sun.'

Onslow sat on the leather two-seater in Jessica's courtyard. Jessica pulled up the garden chair close, so that her feet located between Onslow's, and their legs touched. She chewed hard on her bottom lip. Onslow rested his hand against her cheek and gently prised her bottom lip from between her teeth with his thumb.

'You are one scrummy woman, Jess, but you mustn't eat yourself.'

She closed her eyes, turned her face to kiss his palm and made a deep sigh.

'You want to tell me something, but don't feel you have to, now. Take your time. I will be here for a few days or even weeks.'

Jessica pulled out his mobile from his hip pocket and handed it to him to fingerprint swipe open. She tapped the screen, finding the Al Jazeera phone coverage on You Tube.

'Sorry Ons, I know you are a bit, a bit squeamish.'

'You mean a coward. Let's have a look then.'

Onslow played the video. The first few seconds comprised a slow panoramic of the castle walls around the hotel, with a Turkish commentary. Three shots fired, and the camera spun around to face an emptying square, with faces fleeing towards the lens. Jessica shuddered and walked to her bedroom, returning with a throw. She sat across Onslow's lap facing him, tucking her feet onto the couch. She pulled the throw over her head and body and nestled her cheek against his chest in the dark.

Onslow gasped as the little girl ran to the crumpled body on the ground, almost colliding with the shooter; his arms extended in the shape of a crucifixion, with head facing the sky in ecstasy. Onslow stifled a yelped *no* as Jessica entered the shot, immediately recognising her, despite the distance and poor quality of the footage. Onslow felt her chest heave against his stomach and tears seep through his shirt. He threaded his hand through her hair, drawing her closer as a further shot rang out on the video.

Jessica knelt by the body, performing first aid as the shooter screamed and threatened her with the gun. Onslow saw the volume of vest from under a puffer jacket, with a bright orange length of cable running to his hand.

He spun away from Jessica and shot again towards the bridge. Jessica pulled the gun from under the policeman and the shooter fell forward, a fountain of blood spouting from his shoulder. Police were already running towards the scene from the direction of the camera, riot shields raised for protection against the flash of an explosion. Jessica's shoulder dislocated on the sprint to safety; a fifth soldier grabbing around her shoulder to provide extra support as the detached arm swung limply in the grip of his comrade.

Onslow lay the phone down. Neither spoke. Light snoring replaced the tears. Following fifteen minutes, Onslow stood, carrying the scrunched Jessica against his chest, as he might a sleeping child, to bed.

More than an hour passed when Jessica's phone rang. Onslow pulled it from her back pocket and swiped open the call. The caller ID showing *Mr Bambi.*

'Onslow Dalliance, Company. Mrs Taylors phone, may I help please?'

'Is she there?'

'Mrs Taylor is away from the phone. Can I take a message, or ask her to call back?'

There followed a short pause.

'It is Jason here. Her husband. Is she ok Onslow?'

'Yes Jason, sorry I didn't recognise your voice. She is asleep at the moment; shall I wake her?'

'No. That is ok. Thank you. Are you sure she is ok?'

‘She is fine. She is right next to me. I have only just arrived, she got upset explaining what happened. She will be fine after a sleep.’

‘At least she didn’t ban you Onslow. You must be her favourite, at the moment. Thank you for keeping an eye on her.’

‘I will get her to call you Jason. It is not that I am the favourite, and I think you know that. It is because she loves you so much and I am just an old friend. She doesn’t need to protect me, like she wants to protect you.’

Chapter eleven

Jessica answered the knock at her door.

'May I come in, please? Are you available to run through progress and project status?'

'No Onslow, not in my bedroom. Please book the conference room with reception. I will be there in ten.'

'Sure. I just thought you might … Sure, I will arrange coffee.'

The colleagues sat next to each other, running through the plan on Jessica's laptop.

'I can see where we are, Onslow. Two things: how is the Bridge initial works going and are Comhgall and the Turks suspicious?'

'I don't think so Jess, Jessica, Mrs Taylor. S-400 Compatibility is going well, thanks in part to your management. Comhgall's team are too busy patting each other on the back to notice me spending tremendous amounts of time slipping in my additional work, between running checks and sorting niggles.'

'Don't look so smug Ons, we shouldn't have to lie to the client and our own people. I even wonder how legal this is.'

Onslow rolled his eyes.

‘Sorry Mrs Taylor. I will try harder to do a worse job and not enjoy my work in the future.’

‘Hey Ons, I didn’t mean that. Sorry. It just goes against the grain. Our Sam Smith is a reptile, like those bloody snails he keeps. But I don’t know why Amara is going along with this and dragging me along. And I am dragging you along.’

‘Molluscs, but I know what you mean.’

Jessica rolled her eyes this time, at being corrected. Onslow took her arm in both hands and shook it playfully, as she did when teasing him. She reluctantly smiled in return.

‘It won’t be long before I can leave site for a bit. I have added a tentative line in the plan to return for the end of November, to throw the switch and turn on Bridge. Job done.’

‘Job done for first battalion, Ons. You will have to repeat the work for the remaining three battalions and start again next year on the next tranche of deliveries.’

‘You are a smile a minute Mrs T. Take a month back at Koyaka with Jason – let Comhgall run this end. He now relies on your direction, because it is there, but he is more than capable of running his own show. And I am sure you can backseat drive, from the sunny Aegean.’

*

Jessica collected her hire car from Milas Bodrum airport carpark, the battery flat. A group of junior hockey players stopped boarding their bus to help. After arguing who should drive, a girl, seemingly around twelve years old, pushed her way into the driver's seat, giggling. With half a dozen players pushing, they bump started the heavy pickup. It spluttered and coughed into life and the young driver, barely tall enough to see over the steering wheel, decided it needed at least three laps of the carpark, weaving around parked vehicles with the radio blaring, before it was ready to handover, back to Jessica. Her friends laughed, jumping on the spot and waving, each time the seemingly driverless car sped past the group.

The temperature soared, compared with the mountainous east. Jessica ignored Priti's instruction and drove to the shack, on route, rather than directly to the hotel to see Jason. In her mind, Jessica also worked through the various put downs she might use next time Priti tried to boss her.

Driving the more direct, but much slower, scenic route over the dry interior of Bodrum Peninsula she headed towards the smoky sky above Oren. The mayor, a local man, campaigned hard for election and promised every resident everything they wanted. Once elected, he took a backhander, sold municipal land to an energy company to build a carbuncle of a power station against the beach and promptly moved to a big house in Marmaris, on the proceeds.

Jessica parked her pick-up, leaving the engine ticking over rather than risk it not starting. A lady sold freshly cooked *gozleme* at the side of the road. Jessica drank all but an inch of water from a litre bottle before walking a few yards into the pine forest to pee, stamping her feet to warn off scorpions and snakes, including the feared desert vipers who lived in the ditches and hedgerows. Rinsing her hands with the already warming inch of water, she crossed back to the lady, ordering a cheese and potato Turkish pancake, with a tulip-glass of tea, boiled on a wood-fired stove.

Jessica pointed to the sulphureous sky towards Oren.

'Guc istasyonu?'

'Hayir. Orman yanginlari.'

'Oyle mi? Forest fire? Blimey. Under control? *Tamam?*

The lady shrugged. Jessica ate a slice of the hot pancake as a small, brightly painted lorry, carrying a disgruntled cow, pulled over. The driver walked to the same tree Jessica had used. He did not carry water to rinse his hands. He ordered a minced lamb *gozleme* and salty *ayran* buttermilk drink in a steel cup.

'Where you going?'

'Koyaka. Will I get through?'

He shook his head, undecided.

'Have plenty of petrol, in case you need to turn back. The Coastguard is evacuating residents from Oren. They are cut off and the fire is at the power station. They are clearing forest to break between the fire and Koyaka. He held his face to the scorching breeze and sniffed the air, as Brian her dog would, out of the car window.

'Autumn is very late. Hot wind, no rain. The forests are dry.' He shrugged. '*Ne olacak.*'

He stuffed the last of his lunch into his mouth, half waving and half saluting the women goodbye. He returned from his truck with two fishing line necklaces, each holding the turquoise glass evil eye charm to ward-off spirits and bad luck. He placed one around the neck of each woman and left.

Jessica slowed; workers spilled across the narrow lane. They worked in the blazing sun to clear trees and scrub, using heavy bulldozers. Local farmers worked alongside, clearing debris and ploughing dry grass into the dirt. A young plough-hand used a narrow plough pulled by a mule, to turnover a steep section of inaccessible knoll. She wore only short rubber boots over bare feet, a billowing pair of cotton bloomers, a thin boy's shirt, unbuttoned and tied into a knot and a Formula-One, bright red baseball cap. The mule wore a straw hat. Its ears poked through and protected from the sun by swatches of muslin tied with string. Sweat poured down the backs of the team, encrusted with dust and flecks of vegetation. Even in this more prosperous Aegean region, Jessica knew the young woman earned less than £10 for each day she toiled.

Jessica inched forward. Seeing a friendly, foreign female face, the woman stopped to offer Jessica a wide overhead wave. Jessica continued towards home, the air-con on full and the vents shut against the putrid smoke.

With just a few miles to go, the air thickened and darkened again with smoke. A young volunteer waved down Jessica and held a crude hand-drawn map showing a highlighted diversion. Jessica studied it through the window before mouthing a thank you and pulling off the road onto a dry dirt track. Weaving along a steepening route of mostly logging roads and forest firebreaks, she pulled alongside a small, stranded Fiat. The woman sat in the driver's seat, the car in reverse gear, as the man tried to help push the car up the steep hill backwards. Jessica had a tow rope with her spare wheel. Without speaking to the couple, she fixed the rope and gestured for them to continue reversing up the hill, but to avoid damaging the burning transmission further, by continuing to rev and slip the clutch.

The man jumped into the back of the pickup to reduce weight in the car. Jessica selected four-wheel drive, low ratio and differential-lock. She released the clutch without touching the accelerator and allowed the pickup to creep up the steep gravel road at little more than walking pace.

Over an hour later, with the man occasionally offering directions through the closed side window, they reached the main road. Jessica hung the evil eye charm around the woman's neck and watched them drive up the mountain road towards the city of Mugla. Jessica continued down the mountain towards Koyaka, stopping behind a line of traffic, the road now thick with black and sulphurous-yellow smoke. Blue lights lined the road. A helicopter dropped tons of seawater onto the smouldering downwind side of the road, just a few yards away; the down force rocking Jessica's car.

Volunteers parked SUV's at either end of the opaque section of road, floodlights glaring back towards each other. As firefighters and other volunteers fought the flames, using the road as a natural break, the SUV volunteers communicated by mobile phones to direct small groups of traffic through the smoke, towards the opposite headlights.

Jessica led her group cars, inching towards the headlights, avoiding the firefighters in breathing apparatus, fighting intense pockets of flame as it tried to leap across the road on the wind, and to freedom.

Jessica pulled into the village, stopping outside her old landlord's building supply shop.

Oglan stood at the door with his mother, watching the smoke and embers creep down the hillside.

'Oglan, love. Can I hire a petrol water pump? Do you do those, please? The petrol station is closed; do you have petrol?'

'Yes, we have. For empty holes full of water. No petrol – your car. Money later, lady.'

Oglan heaved the heavy pump onto the back of the pickup and jumped in to steady it as Jessica continued down the hill towards the river and her shack. The bed-and-breakfast staff worked in the grounds and in Jessica's garden to remove any combustible materials, raking the loose grass and throwing rubbish into the river.

The fire burned in the reeds on the opposite bank. Either side of the flames appeared untouched, but a tongue of fire twenty meters wide licked at the river.

Oglan started the pump on the dregs of fuel and syphoned more petrol from Jessica's car. As Jessica walked to the river to position the inlet hose, she felt the fire hot against her head and face. Not trying to tackle the actual fire from across the river, she sprayed the water onto the vegetation and as high up the eucalyptus trees as the water jet reached.

Occasional flames spat across the river, wilting the higher leaves. Jessica lived at one end of a eucalyptus wood, which wound through the houses to keep the land drained. If the fire jumped the river and caught the trees, it would rip through the heart of the village. She doused the higher fires as Oglan and the hotel staff smothered the lower fires. The thin layer of leaves and twigs settled on her tin roof, smouldered and smoked. Unable to leave an area of wilting trees waiting for the opportunity to ignite, she called to Oglan who, scared to disturb the tinder dry debris should it flare, cut the hose taking spring water to her tank and doused the roof; the gentle flow barely coping as the roof steamed with the evaporating water.

Oglan poured petrol into the tank of the running pump. As he moved away, face covered by his T-shirt from the heat of the fire, fumes or drips from the refuelling ignited and Oglan and the pump erupted into a ball of flame. Jessica turned to douse the flames and to cool Oglan's body, but the flash ended as Oglan scurried away, throwing away the petrol can in case that also exploded.

*

Jessica, Oglan and the owner of the bed-and-breakfast sat on rocks close to the river's edge, watching a thick scum of ash and debris flow away to the sea. The reeds opposite blackened. Sahip cracked open three beers. She ignored Jessica's protests regarding Oglan's age. The phone rang.

'Hey Amara. Really sorry I didn't check in. I travelled back today; I clean forgot.'

‘No problem, Vanilla. I don’t mean to chase you. Everything ok? Jason is moaning because you are staying in the shack instead of going straight to Dalaman to see him. You are not doing your *pull the drawbridge up* Jessica thing, are you?’

‘No, honestly Am. Anyway, he detailed his best friend to tell me he wanted me in his bed tonight. I am not sure that counts.’

‘But everything else ok Jess? Promise? What have you been up to, you sound deflated?’

‘Just the journey was tiring, Am. Nothing else. Had a lovely gozleme lunch at a roadside stall. That is about the most exciting thing that happened to me today. Anyway, how are you keeping? How is that gorgeous wife of yours and that sinister bloody cat, Jeffrey? And I don’t want to nag you Amara, but there is still nothing on file about the kerosene plant. I wouldn’t mind making a bit of a start on that as soon as possible, please.’

Chapter twelve

‘Thank you all for attending this video meeting. But, sorry Jason, I am not sure why you are here. Your Dalaman *Damp* job is Contract’s baby, not ours. Even though I realise your wife is going for Company domination.’

‘Because your Area Project Manager told me to attend, Sam.’ Jason pointedly refusing to use Sam’s surname.

Jason mentioned earlier to his wife how he automatically disliked anyone who Jessica dislikes. She asked if that applied to Priti.

‘Mr Smith. I want to touch on the kerosene job at the Incirlik airbase in eastern Turkey. I wanted you to hear Jason’s thoughts.’

Amara spoke. ‘The Incirlik project is likely to go to Contracts as well. I am not sure why you are so interested. I got you access to the file, but I would much rather you concentrate on what we are paying you for.’

‘I have concerns. Jason’s potential involvement,’ Jason closed his eyes for a moment in exasperation, ‘but also security, legal and ethics. I am happy to go to Ethics directly, if you prefer.’

Sam, pleased with the level of patronising he squeezed in, responded. 'No Jess, please continue. None of us have anything better to do. How does this worry your pretty little head? How can we make everything better for the Taylor household?'

Amara intervened. 'Sam! That is enough. Jessica is one of our most experienced *Areas*. If you do not want to hear this, then just kindly leave the meeting.'

Sam sat back in his chair, a smirk on his face.

'Sorry. I forgot how Jess is such the centre of everyone's life, here.' Sam referring to Amara's previous liaison with Jessica, and in front of her husband.

'Jess love, please continue.'

'At the Incirlik kick-off meeting, Jason realised the new plant may process kerosene into military aviation fuel.'

'That is only a guess Jess, I made that clear.'

'Please explain to Amara and Sam the points they said to make you consider the possibility.'

'No, no, no! Please spare us the boring details about a couple of lengths of pipe and a few nuts and bolts.'

'Sam is right, Jess. Just tell us what is worrying you both. Or at least worrying you; Jason does not seem too bothered. I am assuming, this is why you keep referring to Incirlik as the kerosene job? So what, if it is?'

Jessica continued, fighting to keep the emotion from her voice.

'The other week, I saved a dog from being hung. His owner tied a short leash to the wing mirror of a bowser, which then lifted as it emptied. I also shot a man who I thought would blow up a little girl.'

Sam made to offer a snide comment but exhaled a loud sigh instead.

'Sorry Mr Smith, this must bore you. Just another dog, another child, another foreigner.

'The bowsers were emptying paraffin, or kerosene if you like, into a big road tanker. They bullied the poor guy, who I shot, into driving kerosene over the border in small trucks and tractor pulled bowsers, through Turkmen held areas. In other words, with Turkey's consent. I realised they were importing kerosene in small tankers and offloading it into big road tankers.'

'*They* being *who*, exactly, Jess?'

'Islamic-State, Amara. Syrian oil and hydrocarbons, including kerosene, are strictly sanctioned. Nobody except Russia is buying Syrian kerosene. The Russians buy it to help fund Assad and the Syrian Armed Forces.

'But where is Islamic-State receiving funding, do you think? Who is funding Islamic-State to fight the

Kurds? Except for Turkey, who else even *wants* Islamic-State funded, to fight the Kurds?
'Who has access to any Syrian oilfields and refineries? Well, Syria obviously, but also Islamic-State, within the caliphate. Islamic-State even has access to some Iraqi oilfields and refineries.
'Turkey, I suspect, I know, is directly funding Islamic-State to fight the Kurds. The same Islamic-State who keeps knocking holes in European capitals.'

'I am not an expert in the controls, bonded-stores and everything, Jess, but my understanding is hydrocarbons have a DNA. Turkey could not move significant quantities of black-market kerosene onto the markets, especially the international commodities market. And they would be hard pushed to fund a war by hawking heating fuels around a few isolated towns. Even the logistics of where to store bulk quantities of illegal hydrocarbons makes it improbable.'

Jessica held Jason's gaze. The corners of her lips turned up and her eyes twinkled. She willed him to read her mind.

'Shit Jess. They are transporting and storing it in Incirlik – a secure base. Planning to process it through our new plant and burn it in NATO jets.'

'Yes Jace. They are. They don't even have to go to parliament to release funds to fight their covert war with the Kurds. The money or supplies they send to

Islamic-State, is paid for from Turkey's domestic, and NATO's in Turkey, jet fuel bill.'

For the first time in Jessica's experience, Sam sat silent, speechless. Amara spoke.

'Ok guys, this goes no further. We are not whistleblowing on one of our new markets and the very centre of NATO in the middle east. You all leave this to me, to handle. We all know how fragile Turkey's relationship is, with NATO and the west.'

The meeting closed. Not realising the video conference had still to shut down, Jason spoke to Jessica.

'I see what you mean about Sam Smith, love. He is such a dick.'

*

Jason's phase of *Damp* was ending, nine per cent ahead of schedule thanks to Jessica's guidance; over ten per cent ahead would suggest poor planning. Comhgall and the commissioning team finished installing S-400 Compatibility on the four battalions in service. Onslow arranged to meet Jessica in Sehir to activate Bridge project on the first battalion of S-400 Triumph, following his successful, secret, efficacy trials on the carriers for the *Naap* end of Bridge. Jessica could then plan for Onslow to complete Bridge activation on the remaining three delivered battalions of S-400, at a later date.

Jessica and Jason sat in the Ottoman Residence Restaurant, the fanciest boutique hotel in the Koyaka area, just a few hundred yards from the shack. Jason wore a cream silk pullover shirt, a gift from Jessica. She wore a brightly coloured, patterned cotton maxi-dress. She draped the keffiyeh she bought for Jason around her shoulders and chest for their long pre-dinner walk around the village before slipping it off in the restaurant for Jason; the dress cut low and the material thin.

'I like her company and everything, but I am glad Priti allowed my husband to see me alone this weekend.'

Jason snorted at his wife's backhanded compliment.

'So, you like her now?'

'I always have. She is lovely, hot, clever, hardworking, funny.' Jessica glanced from her plate to see the surprise on her husband's face. 'Seriously, I like her. When you first fell in love with me, I was her age. My skin was clear like hers. My tits were perter, like hers. My bum was smaller, like hers. My …'

'I have failed you, if you think for a moment that I love you any less now than when we first met. You are as drop-dead gorgeous now as when you stripped for me on that Italian beach. Is that why you booked the bridal suite here, for the weekend?'

Jessica shrugged. 'Have you told her, you know, that we haven't? You know. Have you told Priti that we haven't had sex since the shooting and all that?'

'Jess darling. First, it doesn't matter. Second, no, I haven't told Priti or anyone. And third, she wouldn't care less or think worse of you. As you kindly pointed out, I am just about old enough to be her dad. Nearly.'

'Nearly? She has the hots for you. You are in nearly every photograph of hers, since she landed in Turkey. I am in only two.'

'She showed you, her photos?'

'Company doesn't mind us taking personal photos on our work phones, anything to encourage us to carry them and stay contactable 24-7.'

'To answer the question?'

'Yes, I saw them in her laptop folders. Backup - iPhone – pictures – personal. She has quite a photographic eye. Jason getting out of the pool, Jason getting in the pool, Jason laughing, Jason in a working-at-height harness, Jason looking studious with a drawing. That kind of thing. Mind you, there is a striking photo of Priti wearing just a coil of rope, reclined on a riverboat. Don't worry, I checked dates – you were here with me.'

'And she showed you?'

‘She swiped me on to her profile on her laptop, when I wanted to update the *Damp* project file. Not supposed to share access, but I shouldn’t have been making the changes, really. So I did them on her log-in; just trying to help.’

‘So, she didn’t show you?’

‘Jace! Stop being so pedantic! I’m just saying, it isn’t healthy. You have a few photos of her and so do I. I mean, she is easy on the eye and everything. But she has just gone overboard with you.’

‘My photos?’

‘You showed me yours.’

‘When?’

‘You were sleepy. You probably don’t remember.’ She looked from her plate and pouted. ‘Really sleepy.’

‘You used my fingerprint to open my phone as I slept?’

Jessica shrugged. ‘Anyway, I brought you here, so you could do me all weekend and catch-up.’

‘Jess, darling, I’d love to do you all weekend in a posh hotel. But would you like to know what I really want to do?’

Jessica shrugged again.

‘I would like to take you home to your draughty shack, light the wood burner and lie in bed listening to the eucalyptus tree shed its seeds onto the tin roof. And if, only if, you want doing, only if you are ready, I will be there. It would be rude not to.’

Jessica beamed back at her husband.

‘Me too!’ She called to the waiter. ‘*Bakar misiniz*. Really sorry, can we check out, please? We have a change of plan. We will pay, obviously.’

‘No madam. Is no charge. You stay another time please, no charge. *Itfaiyecim*. We will pack your bag and walk it back to your house by the river.’

‘Jess, what was that about? And what did he call you?’

‘The shooting has been a terrible experience, but otherwise, hasn’t this been a lovely, shared adventure?’

‘Jess?’

‘The Turks have only had surnames for a few generations. I think they make-up names, depending on what you do.’

‘Jess?’

‘He called me his firefighter. I kind of, you know, by accident, saved the village from burning down. I don’t tell you these things, because you tell me off, for taking risks.’

Jason moved to the seat next to his wife and gave her a long hug.

'Never a dull moment, Jessica Taylor.'

'That is what Onslow says. Which reminds me, I am meeting Onslow back east next week. Let's get this sorted. I want to be home to give Brian the Christmas he deserves. I have left him with my sister for plenty long enough, poor dog.'

'Onslow says strange things. He said you were asleep in bed, next to him, when I called you after the shooting. Discuss.'

'Well, depends how you look at it. Yes, I was asleep, and yes, he was next to me in bed. But not what it sounds like. I cried myself to sleep, and he stayed with me. Clothes on and everything. It's not like he kissed me, or anything like that.' Jessica studied her husband for a reaction.

'Good. If he had, I'd rip his head off. I am being most trustful of you two, with your history; don't let me down.'

Jessica nodded. 'Would you rip his head off, if *I* had kissed *him*, do you think?'

'Yes! Now let's change the subject.'

'What if I just kissed him once, and nothing else?'

'I would just rip his head off once, and nothing else.'

Jessica nodded again.

'Has Amara spoken to you about attending another Incirlik meeting?'

'Yes, I was going to mention it tomorrow. She wants me to go, and act like nothing is up. There is absolutely no way I am helping Turkey to process jet kerosene to pay for Islamic-State to kill Kurds, Parisians, or Londoners even.'

'I spoke to Amara as well. I suggest follow your gut.'

'But?'

'No *but*, Jace.'

'But?'

'But I would go. It is so intriguing. If the meeting is fact finding only and not actually progressing the plant, you know, what harm could it do? Personally, I would go. Just saying.'

'I am worried Company will take it on, or at the very least, not shop the Turks for fear of losing a big customer. Especially with the Russians waiting to jump into NATO's shoes.'

'Hey, listen to you! I might have to stop calling you dumb ass soon.'

'Or just in bed, please? I am not worried about security or safety – it just leaves a nasty taste.'

‘The Egyptian Police used stun grenades against peaceful protestors once. I thought they were my supply, and I couldn’t sleep. Then I found out they were Israeli manufactured, and I was ok.’

‘What does that mean?’

‘It means, try not to follow my moral compass. Follow your own gut.’

They sat next to each other over Turkish coffee and sweet baklava. The manager refused to bring the bill and offered to drive them the few hundred yards to the shack, in the cooling night air; they declined.

The couple planned to stay in the hotel and so had no jackets to hand. Jessica wrapped the keffiyeh around her bare shoulders and lent into Jason.

‘We will light the stove as soon as we get back. I am not tired yet, we can sit and watch the flames together.’

‘Actually Jess, I don’t mind you being a bit cold.’

She stopped to slap his shoulder.

‘Stop looking at my chest! It is involuntary, you know; not for your amusement.’ They continued the short journey. ‘If you fly as far as Adana for Incirlik, well it is only a short hop to Antakya and then Sehir. You could meet Onslow properly. He is a great guy – you will soon see why I… anyway. Driver will pick you up. He took a bit of a shine to me.’

‘Everyone takes a shine to you, Jess.’

‘I don’t think I am his type. No, really, I am not his type. If Priti tags along, we might have to split her room cost. I am not sure how we could justify putting it through expenses. But it might not be her thing. But then, you will be there, so it will be her thing.’

Jessica turned to Jason in the opened doorway, allowing the keffiyeh to slip to the floor. She kissed him fully on the mouth and squirmed her cold chest into his.

‘That is *it* then, Jace. Decided. I will get Trish onto arrangements Monday.

*

Onslow arrived in Sehir a few days before Jessica. He failed to gain the access needed to the S-400 command truck to power up Bridge, and so spent his days tidying Quality Control reports. Jessica’s old suite was already allocated; reception gave her the adjacent first story room to Onslow. On realising, Onslow hinged back the dividing grids separating the two balconies and pushed together the tables and chairs.

They arrived mid-November. The early snow flurried around the square and bridge. It looked picturesque from a warm room looking out, but the biting cold made trips less appealing. They ate early in the mostly empty hotel restaurant, sat on the balcony until the cold sent them early to bed. Onslow took his two spare blankets, wrapping one around Jessica's shoulders and sharing the second across their laps.

'We have access from tomorrow Ons. Driver will collect us at seven o'clock. The working days, for us, will be short because of the weather and long nights, so let's press on.'

'Sure, Mrs T. Thank you for sorting access; I was getting nowhere. I must admit, I am not happy driving through the mountains at night-time; it doesn't feel safe. Are you still dragging Jason down here?'

'It doesn't seem so appealing now the weather has turned. Talking about feeling safe, it looks like Jason is going to rip your head off, for kissing me. Sorry.'

'Shit. Did you have to tell him? And you mentioned it was you who did the actual kissing?'

'To be honest, Onslow, he wasn't really listening. He is so unreasonable sometimes.'

The couple sat, looking over the black nightscape towards Syria. A few lights twinkled in the distance from Tuffahiyeh. Jessica remembered the imaginary curtain driver said hung from skyhooks along the border. She wondered if it was a blackout curtain with just a few pinpricks.

'I know how I report progress, but do you see it panning out the same way?'

‘Yes Jess, I think so. Everything is going fine. My end will be ready to rock-and-roll from 25th November. Bridge is an on-demand service, so I won’t know when it is actually used by the client for the first time, or if ever, but that is not part of our brief. Then I was thinking of having my head ripped off around the same time, perhaps the 26th. Could you ask him not to damage my face?’

‘No point, Ons, he doesn’t listen. Strange to end a project without seeing it work. I mean, I often do, but somebody, commissioning or someone, sees it. Have you heard any rumours about who the end user is? British intelligence, obviously. My guess is Royal Navy intelligence, Room 39. Might even be a dedicated team within a team. Like you and me.’

‘I guess so. I still think NATO is involved. Royal Navy operates it and NATO provide the political will, perhaps. Mind you, Company could have sold the system to China, for all we know. Should I say sorry, to Jason? Even though I really don’t remember doing much wrong.’

‘Sure, it can’t hurt. Don’t whimper though and, whatever you do, don’t hit him back – it will only antagonise him. He is actually a really gentle and sweet guy. Usually.’

Onslow stood, leaving the blankets for Jessica.

‘Sleep well Mrs T. I am only a scream away if you have another bad dream.’

'And you, Ons. Thank you for putting up with me. I am almost back to normal.'

'I was thinking of being hung for a sheep, rather than a lamb.'

'Yes, I don't blame you.'

Onslow bent at the waist, cupping Jessica's face and bringing his lips towards her. She raised a finger across her mouth, as if to silence him.

'I am glad he didn't blow you up Mrs Taylor.'

'Same here, Onslow.' She moved her finger from her mouth and, gently parting his lips, ran the tip of her nail along his teeth, making a faint clicking noise. 'And I am glad I got to see you again, while you still have your teeth.'

*

Onslow headed to work early each day, warming up back at the hotel late afternoon, before preparing for the following day on his secure laptop, analysing data and running tests. Bitter cold, the battalion donated him an artic combat coat. Jessica kept close to the army contact, arranging for Onslow to have the military support he needed and batting away increasingly tough questions about why the two remained, so long after Comhgall's commissioning team had left.

Jessica ran a bath for Onslow, in her own en-suite; one of the few in the hotel with a tub. She wrapped herself in his army coat, topped-it with the Royal Marine beret and sat on the balcony to afford him some privacy. She called down to reception, asking if they had birding binoculars she could borrow.

Onslow dressed, wrapped a blanket around his shoulders and stood just inside the balcony door, the air-con set to heat, gently blowing over his damp hair.

'What can you see Mrs T?'

'A convoy heading from Syria, towards Sehir. Or maybe they will aim higher on the border at Yamamah. They are motoring look, just a dozen old tankers. Suppliers for Jason's new project.'

'How do you mean?'

'Nothing. I am just messing.'

A Russian Su-24 attack aircraft screamed into view midway between the hotel and the convoy. Banking hard left, the supersonic bang crashed into the quiet afternoon, bouncing off the hotel's castle walls and rattling the table where Jessica sat. The jet opened fire, a short burst of its 23mm cannon, towards the convoy. A hidden heavy anti-aircraft gun *ak-aked* tracer fire in the jet's path. It banked hard left again and entered a steep climb, releasing flares and foil chaff.

'Shit Jess! Those drivers had a lucky escape.'

'It will be back. That was just a tap on the roof, to give the drivers and anti-aircraft crew a chance to flee.'

Jessica fidgeted on her seat, watching the stricken convoy. All but two of the tankers stopped, doors left open, and occupants running in all directions. Two lorries accelerated away. From this distance, their escape seemed pathetically slow to Jessica and Onslow.

The anti-aircraft gun fired again, a slow thud of tracer bullets arching into the sky above the convoy. Jessica saw the faintest of silver slither as the jet roared just yards above the rough, hilly terrain. It released two laser guided Kh-29L/T missiles. The anti-aircraft gun exploded into a ball of fire and debris, immediately before the jet reached within range. The jet fired the 23mm cannon again, strafing the road and each of the tankers, including the two which had attempted to speed away from danger.

The Su-24 banked right and climbed steeply over the hotel, over the square and bridge, banking hard right again to re-enter Syrian airspace. As it crossed the border into Turkey, it released more flares and chaff – slithers of silver and golden foil falling from the sky, coating Jessica and the balcony. The sonic boom rattled the hotel, cracking Jessica's window.

Jessica turned her attention to the convoy. All the trucks burned, some gently billowing black smoke into the clouding sky, others burning ferociously as the contents of the fuel tanks mixed with the kerosene payloads. The two escaping trucks had turned onto their sides. One had the driver's door open as the occupant fled. Drivers running to assist the stricken driver in the second vehicle.

A series of explosions sounded from the anti-aircraft gun emplacement as shells exploded.

Onslow pulled Jessica back into the room, discarding the coat and beret outside, as Jessica continued to watch the disintegrating convoy and the driver rescue attempt through binoculars.

'In you come Jess. You don't want to breathe that rubbish.'

*

Onslow fetched a reel of sticky tape from reception, sealing the cracked window. Snow fell across the small mountain plain, which the convoy had almost managed to cross. Jessica had a fit of uncontrollable giggles. She sat on the bed shaking and apologising for laughing. Onslow opened the quarter bottle of local brandy from the minibar. They shared the glass.

'S-400 didn't engage the plane; it was clearly over Turkish airspace.'

'Is that because the Turks let-it-go, or did Uncle Vlad turn it off from Moscow?'

'My guess is the former, Ons. But it would be nice to know for sure.'

‘Should we feedback to Company?’

‘God no. That is espionage. Obviously *Naap* would not engage for a jet knocking out a few tractors in a war zone, but I’d love to know if it tracked the jet. I bet Bridge would have detected something, if only it was operational. Phew! I won’t sleep tonight.’

‘Shock? You have been through a lot these past few weeks.’

‘No! Excitement. I mean adrenalin. I will have to call Jason later.’

She pulled the blanket over her shoulders and covered her chest in embarrassment.

‘More, or less exciting than stopping a shooter single handed?’

Embarrassed, Jessica studied the brandy glass they both held, and shrugged.

‘I can’t help it Ons. I am who I am.’

‘Hey Jess, I am not getting at you.’

He pulled her close, feeling her shoulder tremble against his chest. She rubbed her cheek against his shoulder.

‘Jace and Priti will be here tomorrow. Best we don’t sit too close, or you come into my room or have a bath or …’

‘Of course not, Jess. I want to keep my head on my shoulders for as long as possible. We are quite, attached.’

‘And just because we are all Company and everything, just remember the rules. You do not talk about any projects. Jason and Priti are just doing the Dalaman petro-chem job.’

‘Yes, boss.’

‘I’m hoping Jason can stay a few days. Dalaman is all but finished. Then we can all head back to Koyaka for a couple of days and home to Blighty before the start of December. I can’t wait for a week off and then back to normal office life.’

‘Yeah, right!’

‘Stop teasing!’

She slapped him with her flat palm, leaving her hand to rest on his chest. Her cheek still against his shoulder.

‘It is 24th November tomorrow. I am going to have my first attempt to go live with Bridge. Do you fancy coming to watch? There won’t be anything to see, hopefully, so up to you.’

‘Yes Ons. I would like that, please. It also means we can get both our e-signatures on the sign-off. Jace and Priti will arrive later in the afternoon from Adana, so that fits in well.

'I am dreading it now. He spent all of those evenings with the glamourous Priti, sipping cocktails and frolicking in the pool, only for me to drag him down here to duck bullets and freeze in an empty hotel in the middle of a war zone. I need to be careful Ons, or he might just realise where his bread is buttered.'

'Don't be silly Jess.'

'Look, I'm wide awake now. Have you enough steam left to run through tomorrow with me, please? I would like to witness the procedure, rather than just watch it.'

'Sure. I will get the brandy from my room.'

*

Jessica hijacked Onslow's army coat and wore it herself, with the Green Beret, both now sparkling with shards of metallic chaff, to attend the command truck the following day. The battalion moved a few miles back from the border and perched on the side of an isolated hill, protected by higher surrounding peaks and ridges.

On seeing Jessica in the oversized army coat, a nervous jandarma cautiously body searched her, insisting she keep her arms above her head and her palms showing forward. Jessica enjoyed this start of her workday. Onslow, Driver and a second security guard stood in a group, teasing the jandarma and Jessica for her choice of workware.

The communications officer, Jessica's contact, vacated his workstation in the command truck for Onslow to use, preferring an hour spent practicing his English on Jessica. They sat in the welfare accommodation out of the biting cold – a tiny canvas hut on the back of the parts store, six-wheeler truck. Every few minutes, Onslow called Jessica to witness a stage on the initiation plan.

'Did you pick-up on the jet over Sehir last night?'

The officer continued his flirty smile, leant forward on his knees. He squinted slightly in concentration, hardening his expression.

'Is that not classed as an operational question, Mrs Taylor?'

'Oh dear. Sorry, forget I asked. I like all this military stuff.'

She rolled her eyes towards the beret on her head and tugged on the coat to demonstrate.

'Don't worry, it is not important.'

As the officer spoke, he glanced at his watch and made an entry in his notebook. Onslow shook the canvas flap.

'Mrs Taylor, sir. Please come and make a note of this confirmation code on the screen, then we can make a move.'

Onslow said goodbye to the crew he had got to know over the previous visits. They all shook hands farewell.

'I think a celebration meal tonight Ons. Well done. It will be the whole team, just you and I.'

'And Priti and Bruiser.'

'Of course. I had forgotten for a moment. I will have the hotel make a feast. It will snow a little, in the early evening. I will take Jason by the arm and walk him around the square and over the bridge. You can escort the other one. Then we can return to the hotel for food and champagne in front of the roaring open fire. Make sure you have your earplugs for night-time. Remind me to help reception select a suitable room for Priti. Tomorrow I will make arrangements to have us all transported back to civilisation.'

She squeezed his arm and shook it in excitement. He smiled broadly at this small gesture she seemed to reserve for just him.

'Quite a rollercoaster, Jess. All the complexity of S-400 Compatibility. The excitement of my dip into *Naap* on the carriers. Then the fast-track cloak and dagger of you know what. My life before Jessica Taylor seems so mundane, now.' She squeezed his arm and smiled. 'It is ok Jess, I know you are not actually *in my life*, I am just saying.'

'Hey Ons. Don't look so sad. I am so proud of you.'

‘Is Jason right-handed? I was just thinking, you could hold his right hand, mostly. If that is ok?’

‘Wouldn’t make any difference, Ons. He is like a boxer; both hands are as effective. You’ll be brave, I know you will. To impress me if nothing else.’

‘That is so sweet, thanks. I was thinking of asking Driver to dinner, if I pay him.’

‘I don’t think driver would dare get in the way.’

*

Jessica bathed and dressed, ready to meet her husband. She brought a new dress from the market and had a seamstress make alterations as she waited in the tiny dark shop, heated by a paraffin stove. The smell reminded her of the convoy, as the smoke drifted over the border following the jet attack. The dress fitted perfectly, looking sophisticated; blue linen empire-waist, the skirt hanging just above her knee. Jason may have preferred something skimpier, but she was also dressing to impress Priti. She planned to wear her new slippers and glass necklace, both earlier gifts from the Turkmen stall holders, following the shooting.

Jessica jumped up from her seat in reception and threw her arms around Jason’s neck. Only half undraping herself, she pulled Priti in for a kiss on the cheek. Priti and Onslow shook hands, his palms sweaty. Jason dropped his bag to the floor and stepped forward towards Onslow; hand raised to shoulder height. Onslow spun away, flinching and bringing his hands to protect his head. Jessica leapt to Onslow, grabbing his face and laughing.

'He was high handshaking you Ons, that's all. Sorry, sorry, I meant to say ...'

Jessica giggled nervously.

'You didn't tell him anything, did you?'

Jessica shook her head, bringing her snigger under control.

'No. But I never actually said that I did tell him. I only repeated what he said he *would* do.'

'Tell me what?'

'Exactly Jace. I have to keep reminding Onslow about security.'

*

The four left the hotel to walk off Jason and Priti's short flight, followed by the long car transfer. Jessica swapped her slippers for boots, added a long summer coat, covered over with her long woollen Mongolian jacket. Priti appeared in reception already wearing her coat and boots, so that Jessica was not sure how she was competing for the attention of the two men. She wore the jamana Jessica bought her, as a choker scarf around her neck, and the Turkmen keffiyeh over her hair, tied loosely into a knot around her face. Jessica felt a spontaneous smile cross her lips.

‘You are as pretty as a picture, Priti. You must update me on your young man, when we have some privacy.’

‘Thank you, Jessica. You scrub-up well yourself.’

Jason and Jessica walked a little ahead of Onslow and Priti. They could hear Priti chuckle at a story Onslow told; they now had a few anecdotes he could share – and a few more, which he could not.

‘I love her laugh, Jace, so infectious. I shouldn’t have dragged you both down here, especially in the winter. I forget, everyone doesn’t do war zones and quirky towns, like I do.’

‘Is this *the* square?’

‘Just here. There is still a bloodstain under the frost. We can walk around the square, over the bridge and back. Tomorrow, we can walk over the bridge and then around the square. That is kind of the extent of the things to do here. I feel so stupid telling you to visit.’

‘We love this place, Jess. It is so frontier and dramatic. So different to back home.’

‘We?’

Jason sighed. ‘Yes. We do talk. Priti is quite proud you invited her here, to share this with her. Especially after what happened. She was on the phone the other day, talking to a friend, I think someone in Contracts. She was all, *I stay with Jessica in her villa. Jessica and I work together on this and that. I said to Jessica …'*

Priti chuckled again and Jessica smiled at Jason.

'I know Jace. You know what I am like, I can't let things go.'

They approached the stalls, most closed with tarpaulin or the goods removed for the night or for the winter. The stallholder who sold Jessica's original purchases on the evening of the shooting came to the group, shaking Jason's hand as Jessica introduced them.

They continued their tour of the old town, speeding up after crossing the bridge, to return to the open fire in the hotel. Jessica had thought to have Priti allocated to a room furthest from her own, maybe on the next floor. Eventually, she talked reception in to upgrading her to the now available private courtyard room.

*

Jessica and Jason stayed awake late into the night, making love and discussing their plans together, their return to the UK, and work. They woke late to see Priti and Onslow sat on his balcony drinking coffee. Without waiting for an invitation, Jessica unbolted the dividing grid and hinged it back, joining the two balconies.

'Hey Mrs Taylor. Good morning. Sleep well?'

He held her gaze as she blushed slightly. She wondered if he had heard, or even listened to them making love and if he had told Priti.

'But guess what? Our client is aware of some changes, following our installation yesterday, of you know what, if you know what I mean. They want me to have a look. Shouldn't take long, just a utility path, probably. Bad news is, they want you along as you are the official Company representative.'

'A utility path? Goodness Ons, your utilities are a pain in the butt. Does Driver know where to head?'

'All sorted. They gave us one set of coordinates. Once there, they will escort us to the final destination. Time for a leisurely brunch, first.'

Jason joined the group on the balcony. The bright sun, in a clear blue sky, causing them all to wear sunglasses. Priti took charge of ordering a late breakfast from reception, suggesting Jessica's favourite of spicy egg Turkish menemen and a selection platter of village breakfast.

Jessica saw the approaching Russian Sukhoi Su-24M attack aircraft first and jumped to her feet, pointing out the slither of silver clinging to the low hills at the base of Turkmen Mountain, over the narrow mountain plain near to where the black-market kerosene convoy and antiaircraft gun had been destroyed. This time, there was no resistance or fire from the Turkmen brigade.

Two Turkish Air Force F-16 fighter jets flew in close formation between the hotel balcony and the border, just a few hundred yards away. One F-16 flipped onto its side to flash the under-hanging air-to-air Sidewinder missiles to the approaching Russian pilots. The group on the balcony had time to register clearly the pilots of the Turkish F-16s sitting proud of the fuselage in their Perspex bubbles. The Turkish F-16 looking like a toy compared with the bigger and more substantial Russian Su-24. The roar of the jet turbines hit the balcony, followed by a sonic boom. The Russian fighter banked west to mirror the Turkish jet's trajectory, firing defence flares for several seconds as the three planes flew together, in formation, with just a few hundred yards of separation.

Priti stepped backwards, away from the balcony railings as Jessica stepped forward, to gain a few feet and stand closer to the action; they clashed. Priti spun around, burying her face into Jessica's shoulder as the coffee cups rattled and jumped to the sonic boom and turbulence. Jessica instinctively grabbed Priti's hair, pulling her closer, at the same time straining for a better view of the jets.

The Russian jet continued west and then north along the border until out of view. The roar of the engines eased and became a distant thunder.

'Shit! What was that about?'

‘That, Jace, is the Russians letting the Turkmen and the Turks know they rule the airspace up to the border. They are currently supporting Assad’s Syrian Armed Forces fight Syrian Turkmen brigades, Army of Conquest and al-Nusra Front fighters just a few miles south of here, knocking on the door of Turkey’s allies, the Turkmen’s dominated swathe of Syria. Turkey has avoided occupying this region as the Turkmen are doing *ok*. But Russia is warning off the Turkmen and Turks taking the fight to Assad held areas, further south. I like the way the Turks flashed their Sidewinders to the Russians, as if they didn’t already know. See! It was worth the trip here, just to see that!’

Priti, still hanging onto Jessica, Onslow and Jason, all stared at Jessica with varying degrees of incredulity and disbelief.

‘What? So that wasn’t exciting?’

Jason laughed. He straightened the spilt coffee cups before moving to Jessica and Priti, wrapping his arms around both and kissing his wife’s forehead.

‘Never a dull moment with Jessica Taylor, eh Onslow?’

The Russian Su-24 appeared again, flying in the opposite direction, east. It clung to just yards above the ground, releasing flares, dipping and swerving from side to side before banking steeply vertically and to the right, seeking the protection of the low hills to the south. Two white streams of exhaust closed in on the jet.

A series of sonic booms hit the group. Priti moved onto Jason for protection. Onslow stood rigid, gripping the back of a chair, and Jessica moved to the balcony railings, wide eyed, staring at the unfolding situation.

The first missile bucked to the right and ploughed through a concentration of flares. To find the target Russian aircraft again, the missile dipped and changed course south, crashing into the ground and sending clouds of debris, dust, and smoke into the air.

The second missile completed a seemingly impossibly tight turn, continuing on the tail of the jet. The Russian pilots fired more flares, doubled back on a hairpin loop, rolling the aircraft upright as the missile struck. In the same moment the missile and the aircraft exploded, the two pilots ejected clear; fired at a slight angle up and towards the border and balcony.

The group watched as the white parachutes opened, before a blast of displaced air from the explosion pushed them all backwards. Priti and Jason stumbled and fell. Onslow automatically covered his face with his hands. Jessica shielded her eyes with one hand, as if from a bright sun, and continued to follow the parachute's descent. Blown partly by the blast, the pilots drifted apart. Turkmen forces fired machineguns and small arms. Jessica screamed as one parachute bucked and twisted under fire. The second pilot gained a little height on a thermal, before landing in a rough area of hillocks and boulders.

Jessica held her hands to her mouth, screaming. Jason grabbed her from behind, trying to lead her inside the hotel room. She wriggled away until he gave up, wrapping his arms around her waist and chest as she continued to sob.

They smelled the burning aircraft. The scene now completely silent except for a call to prayer from a nearby mosque and hedge-sparrows chattering in a bush below the balcony. Jessica found her borrowed binoculars and searched the ground for the second downed pilot. She heard and then saw the two Russian rescue helicopters approaching from the south, flanked by Kamov Ka-50 gunship helicopters, their curious twin rotors recognisable to Jessica. Two more Russian Su-24 attack jets screamed across the area, firing cannons at unseen ground targets.

The two Mil Mi-8 rescue helicopters split, each moving to the area of a downed pilot. The first came under fire from the ground. The Russians returned fire from the Mi-8's fixed machinegun and the Ka-50 auto-cannons. The Mi-8 spun around on its rotor, crashing heavily onto the ground, bouncing back into the air, and crashing again onto its side.

The second Mi-8 rescue helicopter landed closer to the second parachute site, discharging the payload of special forces troops running into the rough terrain.

The helicopter immediately took to the air, releasing flares. One of the escorting Ka-50 gunships moved towards the first landing site and completed a sweep of the area, engaging Turkmen ground forces. The gun battle raged for over an hour.

A third rescue Mi-8 helicopter arrived with a single Ka-50 gunship, landing close to the downed first helicopter. Once loaded with the stricken crew, it soared steeply into the sky with the Ka-50s providing cover fire and turned south with a single escort.

The remaining gunships returned to the second site and continued to hunt and attack around the area of rough terrain. The second Mi-8 rescue helicopter returned to the area, landing heavily on the ground as special forces rushed from cover of the rocky terrain. Through her binoculars, Jessica saw the jet pilot running, aided by Iranian Hezbollah special forces wearing the yellow headbands around their woollen balaclavas, and Russian Navy Infantry with bright red arm-insignia.

The Mi-8 soared into the sky with one gunship, as the remaining helicopters provided cover fire before peeling away and also heading south.

*

Priti and the steward cleared away the mess of their breakfast. Onslow sat on the balcony, preparing his workday ahead on his laptop, hands trembling. Jessica and Jason sat on their bed.

‘Priti! Here a sec, love. Look guys, I have a bad feeling about this. Priti, you need to talk directly to Trish. I need you to be assertive. I want you and Jace out of here. As an absolute minimum, I want you back to Dalaman. Better still, back to Europe, if not Blighty. Also, I want Trish to have Onslow and me extracted as soon as we finish looking at the problem with, the problem we are looking at. Seriously Priti, I want us out of here.’

‘Jess, what is going on? And I am going nowhere without you.’

‘Please don’t argue, Jace. I don’t have the time or inclination. You and Priti get the fuck away and let me concentrate.’

‘It doesn’t work like that, Jess.’

Jessica studied her hands for a moment.

‘Priti, I need to speak to Jace, alone. Give us a moment.’

‘No, Jess, Mrs Taylor. What is going on?’

Jessica continued to study her hands. She ran the nail of her right thumb along the nails of her left hand, searching for snags and rough edges. Repeating the process with the opposite hands.

‘Fuck Priti! You and Jason are morphing into one stubborn entity. I am not happy with that shooting down.’

‘I am not sure anyone is, love. But two Turkish jets shot down a Russian jet. Why are we fleeing in panic?’

Jessica called Onslow into the bedroom.

‘Ons. What do you reckon? Were they Turkish Air Force Sidewinders that hit the Russian jet?’

‘I really don’t know, Mrs T. I have never seen a jet shot down before. I have never seen a Sidewinder launched before.’

He shrugged. Both Jason and Priti made to speak at the same time. Jessica held a silencing hand.

‘Go on Onslow. What you saw isn’t going away, just because you don’t say the words.’

Onslow’s face twitched. His eyebrows danced and his forehead furrowed, as if arguing with himself.

‘I have never seen Sidewinders launched. But I have seen 40N6E missiles launched from the carriers. They looked like 40N6E missiles that shot down the jet, to me. Maybe not. Look Jess, I am a fucking gamer who plays with computers for a living and am only here because I fancy the boss!’

Onslow dropped his gaze.

‘Sorry. I just want to go home.’

‘Calm down, Ons. What else? We know the Turks have 40N6Es missiles as part of the Russian bought

S-400 antiaircraft system armaments. But what else did you notice?'

'The operational battalions of S-400s are stationed to the north and east of here. The missiles that downed the Russian jet came from the west.'

'And what is west of here?'

'Fuck off Jess. I am not a geography teacher.'

Jason intervened.

'The Mediterranean is west of here. What is the significance of that?'

*

Driver and Passenger collected Jessica and Onslow from the hotel, for the journey to the S-400 missile battalion.

'Hey guys! Overtime? I thought you finished yesterday.'

Jessica and Onslow sat at opposite ends of the rear seats, both resting against a door and staring out of the window. Jessica stretched her arm to hold the hand of a reluctant Onslow.

'Did you see the news reports? Turkey shot down a Russian jet! I know! What a cluster fuck. First, the Turks denied it. Then they said the jet was in Turkish airspace and refused to cooperate, so they blasted it with F-16 Sidewinders. Now, this is odd – social media is showing an unexploded Russian 40N6E missile with the Turkish flag etched onto the casing, so presumably fired from Turkey's Russian supplied S-400 antiaircraft system. So ironic, so funny.'

'Funny? You prick. We watched a pilot shot dead on a parachute, you wanker.'

'Sorry Mrs Taylor. Sorry, sir. Gallows humour. Sorry.'

Passenger squeezed Driver's arm.

'What else did the news say, please Driver?'

'Well, Mrs Taylor. Yes, it looks like one pilot, Oleg, was shot dead, probably by some Nazi Grey Woolf fighters. It looks like a Russian and Iranian combined effort rescued the navigator, but, sadly, a Russian marine died in a helicopter crash. Shit happens. The Turks recovered the body of the pilot and the surviving missile. It is being laid in state under a Russian flag, ready for repatriation to Russia. The body, I mean, not the missile.'

Driver pulled onto a gravel track; Jessica recognised it as the first site she had seen the S-400 battalion; they had moved full circle. A jandarma sat in a van.

'The weapons guys will send a jeep. We cannot stay here, but we will wait on the road until we know you are safely collected. Have a good day.'

Jessica and Onslow trudged to the jandarma policeman. Jessica recognised him as the Tommy Cooper impersonator from an earlier roadblock. He made to kiss her on the cheek, before straightening and saluting.

'There's a surprise. Jessica Taylor gets to kiss random soldiers in this God forsaken middle of nowhere.'

'Jealous? Let's do this shit and get home Ons. I mean like home home.'

The jandarma walked from the van, talking into his radio. Driver drove away, arm extended in a wave, through the window.

'Lady, sir. Into the van, please. Arms here.'

The soldier zipped plastic strip handcuffs onto the couple.

'Hey! Easy tiger, what is going on? We are allowed here, to work on something for the army. They invited us here. We have permission.'

'Sorry sir. I am told to arrest you and take you to barracks.'

*

The soldier turned off the flashing blue lights and eased onto the road. Turning right, he drove in the opposite direction to Jessica's own transport and security. Once around the first bend, the soldier turned on the flashing blues and sped up. Twenty minutes later, he pulled into an old road construction layby, cut the engine and lights. A *dolmus* minibus parked behind them. The soldier and the bus driver walked to the edge of the layby to talk.

'Jessica, I am not comfortable with this. What if I cocked-up and the S-400 system fired by mistake?'

'Then you are in deep shit. Now be quiet, I am trying to hear.'

They could hear voices, but no words Jessica understood.

'Ons. Something is wrong. Stay calm. Keep smiling. If you have a chance, escape and hide. But don't run away or do anything rash within firing range. Don't worry about me, if you can escape and fetch help, then do so. Otherwise, do as you are told and stay calm.'

The soldier and bus driver returned to the police van, carefully helping Jessica and Onslow out and towards the *dolmus,* still handcuffed. They ignored Jessica's protests. Six women, mostly late teens and early twenties, sat in the *dolmus* minibus. Some wore hijabs, all wore jeans, T-shirts and training shoes. A few looked towards Jessica and Onslow as they were bundled into empty seats at the centre of the minibus. The woman next to Jessica spoke.

'Hos geldin. Nasilsin?'

'Thank you. I am fine. And you? Look, I need to ask, why are we here? Where are we going? Who are you all? I think we are in danger, can you help me, please?'

The young woman smiled, took Jessica's hand, but looked away without answering. The bus driver and the soldier walked to the jandarma van. The soldier shook his arms loose, stood to his full height, and closed his eyes. The bus driver swung a right-hook and punched the soldier in the face, cutting his lip. They both laughed, the soldier playfully pushing away the bus driver. They took up the same positions. A woman, in her late twenties, tutted from the front passenger seat and leant behind, taking an AK-47 assault rifle from the floor of the *dolmus,* and sauntered towards the jandarma. They spoke and shook hands. Without warning, she swung the rifle at the soldier, catching the side of his head. His knees buckled. As he crumpled to the ground, she kicked him in the stomach and hit him on the shoulder with the butt of the rifle.

She leant down, rubbing the soldier's back for a few minutes as he caught his breath. They then helped the soldier into his van, handcuffed his hands to the steering wheel, threw the ignition keys into the bushes, and gave him a few gulps of water from a plastic bottle. She took his service pistol from the holster, fired twice into the trees and threw the gun across the layby. Walking back to the *dolmus*, she hesitated halfway, took aim and shot a tyre of the van with her AK-47. She climbed into the *dolmus* and the bus driver continued the journey.

*

The *dolmus* progressed at a steady pace, staying within the speed limits and slowing to allow other vehicles priority. Pedestrians waved for the driver to stop and allow them to board the minibus, but he replied with an apologetic shrug, wave, and smile. They passed through small hamlets and farms as the sun set against the hills.

Following the assault on the soldier, Onslow showed more fear. Eyes wide, he wrung his constrained hands together, rubbing his wrists sore against the plastic straps. Jessica remained calm, studying the mannerisms of her fellow passengers; looking for any obvious weak spots and trying to see the hierarchy within the group. The women tended to pay more attention to the woman sat in the front, with the AK-47. Each time Jessica made eye contact with any of the women, she smiled.

'Jess. Don't look around. I think I saw our Land Rover in the mirror.'

'If it kicks off Ons, for Christ's sake, keep your head down. If this lot tries to drag you anywhere, just go limp; but don't fight anyone.'

Onslow snorted at the suggestion he might try to fight his way out.

The *dolmus* slowed to allow the Land Rover to overtake, but it pulled behind and continued to follow the *dolmus* for several more miles. As the vehicles negotiated a sharp left bend, the Land Rover sped up as if to overtake, before side swiping the *dolmus* into the shrub. The two vehicles came to a halt in a cloud of dust. Two powerful spotlights illuminated the *dolmus,* from the Land Rover, blinding Jessica, Onslow and the other occupants.

'*Disari!* Out now and on the floor.'

Jessica recognised her bodyguard's voice. The side door of the *dolmus* swung open. The first young woman climbed out, dropping to her knees just as the woman behind fired her AK-47 into the chest of Driver. Driver fell backwards, staring into Jessica's eyes. The remaining women jumped from the rear doors of the *dolmus*, moved along the sides to open fire on the Land Rover and Passenger bodyguard.

Jessica screamed and tried to fight her way to the crumpled heap outside the side door, still handcuffed. As she kicked and screamed at her kidnappers, the slightly older female from the front seat rammed the butt of her rifle into Jessica's temple and she passed out.

*

Jessica realised it was probably a dream. Cavus, her previous holiday romance, helped Driver to sit up. They were laughing at a shared joke. Cavus held his hand on Driver's back. Jessica could see his palm through the gaping wound.

Onslow helped Jessica to sit up from her position on the *dolmus* floor between the seats. He manoeuvred behind her, so that she sat back against his chest.

'Did they shoot both bodyguards Ons? What happened?'

'It happened so quick. They all opened fire on the Land Rover. Passenger fired back a few shots, but he didn't stand a chance. He shot out the *dolmus* windscreen. I am sure Driver is dead. I did not see Passenger, but I can't see how he could survive. But are you ok?'

'Sure. A bit woozy. Have they said anything to you?'

'Nothing. It is like we aren't here. They were actually singing a few minutes ago! Like a schoolgirl's outing. I have got to be honest, Jess, I am shitting myself.'

'Time for that later, Ons. Keep smiling, keep making eye contact, make friends. Concentrate.'

The *dolmus* pulled into the compound of a marble workshop. Enormous slabs sat in steel racks. The women left the minibus, stretching and chatting. One woman helped Jessica to stand and out of the side door. The front seat woman studied the bump on Jessica's head, her brow furrowed in concern. She gently kissed the area. Using a knife from tucked into her belt, she cut free the handcuffs.

‘Sorry lady. I think you will have a big bump and two black eyes. We have to walk now, maybe two kilometres. Is that ok, you poor thing?’

‘To be honest, I think you have the wrong people. My friend and I are administrators working for an English company. Perhaps there has been a mix-up. We are quite happy to just leave it there. We can find our own way back.’

‘Please, lady, you have done nothing wrong. We are looking after you. We have friends in the jandarma. You were arrested, we rescued you.’

‘No, I don’t think so. We are happy to be arrested; there has been a mistake. We will explain to the jandarma. Obviously, we will not mention meeting you, or anything. It is very kind of you to help, but I must insist that we leave you now, please.’

‘The men who tried to take you back, are they friends?’

Jessica nodded. Her eyes stung with tears. The woman pulled her into a hug; Jessica sobbed against the woman’s chest, tears seeping into the T-shirt.

‘Sorry, I don’t mean to cry. They are lovely guys. So caring.’

‘It is very difficult for you, lady. I am sorry for your loss.’

Jessica nodded again. She tried to force a smile; the woman offered her a tissue to blow her nose.

'We must go now. You do not have a choice. This is a dangerous area; you and your friend must come silently and do as you are told.'

The six women, Jessica and Onslow squeezed through a gap in the compound fence at the furthest corner from the gate. The minibus driver waved goodbye to the group, two of the younger girls waved back. The six all carried AK-47s. Two women took the lead, negotiating small tracks in the near darkness, without torches. The group remained silent. Young and light on their feet, the only noise came from Onslow's work boots. Every few hundred yards, the procession stopped and knelt as the leaders strained to hear any warning noises in the night.

They came to a high wire fence, the mesh thick and the steel lattice supports substantial. It hummed gently with electricity. Signs warned of alarms and the risk of electrocution. Jessica saw movement from a guard post, high-up and some distance away. She knew the women were prepared to fight and kill. She knew they had friends and comrades in the jandarma. Sighing, she caught Onslow's eye and shook her head.

One of the leaders rummaged at the root of a thornbush. She lifted a wooden lid, complete with the bush tied to it, to reveal a tiny hole in the ground. The second leader crawled into the hole, headfirst, and disappeared.

'No, I can't. I can't go in there. I am claustrophobic. Please, there must be another way.'

'Hey lady. Look at me. You are with me, and I will keep you safe. Look at me. You must breathe gently, relax.' The main, slightly older woman, who had driven shotgun in the *dolmus*, spoke. 'My name is Lideri. You can stay close to me. I help you first, then I am behind you. Then your friend. There is plenty of room down there. It is big. Lots of space.'

Jessica crawled a little into the entrance. The first woman lay just ahead in the complete darkness. Jessica felt the training shoes. Hands reached for Jessica's and pulled her forward until her torso lay along the woman's legs. The woman wriggled forward, pulling Jessica along by her outstretched arms. Every movement kicked-up dust, the air already thick and stale. Lideri followed closely, pushing Jessica by the soles of her shoes as the leading woman pulled. Jessica heard Onslow behind Lideri, breathing hard through his nose, trying to keep the dust from his mouth. She recognised the noise from the long kiss she had forced onto him in the aircraft carrier cabin.

The lead woman stopped edging forward. She continued to drag Jessica up her own body until Jessica's face was level with the woman's chest. Jessica could hear a muffled conversation from further back. Lideri spoke.

'Further Jessica, we need a little more room for everyone.'

'No! There is no room.'

The lead woman pulled Jessica from under her arms until her head rested under the woman's chin; the woman pushing her own head against the dirt roof of the tunnel. Lideri pulled herself along the back of Jessica's legs, wedging her face against the small of her back. Jessica tried to straighten her trapped leg as it spasmed into cramp. Trying to straighten her painful leg, she panicked, thrashing her trapped limbs. The lead woman and Lideri restrained Jessica. A singing voice started further along the tunnel and the two restraining women joined in. Jessica buried her face into the lead's neck and wept. The woman scrunched her T-shirt around Jessica's mouth to ease her hyperventilating.

'Worse than my fear of spiders and flying, Mrs T?'

Jessica snorted giggles between the sobs.

'You are in so much trouble, when I do your annual appraisal Onslow.'

*

There was not enough oxygen for everyone. Jessica deepened her breathing, consciously forcing out the carbon dioxide laden air from her lungs. The women stopped singing. Some yawned. The lead woman and

Lideri spoke in a few, urgent, snatched sentences – too fast for Jessica to understand.

Lead took a hunting knife from her bag and dug it into the wall of the tunnel, using a small torch to light her work. Lideri passed Lead her own knife to use as a hammer. Lead tapped the handle of the hunting knife in groups of three, waiting in between for a response. Jessica heard dissenting comments from further back.

Twenty minutes passed. It was now pitch black again. Jessica thought her vision blurred, but could not be sure in the dark. She heard Lead's three taps, followed by four faint echoes. Lead tapped three more, followed by four more responses. She tapped rhythmically, once per second; one Mississippi two Mississippi three Mississippi four … Jessica closed her eyes. She searched in her head for the earlier dream of Cavus and Driver. She wanted a happy ending. Jason smoothed hairs back from her forehead. *Darling, I would rather you stayed awake, really, I insist. Wake up Jess, this is not the time to sleep.*

The spade that hit Jessica in the face was a love heart shape. Cold steel. Not much bigger than a garden trowel. She grabbed it. Pushing her lips to the small hole it had made in the wall of the tunnel, sucking in the fresh air it delivered. A hand tried to push Jessica back, but she already had purchase against Lideri, forcing her head, then shoulders through the wall into a larger adjacent tunnel. Jessica, through the hole, kicked back, enlarging the gap. Lideri came through the hole next, dirt falling over her head. Jessica pulled the woman, propelling her on top of herself, laughing. Jessica grabbed the woman's face and kissed her. Lideri consented, allowing Jessica to clamp her lips to her own.

'You see Jessica *Bayan*? I said I would look after you.'

Jessica refused to move. Dragging Lead over herself and then Onslow, holding him in a long embrace, before the two followed Lead and Lideri along the new passage. Barely large enough to crawl, the second tunnel felt enormous compared to the first. Every few yards, Jessica encountered wooden shuttering and props. Two miners remained at the junction, chipping away at the old tunnel, until it collapsed, sending a cloud of dust over the group.

A miner crouched at the end of the new tunnel, his head torch bathing a bell chamber in light. The group huddled around the light like moths. He counted everyone in, including the miners. He extinguished his torch, stood and eased back a wooden lid; designed to hold an inch of disguising soil and gravel.

Lead and Lideri left the tunnel first, Jessica and Onslow next, followed by the others. Lideri led them into an area of low scrub and thorn bushes, waiting for the two women scouts to resume the lead.

Chapter thirteen

'Welcome to Kurdistan. *Kurdistan'a Hos Geldiniz.* Welcome to Al Hol. I am sorry about the journey.'

Jessica smiled at Lideri. Onslow caught her eye and frowned; wondering if she had forgotten insurgents held them captive.

'May we ask who you are, please? And why do you feel the need to …, feel the need to rescue us so forcefully? Where is Al Hol?'

'I am a Peshmerga Commander in the Kurdistan Democratic Party. You are my guests. Our friends in the Turkish jandarma informed us of your circumstances and the rest, as you say …'

'Not really Lideri. What do you want with us?'

'You Brits are so brisque. Ok, as you ask so directly, I shall reply directly. The Russian jet.'

'Nothing to do with us. Turkish Airforce shot it down. We were busy eating breakfast.'

'Not according to Turkish intelligence, Jessica. Our friends in Turkish intelligence informed us you brought down the jet, having infiltrated the Turkish air-defence systems.'

Onslow responded. 'No! Absolutely not. We did not do any such thing. All we did …'

Jessica intervened. ‘My colleague is correct. We did no such thing. We have absolutely no access to the firing sequence of …, the firing sequence of anything. We just reconciled a few interactions with Turkey’s new Russian system. We absolutely are not involved in any military engagements. Lideri, I am going to insist you release us back to Turkey. You can’t just drag innocent civilians into the middle of a battleground. Please return my phone. I wish to call my office and get this resolved. I also need to speak to my husband; he will be worried sick.’

‘Your husband and his friend are perfectly safe, Jessica. I will personally reunite you all, once we have finished here.’

‘You have Jason? This is ridiculous Lideri, this has gone too far. I promise you; you are barking up the wrong tree. My friend and I are bean-counters. Jason is a grease monkey and Priti does supplier assessments and runs ledgers. You killed two decent men, to drag a couple of number crunchers through a tunnel for absolutely no good reason. This is sick. Jason had better be alright, seriously, I mean it and that is a threat.’

Onslow slipped an arm around Jessica’s shoulder.

‘Look, Commander, tell us what you want, and I will explain to you why we can’t provide it. Then we all go home. And in the meantime, you really must send Mr Taylor and Miss Khan home immediately, as a gesture of goodwill.’

'There is little goodwill in a civil war, Mr Dalliance. Islamic State is shadowing you both, your husband Taylor, and his friend Khan. You should not be looking for us to release any of you. If, when, you help us, we will be in a position to offer you a full military escort and hand you over, securely and safely, to Turkey or the European Union, or even the Russians or USA, as you wish.'

'We cannot help you. How long will we all look at each other before you accept, we cannot help you? This is ludicrous.'

'You will help us, Jessica. You will help us tomorrow. If you decide to continue this charade, we will indeed release Jason and Priti. I am sure they will not have to walk far in the mountains before Islamic State offers them a lift. In fact, I can guarantee it. Exactly what happens to them then, you can watch on You Tube.'

Jessica released a scream, short and sharp, as if she had witnessed a car crash.

'No Lideri. You can't do that. Please believe me. God no Lideri, we cannot help you. It was not us who shot down the jet, I promise.'

'Commander, this is insane. We have no access to any air-defence. Britain is a tacit supporter of the Kurds. America is all but a military ally! You cannot threaten four British citizens.'

Jessica sobbed again. Onslow had watched her resolve crumble, since they shot Driver the bodyguard. Jessica needed to hold it together and concentrate if they were all to have any chance of survival.

Lideri pulled a sobbing Jessica onto a leather sofa against the back wall of the concrete room.

'I know, sweetheart.' She hugged her close, wiping her nose with a tissue and brushing stray hairs out of her eyes. 'This is awful for you. May I suggest something?'

'Yes Lideri. Please, anything. You must save Jason. He is so special. You can take me, but please not Jason.'

'You are very upset Jessica. Can you concentrate, for me, please?'

Jessica gulped back tears and nodded, wiping her face with the back of her hand.

'You need to remember how to operate the air-defence system. Do you understand?'

'But we don't know how, Lideri. It is impossible.'

'Shush now darling and listen. You must make yourself remember. Or your husband and his friend will suffer a terrible and humiliating death, for everyone to watch on social media. If you still cannot remember, I will shoot you, right here in this room, in front of Mr Dalliance. If he still cannot remember, then we will deliver him and your body to Islamic

State, to do with as they want. You don't have children, do you, Jessica? But you have parents, a sister and nieces. They will feel so sad when it hits the news that Islamic State kidnapped you and did terrible things, even as us Kurds heroically tried to save you. Do you understand Jessica? It is a lot to take in.'

Jessica nodded. 'What do we need to do, Lideri?'

'Tomorrow, we push into Afrin on the Turkish border and take back the Region from Turkish occupation, permanently. You and Mr Dalliance will release the full force of the Turkish air-defence system against all aircraft in the area – Russian, Turkish, American, European, Syrian. Nothing flies as we attack on the ground. If you fail, there will be terrible consequences for us all. What you are doing is so brave Jessica.'

Jessica nodded again, wringing her hands in her lap.

'I am going to leave you and Mr Dalliance alone to discuss your strategy. Then we will have a little chat around midnight. At dawn, you push the button. Within twenty-four hours, you will all be safely back together. But if it doesn't happen as I request, there will be no reprieve. It is very important you understand, Jessica. Do you understand? Even if you escape, or kill me, or kill yourself, those terrible things will still happen to your husband and friends. It is very important you understand. If you need anything, just speak out – we are eavesdropping.' She smiled at Jessica as if sharing a secret joke.

*

'Onslow. We have no choice. We need to do as Lideri asks. She is on our side.'

'Jess! For fuck's sake, she is not on our side. Lideri is going to kill us. Have you lost it?'

'God Ons, this is so confusing. Of course, I know she is going to kill us. But she has found a solution. You need to arm both systems. S-400 and *Naap*. She is half correct, isn't she? Somebody has used Bridge to shoot down the Russian jet. There were three 40N6 long range surface-to-air missiles left on the HMS Prince of Wales with the Turkish flag etched on the casing, like the unexploded missile recovered from the crash site. Someone fired on the Russian jet from a British carrier, to look like it was from a Turkish S-400 battalion.'

'Jess, you need to shut up.'

'No Onslow, you need to save my husband and yourself.'

'Listen to yourself! You want me to shoot down jets from half the United Nations, including Britain probably, so an internationally recognised terrorist group can overrun a city under the protection of a NATO country. If I could, which I can't, we will be lucky to spend the rest of our short lives in any number of prisons! Possibly in Turkey or Guantanamo Bay.'

‘Or you watch Islamic State mutilate Priti before hacking your head off! Ons, you have to do this. If you don’t, I will call Lideri back in to execute me tonight, if that is what it takes to force your hand. Like it or not Ons, you are saving my husband.’

‘Even if I find the mechanism to arm the system, which I won’t, the Brits and the Turks will just shut them down. Especially after what happened to the Russian jet.’

‘So, we are in the clear and all go home. But you must do it. And you know where to start looking.’

‘Utilities. As soon as we saw the missiles appear from the direction of the Mediterranean, I made the same assumption as you. Somebody has built a hidden path into the system controls, through Bridge, through those bloody ghost utility paths. I have got to say this out loud, Jess. I am the obvious suspect, but I promise it wasn’t me. Pun, my engineer has the skills, but not the opportunity, especially on Bridge. If the development team did it, they would all have to be in on it, and Quality would have found it anyway. And none of us have a motive.’

‘If whoever, did it, did it, then you can do it also, Ons. Especially now you know for what and where you are looking.’

‘This is going to make me a killer and a traitor, Jess. I can’t. I can’t spend thirty years in jail with this on my conscience.’

'You will regret your decision when you feel the knife on your throat. They force you to make a video first, saying goodbye to everyone. I have a feeling; you are not cut-out for this sort of thing. Look, you show me exactly what you are doing. When we get arrested, I will confess to doing it all myself, to save Jason. It is under duress Onslow – I probably won't even serve a custodial sentence.'

Onslow rubbed his hands over his face and through his hair.

'Christ Jess. Never a dull moment.'

'I will see if Lideri has a moment to see us.'

*

'I knew you would make the right decision, Jessica. Thank you. One day, I will invite you to an independent Kurdistan to share kibbeh meat dumplings as guest of honour.'

'Lideri, please let me speak to Jason. Is he near here? Or I can phone.'

'Sorry love. The phones will give away your locations.'

'But so will Onslow's laptop. I am not sure you have thought this through.'

Lideri threw back her head and laughed. Jessica giggled along. She held Jessica's cheeks and kissed her forehead.

'I am going to miss your wacky humour. You should stay and fight with us. First, it will look like the laptop is in Estonia. By the time they crack your location, all aircraft will be downed or grounded.'

'Lideri. I will be honest with you. You probably listened to us talking. Onslow will try to arm the system, but we do not yet know how. You must promise me Lideri, if we fail, you must let Jason and Priti live.'

'Hey come here Jess. Please don't cry again. You are much prettier when you smile. I know in my heart that you will not fail me. But if it is impossible, really really impossible, to do as I ask, I am afraid you will all die as I explained, including Jason. You have a good cry, love.'

*

Jessica lay on the sofa, pulled into the foetal position, her head resting on Onslow's lap. She cried herself to sleep. She spoke softly, Onslow guessed, with Jason. He hoped also to feature in her dreams. He played with a curl of her hair; his mind wandering between how he would approach the task tomorrow, in the limited window allowed, how he would deal with his success or how he would cope with the failure. There came a gentle knock on the door.

'Good morning. Did you sleep well?'

Onslow shook his head in disbelief at the sunny expression on Lideri's face. She carried Onslow's laptop, charger, and a notepad and pencils. She also carried a paper carrier bag with bread and cheese slices and cardboard cups of coffee. Jessica sat, facing Onslow for a moment, before reorientating herself to her surroundings.

'I thought you might be peckish. You have a busy day ahead. We will, of course, monitor the success of your mission. And let's see if we can't get you home before nightfall. Every minute Turkey and the others fly unhindered, my people will be killed and our mission put at risk. I am not trying to add pressure, Mr Dalliance, but I think it is important you do not test my patience. You have two hours to set everything up. At 0500 hours we start our artillery barrage, and the attack begins. Let us all hope you are ready to arm the air-defence system to protect my people.'

Onslow opened the laptop and powered up. The sim had been removed.

'I've fallen at the first hurdle. It is asking for a wifi password.' He twisted the laptop towards Lideri.

'Let me think. My cats name with a zero instead of an oh.' She laughed at her own joke, before tapping the password.

Onslow tapped on the keyboard as various pages opened on the screen. Lideri held her palm towards Onslow.

'Emails? You are joking Mr Dalliance.'

‘I need a password from my inbox.’

Lideri studied the screen as Onslow searched his inbox, opened an email and copied a long password. Lideri relaxed back into her seat. Onslow continued.

Onslow and Jessica both realised she would not be able to convince the authorities she had performed the task. She decided to confess; explain the duress she was under and then go *no comment.* At 0440 hours, he stopped working and sat back.

‘I can’t promise. But I think I am ready to go. I estimate another five minutes' priming. So you say when – 0455 hours?’

‘Thank you, Mr Dalliance. How confident are you?’

‘I absolutely am not confident, Commander. I am not a weapons operator. I definitely found a hidden path and, so far as I know, it will work. I am guessing it worked for somebody who wanted the jet downed. But do you know what, Commander? I hope it doesn’t work.’

Lideri snorted a laugh and pinched Onslow’s cheeks.

‘Oh, stop it. You guys are so funny!’

‘Even if it does work, the operators will close it down as soon as they see it firing without authority.’

‘We both know that isn’t true, don’t we, Mr Dalliance? The systems are locked by your box of tricks. It will take hours to stop the missiles firing.’

Onslow looked at Jessica and gave a slight nod.

*

Jessica sat forward, leant on her knees, wiping the occasional tear from her cheek, concentrating on Onslow running his sweaty palms down his trousers. Onslow stared at the clock on his open laptop, willing time to standstill. He still had time to refuse to fire the sequence which would bring havoc and destruction. Sacrificing his life and that of his friends to benefit others. Lideri sat back in her chair, watching cat movies on the internet, via an Estonian address on her phone, showing Jessica the cuter videos and laughing.

'Lideri, you are barely into adulthood. You have fought bravely for your people, but you are wrong to involve us. I think we should draw a line under this episode and stop the madness.'

'You are correct, Jessica. Sometimes I feel I have grown up too quickly. You have never shot a person or killed anyone.' Jessica dropped her gaze back to Onslow's hands. Onslow snorted. 'The sad thing is, it doesn't matter after a while. We all die one day, so what does it matter if I end a life early or mine ends early? Our leaders keep swapping allegiances; now I just fight for my comrades.' She shrugged and then howled with laughter, showing Jessica a video of a cat refusing to let a large dog pass to eat its dinner.

'Our lives are no more important than other people's, Jess. This is wrong at every level.'

‘Our lives are no less important either, Ons. Don’t try to justify this, it will send you crazy. Everyone else is a soldier,’ she glanced at Lideri, ‘or a freedom fighter. We are just innocent civilians.’

‘Innocent? You really think so?’

Lideri sat bolt upright and then stood. Jessica heard the clatter of helicopter blades.

‘Do it Mr Dalliance. Do it right this second, now.’ Lideri levelled her AK-47 at Jessica. ‘Three, two, ..’

‘I am doing it Commander; it takes a few minutes.’

Jessica fixed her eyes on Lideri and softly sang an Adele song, *Make You Feel My Love.* Jessica had sung it for Jason as he fought for his own life the previous year, racked with virus. He had survived that situation and perhaps he would survive this, even if she, herself, did not.

She maintained eye contact. She could not stop the other woman from killing her, but she would not make it easy.

‘Nearly there Commander. Just a few more minutes. Nearly there. Keep calm.’

Lideri giggled. ‘*Keep calm*. You are both so funny. Like your French and Saunders act.’ She snapped back the bolt on the assault rifle.

‘We are seconds away Commander.’

The door came off its hinges and landed onto the floor with a whoosh, expelling air across the room. A stun grenade flashed and banged, forcing the three away from each other. Onslow ducked and immediately resumed working on the laptop. Red dots moved around Lideri's chest and face. Two marines screamed orders at Lideri. She smiled, a genuine open grin. Holding the muzzle of the Kalashnikov, she rested it against the wall.

'Careful guys. It is cocked. It has a mind of its own. We don't want an accident.'

A marine pushed passed Jessica, knocking her back against the wall. He pointed a semiautomatic pistol at Onslow's head.

'Get away from the laptop or I blow your fucking face off!'

Onslow raised his hands and stepped backwards.

'It is safe. It was never armed. I have locked it safe.'

The warrant officer pointed his pistol at Lideri.

'Who are you?'

Lideri snapped to attention.

Commander Lideri, marine. YPJ.

The warrant officer shot her twice in the chest, lifting her off the ground and against the wall. She slid down the wall until she sat like a floppy doll on the floor.

Jessica launched herself across the table, knocking the laptop to the floor. She straddled Lideri's legs and cupped her face. The red dots jumped around the wall, Jessica blocking the line of fire.

'Hey Jessica. That was a curved ball, as you say.' Her smile still bright. 'It is my turn to die today, not yours. Fancy that.'

'No Lideri. I think you are ok, just a flesh wound.'

Lideri snorted a laugh. The stream of blood from her mouth changed from bright red to globs of sticky black.

'You are so funny, Jessica, always joking. I know you are busy, and you want to see your husband, but can you stay for just a moment? I am quite lonely. Don't be too sad sweetheart, I was going to shoot you, if necessary, you know that?'

Jessica nodded. She tried to smile for her friend, but her eyes already looked back dead.

*

The Westland Wildcat helicopter landed on the tarmac apron of Incirlik NATO Base. Two Apache attack helicopters hovered above slowly rotating, noses and canons pointing to the ground to provide air-cover. The pilot killed the Wildcat's engines; the rotors spun gently to a halt. Jessica spoke to Hawaiian Shirt marine.

‘Why did you do it? Why did you shoot her?’

‘She posed a threat, Jess.’

‘But she didn’t, did she? You murdered her.’

Hawaiian shirt marine shrugged. The main door opened, ground-crew assisted Jessica and Onslow to release their harnesses and clamber out. Jessica stopped to punch the marine in the face; slicing open her knuckle on his helmet chinstrap. Pitt and Brad sat further along the seating, both sniggered.

‘You are welcome, Mrs Taylor. Come again.’

A military jeep drove Onslow and Jessica for fifteen minutes around the perimeter road to the office and accommodation blocks. Jandarma escorted Jessica and Onslow to separate rooms; medics checked them over. They gave Onslow a mild sedative.

‘Mrs Taylor. We need to have a chat, before we settle you down for the night. You must feel tired.’

‘Where is my husband?’

‘All in good time Mrs Taylor.’

‘Where is my fucking husband?’

The interviewing jandarma looked to the officer, sat next to her. The officer nodded.

‘He is here at Incirlik, Mrs Taylor. You will see him later, I promise.’

‘I don’t believe you. I want to see him. You have left him rotting in Syria. You have recovered Onslow’s laptop and neutralised the threat. Now you have washed your hands of my husband.’

The officer spoke softly into the phone on the desk.

‘Mrs Taylor, let us have a cup of coffee in the canteen.’

The jandarma and Jessica entered the canteen, Priti and Onslow sat at one end of a long empty table. Jason paced along the length of the wide window.

‘Christ Jess. What happened to you?’

The couple met in the middle of the room. Jason hugged her around the waist as she spread kisses over his face.

‘What happened to your face? Are you injured?’

‘Mr Taylor. Your wife is under caution still. I must insist …’

‘My wife has been injured when she was supposed to be in your custody. I will ask her what I like, now piss off.’

Jason led her to a chair at the opposite end of the table to their colleagues. As Jason sat, Jessica slipped onto his lap, wrapping her arms around his neck.

‘I thought you were dead, Jace. Twice in less than two years I thought you were dead. You need to stop this.’

‘I am ok. Priti and I have spent the past couple of days plane spotting and watching telly in the warrant officer’s mess. Where have you been? They said you were helping them with a problem on the air-defence system. What happened to you? Where did you find two black eyes?’

‘Ons and I have been to Syria. Lideri hit me with a Kalashnikov. She was lovely Jace, so full of life. You’d have loved her. I held her hand as she died. I miss her so much.’

‘Mrs Taylor, please. Keep the specifics for the interview room.’

‘She said they were handing you to Islamic State.’

‘Islamic State? The jandarma came for us within an hour of you leaving the hotel. We have been fine, honest. How did you end up in Syria? This has got to stop Jess. You have a nerve complaining about my being ill! You go to work in the morning and end up in a war zone!’ Jason kicked his leg out, sending the chair opposite flying across the room. ‘I can’t handle any more of this Jess.’

Jessica tightened her grip around his neck. She mumbled into his chest.

‘I can’t help it, Jason. I don’t mean to. I kicked a Peshmerga fighter for shooting Driver in an ambush and the Commander hit me with a Kalashnikov. These things just happen sometimes. You can’t blame me.’

'No Jess, these things don't *just happen*! At least, not to anyone else.'

'Maybe not to your Perfect-Miss-Priti.'

Jason released a long sigh.

'Mrs Taylor, Mr Dalliance. I insist we resume our interviews now, please.'

*

Jessica returned to the interview room. A woman of her own age sat waiting in uniform.

'Mrs Taylor. It is kind of you to help the military investigate a serious security situation. You are not under arrest; you are here voluntarily. Thank you. My name is Avukat, I am an advocate for you, appointed by the jandarma. Because of the nature of the conversations we are having, you may not have your own embassy or legal representative present.'

Jessica felt more confident having seen her friends and husband safe.

'*Here voluntarily*, as in, I can leave at any time?'

'Absolutely Jessica. May I call you Jessica? I would just counsel on one point. For so long as you kindly volunteer, the jandarma has decided not to arrest you for crossing into a restricted area, making contact with a prescribed and internationally recognised terrorist organisation, before re-entering Turkey without a valid visa.'

‘I was kidnapped at gunpoint and taken to Syria. I was kidnapped at gunpoint and returned to Turkey.’

‘Again, absolutely agree Jessica. And, if you are arrested for these crimes, I will make a strong case for your full legal representation to defend yourself. You were wronged. It is a shame these processes are so slow and time-consuming.’

Jessica released a sardonic snort.

‘I saw an unarmed woman murdered or assassinated by a Royal Marine. I want this addressed.’

‘Agreed Jessica. All life is important and what you describe is a war crime. My understanding is the event involved the UK military working under NATO auspices, involving a Syrian citizen, in Syrian territory. The Turkish jandarma are not looking to investigate this event, which is not in our jurisdiction, but I absolutely do advise you to report it to the appropriate British authorities, perhaps when you are next home in Briton or through your consulate in Ankara.’

‘I know you all think I am crazy, my husband does, but I miss her terribly. I was so scared for my husband, and she had all the answers. She was brave, beautiful, and funny. God Avukat, I make it sound like a girl crush.’

‘The woman you describe is yourself, Jessica. They say you stayed with her at the end. She was very lucky to have you.’

Jessica nodded, fighting back tears.

'Ok Jessica. Are you ready?'

Jessica nodded again.

*

The officer and interviewer returned to the room.

'Mrs Taylor. I am going to apologise in advance. We arrested you and, whilst in our custody, you were ambushed and kidnapped; we should have kept you safe. Please tell me everything you remember. At the road, did the jandarma turn left or right? How long were you travelling, before the ambush? What do you remember about the ambush? How many people were involved?'

Jessica remembered the Tommy Cooper impersonating jandarma laughing with the kidnappers and the charade of the ambush.

'I was hit in the head. Sorry, I remember nothing. I can remember having breakfast in my hotel, then being dragged through a tunnel. Sorry.'

The jandarma studied Jessica; she held eye contact.

'Ok. We have your friend's account. Perhaps it will come back to you. What are you working on in Turkey, exactly?'

'My guess is you know, already. I am not at liberty to discuss any details. What I will say is, I am subject to the official secrets act in the UK and confidentiality agreements with authorities here in Turkey. Anything I may have been working on is completely legitimate, meets UK laws, international laws and complies with laws of the jurisdiction I am working in – Turkey. You need to refer back to Company for more details. My guess is they will contact the Turkish authority involved to discuss with you directly. I have done nothing wrong.'

'What did the YPJ want with you?'

'You need to ask them. All I can say is what they told me. They told me to arm defence missiles inside Turkey, from a work laptop. Ludicrous. We played for time until the cavalry arrived.'

'You were not in a position to arm the missiles from the laptop?'

'God no! The laptop is used for commissioning purposes only. We can't go around firing missiles, it isn't a video game. Look, you need to refer back to Company.'

'A Russian jet was shot down, are you aware?'

'You know I am aware. I saw it happen, but you need to talk to your air force about that.'

'It wasn't a Turkish Sidewinder, Mrs Taylor.'

'Then the army, or the Turkmen brigades. Or NATO. Or the Syrian Free Army, or Islamic State …'

'Sam Smith?

'Yes, I know Sam Smith. He is a team manager at Company. Look on LinkedIn or Company's website.'

'And he has access to fire missiles remotely?'

'What? No! Of course not. If you shot down a jet by mistake, you need to own up to it, not blame the first foreign office worker that springs to mind. Ask Sam Smith yourself!'

'If our forensic IT team has identified a spurious path between our air-defence system, your aircraft carriers and with remote access, what would you say?'

Jessica stared at the interviewer. She remembered the promise she made to Onslow, to divert any flak from his direction.

'Look, I know what you are getting at. I am the only Company employee with full access to both the carrier system and to the improvements to your Russian made ground system. Nobody else has, that I am aware of, not even my manager, Sam Smith, certainly not Onslow Dalliance, my husband or Priti Khan. So I absolutely understand why you are grilling me. But listen to me – I did not arm anything against the Russian jet and I did not arm your defence system for the Kurdish YPJ. I am not helping you investigate an event, am I? I am defending myself against an accusation. You need to arrest me, and I need to go *no comment.*'

Chapter fourteen

Jessica sat in her room as Avukat sat on the edge of her bed, jacket over the back of a chair, shoes off.

'Who am I meeting now? And when can I see my husband and go home?'

'I am not sure, Jessica. I am told it is a civilian dignitary. Keep still.'

Avukat gently rubbed makeup over the bruise on Jessica's temple. The black around her eyes now mostly gone.

'You look gorgeous, Jessica. Our dignitary will be impressed.'

'I couldn't give a fuck about your dignitary, to be honest.'

'And your husband will be proud of you. I see Mr Dalliance keeps a close eye on you, as well'

The women smiled.

'Ok Jessica Taylor. Let us do this.'

They walked together across the parade ground and into an auditorium. One corner of the stage was set with Turkish flags, tables, and a podium. Jason, Priti and Onslow sat along one table, flanked by Turks in dress uniform and an Anglo-Saxon wearing a suit.

The second table held more Turks in expensive dress suits.

By the podium sat a moustachioed Turk. He wore the shiniest suit and used the darkest hair dye or wig and slickest hair oil. Jessica wondered if it smelt nutty, like Onslow's. He stood and clapped as Jessica entered. Everyone else stood and joined the clapping. Avukat placed her hand on the small of Jessica's back, gently propelling her forward towards the moustache and wig. She peeled off to sit with the audience. The jandarma officer, who had sat in the interviews, introduced Jessica.

'Mrs Taylor. Please let me introduce you to the Governor of Turkey's Hatay Region. Hatay Valiligi Ercan Toupee.'

Ercan shook hands, grinning widely.

'It is a pleasure to meet a hero, Mrs Taylor. Thank you for taking time to see me.'

On first entering the room, she wondered if she was to be condemned to death for conspiring against the Turkish Republic. She was still held against her will, and certainly had not *taken time* to meet this man – she had no choice. She mumbled.

'Well, Lideri, this is a bit of a curveball.'

Ercan looked to the translator, who shrugged. Ercan began in English, the translator speaking in Turkish.

'Mr Ambassador,' he gestured to the suit adjacent to Jason, 'friends, family and guests. It is not often we are fortunate enough to welcome a foreigner into our midst, who then goes on to put herself between a threat and Turkey. Literally between an insurgent and a wounded Turkish soldier. Between an insurgent and a little girl – a Turkish mother of the future. Between an insurgent and a whole community. Between an insurgent and the Turkish Republic. Mrs Taylor is a brave, inspirational hero – and now she is ours. Mrs Taylor, please accept my heartfelt gratitude and this State Medal of Distinguished Service for your gallantry and service to the Turkish Republic. On behalf of the President of Turkey, the cabinet, parliament, the Chief of General Staff, every Turkish man, woman and child, I thank you.'

He placed the golden medal, on a long ribbon, around her neck and kissed her on both cheeks.

'Please, Mrs Taylor. Say a few words.'

Jessica looked around the audience and settled on the beaming face of Jason, before snorting into a fit of uncontrolled giggles.

*

The military airbus a319-100 had the full military livery. Inside was plush business class throughout – four fully reclining seats across the fuselage with a centre aisle. Priti wore her body-hugging travel dress with matching jacket, handing her coat to the steward as soon as they boarded. She smiled at the others, excited. Less than thirty other passengers boarded; a few senior officers in uniform and some young officer families, heading home or on holiday. The flight was scheduled to land in Antalya, Dalaman and Istanbul; collecting and delivering military personal on route. Jessica squeezed in front of Priti and sat next to Onslow. Jason sat across the aisle with Priti taking the fourth window seat. The engines fired-up. Onslow closed his eyes, starting his regime of rubbing his palms along his thighs. Jessica lay one hand on his bicep and one on his inner thigh. She lay her cheek against his shoulder.

‘Come for a laugh?’

‘Wouldn’t miss it for the world. Still scared of spiders?’

‘Fuck off Jess. No wonder she hit you with a Kalashnikov, you are so annoying.’

‘At least I have a medal.’

‘Not a medal for crawling through tunnels, wimp.’

The engines roared and Onslow grabbed Jessica’s hand, cracking her knuckles.

‘And I remember you as such a gentle lover.’

The plane levelled and the engines quietened. Onslow relaxed. Jessica snuggled her face into his shoulder.

‘I asked the jandarma how the Royal Marines knew where we were, for the rescue. They didn’t know or wouldn’t say. But Avukat, my appointed advocate, suggested I ask you. So, how did they know?’

‘I was a gentle lover. I still am. But you will never have it confirmed, not now I have seen the size of your husband. I think the important thing is, they found us in time, just.’

‘If I scream and slap your face, Jace will be over here to punch your lights-out, before you can shout, *wasn’t me!*’

‘Ok. I took a screenshot of google maps and saved it to my outbox, addressed to Amara. When Lideri supervised my opening emails for the password I needed, it auto-sent.’

‘You had no right Onslow. You put Jason’s and Priti’s life in danger. Did you prepare Bridge to arm S-400 and *Naap* against NATO and everyone?’

‘Not exactly, no. Sorry.’

‘*Exactly* what did you do, then?’

‘I exactly spent the time locking down the system so I couldn’t do it, even if they shot your pretty face off.’

‘You unilaterally went against my instruction? You put me, you, Priti and Jason at terrible risk?’

‘Exactly, yes.’

Jessica called to Priti, asking to be allowed to sit back next to her own husband now. As Priti stood in the aisle, providing a screen between Jason and the couple, Jessica lent forward and kissed Onslow softly on the mouth, making sure Priti saw, and hoping Jason did not.

'You are a brave man Onslow. And you accuse me of living life on the edge. You will never know how many times you came close to showing me how gentle you still are, but never mind.'

Onslow shrugged a reply.

'What was that all about?'

'He is petrified of flying, Jace. Just holding his hand.'

'He seems like a nice guy. Not sure why he is so off with me?'

'He is worried, a bit nervous of you. I kissed him.'

'Obviously, Jess.' Jessica turned to face her husband. 'Why else would you ask how I would react to you kissing him? Is that all?'

'Yes darling, promise. I was lonely.'

'And that makes it ok?'

'No. Of course not.' Jessica studied the cabin safety information showing on the screen immediately ahead. She did not want Priti to see her being told off.'

'No, of course not. Fuck sake Jess. It is not alright to kiss another man. It is not alright to shoot a man wearing a suicide belt. It is not alright to intervene in a gunfight between insurgents and mercenary bodyguards. It is not alright to shield a dying *freedom fighter* in the middle of a battle with commandos. None of it is alright.'

Jessica nodded. They both studied the safety information, the aircrew in the video acted by children dressed in uniform, with subtitles.

'Good kisser?'

'Not bad.'

Onslow retrieved a blanket from the locker and spread it over Priti and his lap. She pulled it up to her chin, giggling. Jessica glared at Priti, who held her gaze with a smirk. She shuddered a little as Onslow touched her under the blanket.

'Oh, for goodness' sake, Jace. Is she just working through my back-catalogue?'

Jason turned to watch the couple. Priti closed her eyes, resting her chin on her shoulder, breathing heavy and regular.

'If she works through your whole back-catalogue, she will be busy for a while. Do you remember your old boyfriend, Chris? Remember what you told me about him?'

‘Shit Jace, did I? I must have been drunk, sorry. Size isn’t everything.’

‘No, not that. You said he would fancy you dressed in a bin liner with a facemask of duck poo.’

‘Yes, I do remember saying that, although I said it in context. Why?’

‘Just that I would fancy you more if you didn’t wear your green beret and your medal everywhere. Maybe just around the house?

*

The plane landed in Antalya. Onslow, preoccupied with Priti under the blanket, landed without tears. A dad and two children stood to disembark. Two officers stood in uniform on the apron, waiting to board.

‘Come on, Jace, we are getting off. I have had enough of watching Priti in the mile high club. Priti love. If you can still walk by the time you land in Dalaman, would you collect our luggage please and have it sent to the hotel? There’s a dear.’

Priti struggled to straighten her clothes from under the blanket, using her chin to stop it from slipping. Onslow laughed, shaking his head at Jessica. She gripped Priti’s wrist through the blanket as she tried to pull up her top.

'Now listen to me, love. I want you to find out what our Mr Sam Smith has been up to. Whose balls has he been juggling? Ask your friends in Contracts, not Projects or HR.'

Forty-five minutes later, Jason drove the hire car to the main road. Jessica reclined a little, her feet on the dashboard.

'Where to, boss? And take off that bloody medal!'

'Head south. If there is a glimmer of sun or ounce of warmth left, I want to find it, please.'

'We have no clothes or anything. Should we have collected our bags, do you think?'

'For everything else, there is MasterCard.'

They followed the coast road. Mount Olympos loomed above them. The terrain hilly, the road clung to the cliffs, tiny plateaus and slithers of coast. A junction offered signs for Mugla ahead, towards the shack; to the left, Olympos and Cirali.

'Here Jace. Let's go to Cirali. It has a beach sign and hotels. Follow me.' She grinned at her husband.

'Tallyho!'

Jason turned off the trunk and headed down the winding, improbably steep road. At each hairpin the couple made roars and whooshing noises; laughing at each other and themselves. Steep terraces grew tiny market gardens or a fistful of fruit trees. Narrow farm cottages clung to the cliff faces over several levels. Jessica waved to the locals and small children playing marbles on the road. Jason took each hairpin cautiously, allowing the occasional car or van plenty of room to pass. Despite his caution, Jessica squealed and clamped her hands to her face as she felt her husband was dangling her side of the car over the edge. They eventually arrived at sea level, the metalled road disappearing into a flattened sand track, indistinguishable from the wide sandy beach. Jason parked the hire car in a rough patch of scrub and paid the attendant. They walked towards market stalls lining the parking area. A small girl wearing a grubby summer dress and puffer jacket, with odd colour wellington boots, ran to Jessica and squeezed her hand.

'Good afternoon, miss. It is very nice to meet you. My name is Kucuk Kiz. What are you buying today, please?'

'Hello Kucuk. I am buying some long shorts, beach shoes and a jumper for my husband. I am buying shorts, beach shoes, jumper and a pretty dress for me. Oh, and I need the prettiest pair of rubber boots for a little girl with your size feet. Can you help please?'

'Of course, miss. Follow me.'

The little girl took them to the first stall, it sold cleaning products. The couple laughed behind their hands. The second stall sold toilet seats and a few plumbing items. By the time they reached the stall selling live chickens, the couple were in fits of giggles. Eventually, they purchased the supplies needed for a few bright days, collecting shells on the beach in the wintery sun.

'Oh, I forgot. My friend already has a pair of boots. Would you like these Kucuk? Now, when you are grown up like me, what hotel would you take your favourite husband to?'

The little girl's face beamed with pride at the gift of shiny pink boots with a Baby Shark design.

'I would take him to a house in the trees!'

Kucuk pulled Jessica by the hand until they were almost in the sea. The beach met a spit of cliff and disappeared. She pointed out into a shallow bay.

'I must stay here. But you must walk over the water and live forever in the trees.' She turned and ran towards the stalls, head down, watching her new boots flash over the sand.

'Good at retail. Poor at hospitality.'

Jason and Jessica smiled and waved to the disappearing girl.

'Sorry to interrupt. The little girl is quite correct. If you stay close to the cliff, you can paddle through the water. When you find the beach, follow it to the Lycian ruins of Olympos. Through the ruins is a campsite.' The stranger was a young Turkish man.

His wetsuit pulled down to warm his chest in the weak sun. He studied the office clothes worn by the couple in front of him. 'I guess you haven't got a tent. You can hire a tree house.'

'Yes, yes, yes Jason. Let's do it. How long, roughly?'

'I couldn't say. But it was abandoned in the fifteenth-century.'

Jessica laughed. 'How long to walk to the campsite?'

'I am playing. What is the hurry? The longer the journey, the more you live it.' He grinned back at Jessica. 'Ten minutes in the water. It really isn't deep. Ten minutes to the ruins. Then ten minutes to experience the ruins, or ten years, it is up to you.'

Jessica pulled off her shoes and slacks, folding them in with her shopping. Her smock top just covering her lacy underwear.

'No Jace! I am not appearing out of the sea at Olympos like, I don't know, Cleopatra, with you wearing rolled-up trouser like Reginald Perrin! Get'um off.'

The young man laughed at the argument and wolf whistled as Jason stripped to his boxer shorts and linen long-sleeved shirt. The water felt much warmer than they expected and soon they had paddled to Olympos beach. The ruins spilt onto the sand; Jessica continued to follow the water's edge until they could look back at the ruins and Mount Olympos behind.

They sat on the warm sand. A couple threw a ball to each other along the beach. In the opposite direction sat the young man, waving. Jessica gave him the thumbs up. The sun was warm on their backs, the cliffs like a storage radiator to their front, protected from the breeze. The couple looked at each other. Jessica's nose crinkled and her cheek bones rose on her grin. Jason smiled back, nodding slightly. Without a further word, the couple spontaneously pulled off their remaining clothes and raced each other into the sea. Up to their knees in water, Jessica tripped and fell headlong. Jason grabbed her by the waist to break her fall and they both stumbled into the Mediterranean Sea.

*

Jessica stood at the reception hut in her wet smock top and Jason's boxer shorts, the waist band twisted and tucked in to stop them falling down. Jason wore his work clothes, carrying his shoes.

'Oops! Fall into the sea with your clothes on?'

The couple looked at each other and back at the receptionist. Jason blushed; Jessica grinned.

'Oh, I see. Your clothes all fell off and then you fell into the sea. Even better. Six British Pounds, including breakfast, if there is any left. Is that ok? If you can't afford that, you can pay less. Or pay next time. Or go to the bar and see if anyone wants to share.

Or at a push, sleep on the sofas in the bar, by the firepit, for free. Breakfast included.

'That is perfect. The tree house for the full price, I mean.'

The receptionist handed them a large wooden key fob with a number six burnt into the wood.

'Um. Sorry, there is no key.'

'Number six hasn't got a lock. I can find you one with a lock if you like?'

'Has it a door?'

'Oh yes, they all have doors. Six also has a loo and air-con. Make sure you set it to heat, obviously.'

Carrying their shopping and with Jessica holding up the boxer shorts, they found number six, around the corner from twelve and between seven and nine.

'Chronological order perhaps.' Suggested Jason.

The steps were rickety and steep. Inside stood a small double and a separate single bed. The light electric, the empty window shuttered. The en-suite included a shower. Jason pulled down the flap on the air-con and sent a welcome stream of hot air over the couple.

'Beer and early to bed?'

'Or bed, beer and early to bed?'

Jessica draped her arms around her husband's neck; the boxer shorts slipped down.

'Sorry, I want my beer as much as I want my man.'

The bar comprised a high wooden roof over a lit firepit, floor cushions, low tables and a few picnic tables.

A group occupied the cushions near the firepit. Jason sat on the edge of a picnic table. A woman sat on the cushions.

'Please, join us.'

The group shuffled around to make room.

'Are you guys all together?'

'I am alone. My name is Alona. These guys … Oh I forget, some are together.' The group laughed. Some lent over to shake hands and introduce themselves.'

'How does the bar work?'

'Help yourself, tick against your treehouse number in the book. Same for crisps. It all goes a bit Pete Tong as the evening proceeds. In the morning our barman tots-it-up and we have a whip-round for any missing cash at breakfast. Sometimes there is too much, so bartender leaves a few bottles on the table.'

'Cool bartender.'

A man in his forties raised his hand, his hair blond and dreadlocked.

‘I am.’

The first man spoke again, with his slight London accent; a visitor, possibly from Essex.

‘You guys been to the fire-mountain?’

Jason and Jessica shrugged.

‘Is that a restaurant?’

The group laughed again.

‘You can paddle to the neighbouring beach. From there, grab a lift to Mount Cirali, as in Chimaera. Spend an hour walking up the mountain path. Hey presto. My God! You don’t know about this? Like the mountainside is alight. Flames pour from the ground.’

‘A scrub fire?’

Bartender spoke. He had a nasal tone. Jessica suspected a life of drugs and rock ‘n roll.

‘It’s like crazy. Gas erupts from the mountain and whoosh! Bursts into flames.’

‘Methane or volcanic?’

‘Really gentle, you can run your hand through it. Like making love with dripping candle wax. No? Really? Try it, but only white candles or it burns. Anyway, the gasses spontaneously ignite. You smother them with a towel, then a few seconds later, whoosh!’

'We have a car at the beach. But …' Jason held up his beer to demonstrate.

'I can drive.' The barman slurred. He saw Jason's sideways glance at Jessica. 'Don't judge a book, man! I've been clean for years. You have more shit in your system than I have.'

'Sorry. I didn't mean …'

Alona spoke again.

'Let's do it!'

*

With Jason and Jessica both wearing long surfer shorts and jumpers, the group paddled to Cirali Beach, and the parked car. Jason half lay in the boot of the Dacia Duster. Five Estuary hippies squashed into the rear seat, Bartender drove, Jessica rode shotgun with Alona sat on her lap. Bartender slowly reversed into the market stall, knocking away one corner strut. Once propped back up, he eased the Duster onto the sandy track and crawled along the narrow road between the rustic bungalow hotels, set in magical candle and fairy-light lit gardens, and the beach. Leaving the hotel strip and village behind, the sand track became a dirt track at a slight incline.

'I love your braids Alona, I thought they were extensions. I love the beads; it must have taken forever to have them done.'

‘I do them myself. Each braid and bead mean something, to me, anyway.’

‘Wow! I can’t even brush my hair without missing a bit. What do they mean?’

Jessica fiddled with the braids, running the beads between her thumb and forefinger like prayer or worry beads.

‘You are most perceptive, Jessica. I fidget with them when meditating. Each bead on this braid represents an argument I had with my mum, the year she died. She wasn’t important to me back then, or so I thought, but now I can remember every argument we had, word for word. Although, presumably, I can only remember the arguments I remember, if that makes sense. These beads are one for each lover. Blues and greens for boys, pink and orange for girls. Can you see the dark bead set alone? He hit me.’

Jessica kissed the back of her head and squeezed her shoulders.

‘Some others are countries I travelled, pets I owned, nieces, nephews and cousins. I can see auras as well. I won't mention it again, but if you want, tell me tomorrow, when we are alone, and I will tell you what I see around you and Jason, but only if he agrees. Some people don’t want to know, but I can’t not see it.’

Jessica’s blood ran cold, and she shuddered.

‘Hey sorry Jessica, I didn’t mean to freak you.’

Bartender pulled into the carpark. Essex hippy, David, paid the pennies for the group to park the car and enter the path up the mountainside. Jessica took the torch from the glovebox, and bartender produced one from his hoodie. Bartender led the way, Jessica, Jason and Alona bringing up the rear guard to help illuminate the path. Bats darted overhead and between the group, snatching insects from the blackness.

The path was steep. When the group halted to rest, they turned off the lamps and the milky way slowly illuminated the heavens as their eyes adjusted. The bushes clinging to the mountainside rustled occasionally – bartender shone his light; he carried a four-feet long stick.

‘People, especially the locals, it seems, drop their rubbish over the side and it attracts bears and wolves. These are more likely to be foxes or squirrels, but it is best to keep an eye out. They are more scared of you than you are of them.’

Jessica thought of Onslow and spiders, smiling to herself. Rounding the bend, the group stopped to face the whole mountainside, a mass of flames. Pockets of fire gently burning yellow-orange or flashes of fire in a weak cloud. The experienced members of the group sat and chatted between the flares. Jessica, Jason, Alona and bartender wandered around the mountainside, climbing further to see the forest of fires disappear over the ridge.

The mountain side comprised bare rock and shale, the flames flickering from between pebbles or fissures in the ground. Bartender found a dried blade of grass, holding it to the centre of a flare, engulfing his entire hand. The grass failed to ignite. He pulled off his hoodie and covered a vent, to extinguish the flame; calling Jessica to lean close and smell the gas. With her face just inches from the ground, the gas flared again, engulfing her face and head. She jumped backwards with a yelp and laugh, bartender grinning.

'Wow! It felt cold, not hot. How weird.'

They rested. The hippies produced food and beer. Jessica playfully sang the Doors *Light My Fire.* Her eldest niece had given her the CD for Christmas and she had gone on to use it for her first dance with Jason at the wedding. Alona then sang Hippie Sabotage *Play With Fire.* She kept eye contact with Jessica, her innocent, clear voice making the aggressive lyrics seem more menacing.

*

'Supper guys? Cheese and mushrooms on toast?'

Alona appeared from behind the bar with a single slice of toast and melted cheese on a plate. She sat cross-legged by the firepit, a twinkle in her eye. She opened a ziplock bag and shook the dried woody pieces of magic-mushroom over the cheese, followed by a generous helping of black pepper. She sliced the toast into six pieces and held out the plate. Jessica took a piece but waited for Jason's reaction.

'Yeah, why not? Jessica Taylor on hallucinogens. What could possibly go wrong?'

He took a piece himself. It tasted bitter. The three shared Jason's bottle of beer to wash it down.

'You two need to be careful, you've had some beer already. I never mix stuff, but that's just me.' She offered round the plate again.

'Jess and I don't really do stuff like this; especially now, with tests at work. But it has been a tough few weeks. We are both wanting to let our hair down. A week from now, we will be back in corporate England preparing for commercialised Christmas.

'It isn't a problem, but I was just wondering. Could I crash with you guys tonight, please?'

Jessica cleared her throat.

'Alona, you are a really lovely girl and dead cute, but I am actually a bit jealous like that. I don't really share Jason ...'

Alona smiled and sat back. Jason interrupted.

'Jess, sweetheart. I think Alona is asking to sleep in the spare bed.'

Jessica clasped her hands to her face and giggled.

‘Sorry, I thought you meant … I mean I would consider it if … but anyway, yes of course, you are welcome.’

‘I slept out here last night, but it got bloody cold. I need to make my money last. I am heading east soon, maybe Kerala. Are you ok Jessica?’

‘Mmm. That tasted like strawberries.’

Jason and Alona laughed out loud, tossing back their heads and whinnying like ponies. Jessica tried to tell them to stop, but she laughed so hard the words would not form. She started braying and had a moment of intense realisation that she had been a donkey all of her life.

Jason bought two more beers, one for Jessica; Alona shared a few sips of his. Jessica concentrated to stretch her arm out to reach the end of her elongated face. She followed the conversation the two ponies were having but struggled to join in because of her braying. She managed a joke about Jason being her stallion.

The three negotiated the stairs to the treehouse safely, despite the steps extending in front of Jessica; the journey seeming to take several weeks of climbing. The planks making the treehouse now shone different colours. As Alona and Jason talked, the planks illuminated and repeated their words in an echo. After a few minutes, the planks took over the conversation altogether, shining brightly in green and blue for

Jason and pink and orange for Lideri. She now realised Alona was also Lideri and it frustrated Jessica when she tried to ask her questions about being dead, but the planks shouted over her and shone brightly in a colour she had never seen before.

*

Jessica lay on her back, woken by her own snoring. She wore only pants; the blankets pushed off; she shuddered with the cold. Checking her face to ensure the long donkey nose had returned to normal, she peered under the sheets to check Jason was also wearing shorts. Alona lay in the spare bed, the blanket tucked around her waist and wearing Jason's jumper.

'Jace? Are you ok?'

'Sure. What a weird night. You had a good time; we couldn't stop you laughing.'

'So strange. But not like a dream; like it actually happened. I am assuming we saw different stuff. Like you didn't realise you were a pony?'

Jason's laughter caused Alona to stir, pulling up her blanket against the chill.

'Shit Jace. Did the three of us, you know?'

'I certainly didn't Jess, I went straight to sleep.'

'No, you and I definitely did it. A girl can tell, you know. I won't forgive you, if you did it with Alona.

‘I’ll forgive you, Jess, if you did.’

‘Wipe that smirk off your face, pervert. This is serious.’

Alona sat up in bed.

‘Hey guys. Wow, sorry about that. I had twice that amount from the same bag, last week, and it did nothing. Everyone ok?’

The couple nodded. Alona stood, a little uneasily, and filled the kettle. She drank a pint of water in the time it took to boil the water for three coffees, climbing into bed next to Jessica. Jessica yelped and recoiled from her cold feet, Alona purposely rubbing them against Jessica’s thigh.

‘So how did it go, guys? What did you see?’

Jessica explained about the ponies, donkey and the shouting planks of wood. They all laughed, Alona wide eyed.

‘But after that, I can’t remember. You were right, I shouldn’t have mixed in the beer. Like, did you just go straight to sleep or something?’

‘Yes, straight after.’

‘Straight after what?’

‘After the sex.’

Jessica gulped. ‘Oh, ok. What, both of us?’

'Yep.'

Jessica dropped her chin to her chest. Jason tried to find her hand under the blanket, but she shook it off. Alona placed her cold foot onto Jessica's thigh and started tickling her ribs as she pulled away.

'You with each other, I mean. Not with me, silly girl! You were riding him like a cowgirl and saying he was your horse. So funny.'

Jessica pulled the blanket over her head in embarrassment as the women laughed together. Jason refilled the coffee cups, turned the heater on, and climbed back into bed.

'I had another thing happen. I thought my dead friend Lideri was here. I was a bit sad, because she couldn't talk with me.' Jessica allowed Jason to hold her hand this time. 'But I know she wasn't really here, and I know she isn't a proper friend as such. You know, not in the true sense of friendship, and all that.'

Jessica found the lone dark bead in Alona's hair and rubbed it gently with her thumb.

'Tell me about my aura, Alona. What does it show you?'

'I think you need help, Jessica. You need to see someone.'

Chapter fifteen

Jessica collected Priti and Onslow from the pedestrian tunnel at Gunwharf Quays. Onslow wore a heavy trench coat with small Italian military insignia stitched to the collar. Priti wore a black tunic with gold buttons, a white billowing blouse, high-waisted black slacks with a cavalry red stripe down the leg and high-heeled leather cowboy boots.

'Do you remember when I would rather feel cold to flash my tits, instead of dressing against the weather?'

Snow flurried in the late December morning; not forecast, it was unlikely to settle. The sun bravely battled the leaden sky but held out little hope of victory.

'Looks like Adam Ant meets The Who. Or am I just getting old?'

Jessica turned to ask Lideri to make room on the back seat before remembering. Instead, she shooed Brian into the boot of the Porsche Cayenne.

'I don't like that bloody dog in my car, Jess.'

'Likewise, Jace, he doesn't want you in here, either.'

The couple slid into the rear seat. Onslow lay a hand over Priti's red nose for a few seconds to warm it.

'Hi Mr and Mrs T. Brass-monkeys today.'

‘Now listen up. Amara does not do committees, nor does she make excuses or explain herself. This meeting is an absolute one-off. Damage limitation. So, make the best of it. You will only get this one opportunity; understood Priti? If you don’t ask something today, don’t come whining to me for an explanation tomorrow.

‘Yes Mrs Taylor, no Mrs Taylor,’ looking out of the window she mumbled ‘three bags fucking full Mrs Taylor.’

‘Don’t put her on the spot, though, or the shutters will come down. Jason, listening? And only ask relevant questions Onslow. Nobody is interested in your software angst. Keep it grown up. Don’t make notes. Keep your phones off; I don’t even want to hear any vibrates. If anyone will get away with holding the bitch accountable, it will be me; her very own agent provocateur.’

Security checked the handful of ID cards Jessica handed over.

‘Not many of your lot in; mostly split for Christmas.’

‘Just us sad five with nothing better to do.’

‘Five? Only four cards here.’

‘I mean four. Sorry, I … Just four.’

‘Well, I am supposed to do a full search occasionally. Why not all jump out, it won’t take a moment.’

*

The carpark for the training centre was almost empty. The main roller doors closed. The four walked in formation to the side pedestrian door, entered the vast workshops and fell back into formation – Jessica led, Jason two feet behind and to her right, Priti four feet directly behind Jessica, Onslow four feet directly behind Jason. Brian padded one head in front of Jessica. A tall figure of a man strode towards them. His march purposeful. Jessica decided not military, probably a sportsman, fast bowler or Sunday league footballer.

'Sorry. No dogs in here, it isn't safe.'

'He is with us. He has had a traumatic time with my sister. He shouldn't be left at home alone, poor mite. If you knew my sister …'

'Look, I can't have people and dogs just wandering around. This is a welding shop, not the beach.'

Jessica took in the neat rows of empty steel benches, each with a welding set, air extractor unit, and anti-flash screen. All empty, a light dusting of metal particles settled over the polished floor and cleaned surfaces.

'Well, you are doing a good job of keeping people out. We are booked on a Welding Appreciation Course. We were told to report to a Teresa Green.'

The man rolled his eyes, white against his olive skin. Jessica wondered if he had a little, distant, eastern mixed heritage like herself. Persian perhaps.

'My name is Woods, I am your instructor. *Trees are green – Woods*, get it? We have more natural comedians in this year's apprentice intake than we do natural welders, that is for sure. But no dogs. Although he could probably weld better than the apprentices.'

Priti made a loopy gesture, circling her finger around her temple and pointing at Jessica. 'Brian is a PAT dog, a Pet As Therapy dog.'

Brian peed up the leg of a bench, the puddle spreading as the group watched; the trainer transfixed. He sighed.

'This way.'

*

Most of the chairs already stacked on the desks and tables for the Christmas break. Amara and Trish sat at one long table. A figure walked from the kitchenette area at the rear of the classroom with a tray of coffee and a plate of pastries. She wore a red pencil skirt with matching jacket, white shirt, seamed stockings and patent heels. Jessica recognised the woman, despite her wearing a full, black, welder's helmet.

'Like the hat, Stace. Suits you.'

Stacy mumbled an incoherent reply and nodded, sitting next to Amara. Amara made a gesture, brushing her own face as if warning Stacy she had a chocolate smudge on her lip. Stacy removed the helmet.

'Sorry. I just wondered ...'

Woods cleared his throat.

'You aren't here for welding appreciation training, are you?'

Stacy smiled back. 'If you can, just email me the certificates. We will be an hour or two, then you can lock up please and enjoy the rest of your weekend with the family.'

'My eldest daughter is expecting ... Anyway, I will leave you to it.'

They watched Woods leave. Amara spoke.

'One way or another, you have all had a bit of an adventure. I want a debrief. I hear a lot of people around here meet in the Pilgrims Bar for secret rendezvous,' Jessica and Onslow blushed, avoiding eye contact, 'but I left these arrangements to Stacy. Talking of which, Stacy has prepared some extra-ordinary remuneration for you all. Bonus for Onslow, paygrade increase for Priti and extra overtime payments for our two overpaid contractors. Now, I want to put to bed any concerns you have about the past few months and Company's involvement in

Turkey. I also want to talk about your next job. Please feel free to ask anything and I will answer if I can. Everything is off the record and stays within these walls. In the New Year, we start afresh.'

Jessica raised a hand. 'Where is Sam Smith? Surely he is crucial to this discussion?'

'Ah Vanilla, darling. You forget I know everything. You had Priti do a little snooping, didn't you? I got to hear all about it.' Trish fiddled with her fingers. 'Mr Smith left Company quite suddenly, as well you know. It was a sad day for Company, but these things happen. I have taken over the close-out of my carrier defence system *Naap* and Sam Smith's Turkey Russian S-400 Compatibility air defence system.'

'And Bridge?'

'Bridge doesn't exist. It never did.'

Onslow replied, his incredulous voice high. 'Of course it existed Mrs Pebbles! I worked on it for months and went halfway around the world installing it, with Mrs Taylor.'

'No Onslow. You did not.'

Onslow scoffed and raised his hands in disbelief.

'Who shot down the Russian jet, Amara?'

'Jess! Please don't move on yet. I want to talk about Bridge!'

‘I am not moving on, Ons. I am talking about the same thing. Mrs Pebbles just told you that the Bridge project never existed. Amara?’

‘How is therapy going, Jess? How is the paranoia?’

Jessica took a deep breath, counting down from ten in her mind to the rhythmic snapping of a rubber-band she wore around her wrist.

‘Fine, Amara. I have seen Dr Stockholm four times. She says I have a syndrome and possibly a disorder. I present with high self-esteem which veils my low self-esteem, with a predilection for hero-worship. I have had trauma. But she says if Company keep throwing money at her, she can cure me. Thank you for asking.’ Jessica’s outburst caught everyone’s attention. ‘But the questions I am asking today are valid. Where did Sam Smith move to?’ Amara shrugged. ‘Priti? Can you fill us in, please?’ As Priti spoke, Jessica maintained eye contact with Amara, repeating what she had already told Jessica.

‘I believe Mr Sam Smith left Company on the day the Russian jet was shot down, Mrs Taylor. He moved that same afternoon to Washington, in the USA, not the one in West Sussex. He took the position of Special Advisor in NATO’s ISR department, Intelligence Surveillance and Reconnaissance.’

Amara shrugged again. ‘I always felt our Mr Smith was in a transition to somewhere else, didn’t you?’

‘If Bridge had ever existed Amara, I believe our Mr Sam Smith personally created a hidden, remote access path, probably through the mundane software utilities sections. I believe you, Amara, you, yourself, sent Onslow and me to install the system. The thing is Amara, you know I trust you implicitly; more than anyone else docs. You know you can trust me, more than you can trust anyone. You manoeuvred my old love interest into the frame to keep me sweet; knowing he would follow me around to get back into my knickers. And to make sure I stayed focused and didn’t run home for cover, you sent the person I love more than life itself to Turkey with a rampant supermodel hanging off his arm!’

Priti blushed. To support Jessica, she kept her chin high and continued to look towards Amara. Jason flicked his stare between Jessica, Amara and Priti.

‘Jess love. I am glad it is going well with Dr Stockholm. I want to assure you …’

‘Please don’t do that Am. Don’t fucking patronise me. Sam Smith signed off a shipment of 40N6 anti-aircraft missiles with the Turkish flag etched to the casing and delivered them to the carrier. Using Bridge, he tracked a Russian jet on the S-400 system and blew it from the sky, in Syrian airspace, not Turkish, killing a pilot. The missiles launched from HMS Prince of Wales, but the software trail makes it look like the Turks fired the missile from their own S-400 missile system. The Turks know they still have a full complement of unfired missiles, but it looks to the Russians like the missile came from Turkey. And who else worked this out Amara? Who else had access to Turkish military intelligence? Who else tried to use this information and could have exposed you to the world? Who else Amara? Who else? Say her fucking name Amara, say it!'

Amara sat patiently, listening to her friend; no one else prepared to comment.

'People die in wars, Jessica. People die. Lideri was a soldier. A young, brave, clever soldier.'

'You murdered my friend, Amara!'

Amara lowered her voice. 'It wasn't me who ordered you all killed. It was at Sam's request from his new NATO position; I am an arms dealer, Jess, not a General. I had no idea. He wanted the only other three people, who knew about Bridge and the shooting down, eliminated. I swear I didn't know.'

'Three?' Onslow shouted. Amara nodded.

'The Royal Marine warrant officer disobeyed a direct order. He was to eliminate anyone and everyone in the immediate vicinity of Onslow's laptop and drop the laptop into the sea when returning to the carrier. When he saw it was you and Jessica, he had a change of heart.'

'Why Amara? Is the man crazy?'

'No Jess. Sam is far from crazy. He had a few of you busying themselves with a project that never officially existed. He pushed a couple of buttons and changed the future of the world. Turkey was hours away from giving notice to NATO and allying with Russia. Turkey, seeming to shoot down a Russian jet, made it politically impossible for Putin to proceed with the plan. Putin was set for direct reprisals against Turkey, even following a protocol to warn NATO; to avoid World War Three. NATO, already knowing what was happening, threw its full force behind Turkey, bringing *Naap* to the party on both Elizabeth Class carriers in the Med and Black Sea. Without involving the CIA, British Intelligence or even NATO intelligence officially, Sam Smith saved NATO and strengthened Turkey's resolve. And as a thank you, landed himself a plum job in the US of A.'

'I am not having this, Amara. Company is complicit, directly or by reckless omission. A Company employee manoeuvred and then executed a military strike against Russia. Russia, for fuck's sake.'

'Company did not know what Sam was up to. C'mon now Jess, you, as much as anyone, know Sam is in a constant state of transition. Let's be honest, his choice of Friday night clothes is a bit of a giveaway.'

'Sorry Amara? Sam fancying a job in NATO intelligence justifies him being able to cook the books and fund a whole personal project? How did Company not notice?'

‘We were all fooled. You are correct, we are embarrassed, and Finance has mobilised a team of forensic accountants to investigate. We have warned UK Ministry of Defence procurement, and The City, that we will have to set aside funds for a possible lawsuit, without giving details of course. Because of the involvement of *Naap* and S-400 compatibility projects, Legal is putting forward a case that our little problem falls under the Official Secrets Act; we will just go *no comment.* Strange, we might be using the Official Secrets Act in defence against the UK government. But we all do it, *Miss plus or minus Nine Percent.*’ Amara mindful if Jessica decided to whistle blow at this point, it would be impossible to dissuade her.

‘Meaning what? I manage my projects so that they all come in on target. I don’t finance my own personal battles between superpowers!’

‘So, you booking costs from a failing project supplying armoured vehicles to the South African police, onto a profitable project supplying sniper technology to an eastern European National Guard, is somehow different? What, more acceptable? You make sure everyone gets their killing machines at a cost they can afford – *so that’s ok, then.* At least Sam did what he thought was morally right for the world.’

‘That is unfair Amara. I try to do my job, that’s all. Everyone wants to work with me because I fulfil your expectations, Company’s expectations! I make everyone in my team look good by meeting targets, interpreting and following orders.'

'You are only following orders? Isn't that what the concentration camp guards said?'

'Oh, for God's sake Amara. Now who is being dramatic?'

'All I am saying is we all cook the books. And in our business, that means we are all facilitating conflicts around the world, with human costs. Don't go soft on me Jess.'

Jessica stormed to the back of the room. She drank a glass of water from the tap and leant against the counter, staring at a blank wall. Jason stood to follow. Amara grabbed his wrist, and he shook her off.

'Please Jace. Please, let me.'

Jason sat again, allowing Amara to follow her. She rested her hand on Jessica's neck; she squirmed away.

'Don't push me away, Vanilla. You do this to Jason as well; keep your friends close.'

'And my enemy closer?'

'The west is in a better place because of what you did. Even if you hadn't realised you were involved. Lideri will be proud of you. Turkey, allied with Syria, Iran and Russia, against the Kurds, is not the outcome she looked for.'

‘Don’t you dare speak on her behalf.’

Jessica spun around, expecting to see Lideri, listening. She coiled the rubber-band around her wrist until it snapped. Without speaking, she walked back to her seat, avoiding eye contact with Jason.

*

‘I want the four of you to have a think, please. Jason might want to go back to joining pipes together. Onslow probably can’t wait to get back to his X-Box. Priti wants to return to the office and gossip about her times with the Taylors. I expect Jessica will want a quiet spell to recover. No, actually, forget I said anything, it is way too soon.’

The four watched Amara. Trish and Stacy allowed their eyes to wander around the classroom, studying posters depicting oxy-acetylene flames and welding arc lengths. The silence continued. Amara bit into a Danish. Flakes of pastry cascaded to the floor. Jessica broke the silence.

‘Amara! Stop playing mind games.’

Amara broke into a huge grin. Flakes of pastry stuck to her lips with syrup.

‘It is not exactly official or legit or anything like that. But a client of ours has taken an interest in Turkey buying the jet fuel from Islamic State, which you identified, Jessica.’

‘I don’t suppose this client is a Special Advisor to NATO’s ISR, by any chance?’

‘Oh, I couldn’t possibly say, Vanilla.’

*

The team of seven humans and a dog left Woods to lock-up the training centre and headed for the carpark. Amara went to take Jessica’s hand, but she shook it off.

‘You seem to have Mr Woods’ welding helmet, Stacy.’

‘No, I don’t think so, Jess. It is just a spare, I think.’

‘It has his name on it.’

‘Woods is quite a common name.’

‘You are actually quite weird Stacy.’

‘At least I don’t need a shrink, Jess.’

They linked arms.

Printed in Great Britain
by Amazon

70151190R00180